COYOTE ALIBI

J. & D. BURGES

Naaltsoos Press

Published by Naaltsoos Press

Print ISBN 978-0-9998573-3-5

Typesetting services by BOOKOW.COM

Acknowledgments

We wish to give high praise to graphic artist Paul Burges for his spot-on cover design. Our writer lives were also made better by expert editing assistance from Dr. Susan Booker. Thanks to Dr. Lynn Stevenson and Paul Burges for their excellent suggestions and encouragement.

CONTENTS

24   **Chapter Twenty-three**   273

PROLOGUE

THE lights came out of nowhere as he was concentrating on the still-distant rabbit. He hadn't heard the engine until it was almost too late. Without pausing for breath, he leaped wildly from the pavement and landed on all four paws, scrabbling awkwardly through the sand and shale, halfway off the shoulder of the narrow road.

The brakes and tires were squealing. The smell of hot tire tread and worn-out brake pads swirled with the dust. The wheels had come to a sudden stop, but no one opened a door. Motionless, he waited, watching.

Chapter One

Everybody does good things and bad things—smart things and stupid things.

My law professor, Joseph Shelby, said that once. He said that was the reason we make laws and have courts and attorneys and sentences and settlements. He also said that was why the law was a secure profession that would really pay off for us when we finished our certificates. It was music to my ears. But our little paralegal extension program got canceled when Shelby got caught drinking ninety-proof "milkshakes" for supper during his night classes. It had taken the university three semesters to figure out what I could see in the first week of class.

That's why today found me with only half of a paralegal certificate, sitting on a bench in downtown Sage Landing, waiting for a lawyer. Downtown Sage Landing meant the old shopping mall. Looming over my head was the dusty and faded marquee of what used to be the town's movie theater. I remembered taking my kids to the last movie that played there. That would have been about five years ago, 1980 or '81 maybe. When they were still young enough not to mind being seen at a movie with their mom. Superman II, with adventure for them and Christopher Reeve for me. Now the old theater was an insurance office, but it still used the marquee. A stranger driving down the street would have thought that there were recent movies titled such things as, "Whole life is for loved ones—and for you!" Today's offering was, "Get a Quote for Your Boat."

You might wonder why there are boats needing insurance out here in the middle of the Arizona high desert, if you didn't know about the big lake, or if you didn't call to mind the mighty river on the other side of the dam that had made the lake. As dry as this mesa is, and as tiny as the town that's perched here is, there are still lots of boats.

Unfortunately, the marquee didn't provide much protection from the midmorning sun that had already started to wilt me. I was as spruced up as anybody ever gets in Sage Landing, wearing a new long-sleeved white blouse with freshly-pressed khaki slacks. One of my more understated turquoise necklaces added just a touch of color. My shoulder-length dark hair was having a good day, and my touch of makeup would add polish if I didn't have to sit out in the sun too much longer. I knew that if I got a chance to talk to this lawyer about a job my looks would be a plus. With only three paralegal courses behind me, I needed every plus I could get.

Each time a car turned into the largely empty parking lot, I scrutinized the driver to see if it was a man who matched the descriptions I'd heard for Grant Carson. He was reported to be in his late forties, athletic, suntanned, and rugged. He had been described to me by two different women I knew, both of them with a certain dreamy expression on their faces. After I'd spent forty-five minutes sitting on the bench, no such hunk had arrived.

An aging delivery van drove into the lot, and I looked into the side windows with mixed feelings. Seeing my friend Ellen in the passenger seat made me happy, though it reminded me that we hadn't touched base for quite a while. Seeing that the driver was her husband, Willard Highsmith, irritated me. But what made me really angry was seeing that Ellen's two children were in the van on a school day. I watched as everyone climbed out of the van and the two children opened its back doors and began to lift out cardboard boxes.

Before I could muster a cheerful greeting, a small, dilapidated pickup truck drove in and parked at the other end of the parking lot. An older-looking man got out. He didn't fit the mental picture I'd conjured up for the guy I was looking for, but something about him caught my attention. His salt-and-pepper hair was a bit shaggy, and his threadbare green T-shirt stretched over the slight beginnings of a beer belly. Dressed in faded and slightly grubby denims, he didn't warrant much interest, and I didn't look in his direction again until he began to unlock the office that I had been watching. Then I got up from the bench, picked up the tan blazer that was folded neatly beside me, slipped into it, and smoothed my hair.

As I approached the door, he flipped a switch and flooded the front office with fluorescent light. The office had a large window across which hung the open slats of old-fashioned Venetian blinds—the big wide metal ones that you don't see any more. The room was furnished with three thinly padded armchairs and a small reception desk that held both a computer and a grungy beige telephone. The computer, though, was state of the art —a brand new IBM 286 that took up almost half of the desk's surface.

He passed through the front room and into an inner office just as I reached his door. I walked in and followed him. His inner room was only slightly less Spartan than the outer one, but its desk was larger and had some genuine wood in its pedigree. Behind it was an inexpensive executive chair. On the other side of the desk sat three comfortable, unmatched armchairs that looked like garage-sale stuff.

He had just turned on the light in this inner room when he turned to see me. I could read the nagging thought he was having—the feeling that he might have forgotten some kind of appointment this morning

I couldn't help but stare at his clothes. His denims looked cleaner than I'd originally thought, but I was surprised that he'd wear an old T-shirt if he was expecting a business meeting. Also, he might have worn a belt, and probably not those sandals. He could have washed his feet.

"Grant Carson?" I said.

"Yes."

"The lawyer?"

"Attorney."

"Pardon me?"

"Attorney at Law," he said. "We call ourselves attorneys. May I help you?" At least he remembered to smile, and when he did, I could see more of the image my friends had described. I mean, he was no Tom Selleck, but he did have a similar moustache, under which gleamed white, even teeth. Like most of the outdoorsy types around Sage Landing, he was deeply tanned. His eyes were looking me over with a definite bit of the devil in them.

"Everybody else calls you lawyers," I said and then regretted it. I looked at his sandals again, but tried to put them out of my mind. "On the commercials, too, you guys advertise using the word lawyer. 'Need a lawyer? Call So-and-So.' Then there's TV shows, you know? All those guys call themselves lawyers." I paused only to take a breath.

Then my mouth started up again, seemingly out of control. "Oh. You mean to each other?" I asked. "You call each other attorneys when you're talking to each other, even though everyone else calls you lawyers? What's the point in that?"

The lawyer extended his hand. "I'm Grant Carson, and you are?"

"Naomi Manymules." I barely touched his hand, as is the Navajo custom. "Dr. D. told me to be here at ten o'clock, and I was. I think it's after eleven now. What time do you normally open?"

"Dr. D.?"

"Sorry. Dr. Moreno, the community college president. The sign on her office door says Dr. D. Moreno. Nobody knows what the D. stands for, and everybody thinks it's funny so we usually call her Dr. D." I knew I was babbling again so I shut up. I have a tendency to babble when I'm nervous, which certainly described this situation.

Grant Carson seemed to remember. Dr. D. had already warned me that he had probably had one or two drinks too many when she had talked to him about me a couple of nights before.

"Desiree," he said. "It's Desiree, but she'd kill me if she knew I told anyone. I might be the only one in town who knows her name, and I'm forbidden to use it." He smiled again, and I had to agree with my friends that he was sort of handsome, but not at all in the Adonis way I'd expected. I could see a little of a former Adonis—very little, but still.

For once I kept my mouth shut instead of responding, but I mentally filed this valuable information. Later, I would reflect on its best possible use.

"You said something to Dr. D. about needing office help?" I said, hoping to prod his memory.

I should explain here that what Dr. D. actually said was that this new lawyer Grant Carson had been complaining about the burden of keeping his practice small enough to allow time for fishing but large enough to earn enough income to pay for his boat. His boat, the *Deep Inn,* was already infamous in Sage Landing. During the past few months its reputation had divided the town's women into two groups—those who were disgusted by its rumored goings-on and those who were curious and would maybe like to see for themselves at least. Most women under seventy fell into the latter group.

Dr. Moreno, with whom I gathered Carson had a special relationship, said that she told him about me and told him I could be just what he was looking for. Grant Carson clearly didn't remember any of that. He had told Dr. Moreno that the student should drop around to see him at ten o'clock, Monday. Today was Monday. That conversation had been on Saturday night.

I tried to keep the exasperation out of my voice. "You weren't expecting me? Dr. D. said that you would be expecting me this morning at ten o'clock."

I could see him thinking. Buying himself a little time, he walked behind the desk to sit down in the big chair. I leaned against the door frame and waited quietly as he toyed with a pen that was sitting on his desktop.

He cleared his throat and, still looking intently at the pen, resumed the conversation. "Naomi Manymules, you said?"

"That's right."

He finally looked up and said, "That's an unusual name... a unique name."

This seemed rather rude, mostly because it was hard to believe that he'd been here in Sage Landing almost a year without coming across a number of people whose last name was Manymules. So I locked eyes with him in silence for a moment before blandly saying, "Not really. Naomi is actually a very common name on the Eastern Seaboard—there are lots of women named Naomi in New York and New Jersey, not to mention Florida." I maintained eye contact with him, waiting to see if he wanted to continue in the "you're so exotic" theme.

He didn't. Instead, smiled faintly and changed conversational direction. "You're a secretary?"

"Office manager."

"I only need...."

"When you're the only assistant in a small office, you're usually called the office manager. Nobody's a secretary anymore." I walked in and sat down in the closest of the three chairs facing the desk. Normally, I would have awaited an invitation, but I was afraid that none would be forthcoming. I remembered that white businessmen valued getting a foot in the door. He would probably admire my assertiveness. "What type of help do you need, Mr. Carson?"

Without offering an immediate answer, he leaned back in the big chair and appeared to be trying to remember what was said Saturday night when he had been having a drink or two with friends at the Lunker Room out at the lake. I should point out that I can usually figure out most of what a man is thinking by merely looking at him. Most women can do this pretty well, but I'm especially good at it.

The attorney's face lit up, and I could again see what my friends had said about his looks. When he smiled, he *was* handsome. His face registered some recall and he said, "I was with Abraham Bingham celebrating a pretty damn good day of fishing on Abe's boat when one of his wives—I think it was the younger one—stormed in and raised holy hell and took Abe away. I don't remember what she said, but Abe didn't put up much of a fight." He smiled again and nodded as his memory gradually recovered. "Just after that, Desiree Moreno came into the bar and sat beside me. I had the impression that she'd been looking for me."

He paused, apparently trying to remember just what had happened next. Then he said that Dr. D. had accepted his offer of a drink and had been warm and friendly—quite a surprise to him considering they had had a recent tiff. Along the way she said that she'd been thinking about his problem of having too much business and too little time. She'd suggested that if he had a *secretary*—he made a point of emphasizing the word "secretary"— he could slough off a lot of the work at a reasonable cost to himself and thus gain additional fishing and drinking time. She had said this as if she approved of fishing and drinking, even though he knew for a fact that she did not much like either one. Now *he* was kind of babbling.

His memory of most of the rest of the conversation had grown fuzzy. He was sure, though, that Desiree had not accepted his invitation to go home with him. She hadn't done that in quite a while, he said.

I thought he had just told me more than I wanted to know, so I interrupted his recollection. "I've had training."

He focused on me and resumed his appraisal. I knew what he was seeing —and thinking. Before him sat an attractive Navajo woman about five-and-a-half feet tall. Minimal makeup; short, rounded fingernails; abundant, shoulder-length dark hair—wavy, no gray. Age was harder for a white man to assess, and I couldn't tell if he pegged me at more or less than my thirty-something years. But I would bet that on an attractiveness scale of one to ten, he'd put me at a seven—maybe an eight.

"In a law office?" he asked, probably proud of himself for replying with a businesslike question instead of some remark laced with innuendo.

"In three courses at the community college, extensions from U of A. They were going to sponsor a paralegal program up here, but they dropped it. I made A's."

That actually seemed to impress him and was probably much more than he expected to find in an office assistant, but I knew he wouldn't want to appear impressed. "I'd only need a few hours a week, Ms. Manymules. I tailor my legal practice to a small clientele."

"Dr D. *said* that you didn't have much business, but that you needed a lot of help anyway. I need a job, Mr. Carson." I remembered that the correct white protocol was to ask directly for what you wanted, though this always struck me as somewhat uncouth. "How many hours a week did you have in mind?"

Carson said, "Maybe fifteen or twenty," but it didn't seem to me that he could have given any organized thought to his needs at all. Immediately, he added, "If things work out. Of course, I don't know your expected rate of pay."

"Twenty hours is good enough for now. Whatever you normally pay a paralegal will be fine, Mr. Carson. When can I start?"

He stalled as if he had no idea what would sound reasonable for pay, and maybe he had no idea what to have me do or when to start doing it. He seemed lost for a moment.

Suppressing a sigh, I gently asked, "What were you going to work on this afternoon?" If he would tell me that, I'd have a better idea about what to suggest next.

"Uh, a trust. I was going to make a few notes about a living trust for a client who's coming in tomorrow morning."

I nodded my understanding and decided to try a little legal vocabulary on him. "Revocable or irrevocable? Is it mostly boilerplate, or is it specialized?"

"What? Oh, revocable. Somewhat specialized."

I was glad to have stumbled into a project about which I actually knew something. I'd done a case study on revocable living trusts. "Why don't you just have me plug in the basics and you can concentrate on any specifics. I can start on it this afternoon if the new computer out there is ready to go."

"Uh…" He looked confused.

"Oh, you probably already have the core document prepared since the client is coming in tomorrow."

Grant Carson shook his head, and I could see that he had not yet started on the trust at all. "Actually, I'm a little behind. A lot has come up lately," he said. "I wanted some sample provisions to show him, but we're just in the preliminary stages."

I could tell that he knew I wasn't convinced about his having been too busy. "So shall I get started?"

"We haven't discussed pay yet. I'm afraid that I haven't had an assistant in quite a while…."

"Dr. D. suggested that I start at fifteen dollars per hour," I said. I was pretty sure that Dr. D. would back me up on that. I didn't know what paralegals made, but I got fifteen dollars an hour when I got temp work at the power plant.

"To start?" he asked, sounding surprised.

I continued with a frown. "If you just want someone to answer the phone and file things, you don't really need a legal assistant. I guess Dr. D. got it wrong. Are you just looking for a part-time file clerk? Maybe the high school could help you find a student who could come in after school. You probably wouldn't want to leave them in charge of the office in your absence, but I'm sure you could arrange your schedule to be here most of that time."

I could almost hear the thoughts running through his head. He was behind on the little work that he actually had. Things were piling up. He wanted to spend less time in the office, not more. I would have bet that he was actually about to hire me when the unmistakable sound of squealing tires and an overpowered and over-revved engine interrupted his train of thought—just my luck.

This racket was followed by a rapid succession of four sharp explosive cracks.

I jumped to my feet and started toward the door. But before I could reach the outer office, a surprisingly nimble Grant Carson had scurried around his desk and grabbed me by the shoulders. He muscled me back into his office and all the way into a space behind his desk where he pressed me downward, and I found myself crouching with him behind it. I knew a few women who might have paid good money to be in my position, and I'll admit that it gave me a little thrill.

"Don't get up, Naomi!" Carson released my shoulders. Still hunched down at an awkward angle, he leaned over me and opened the lower left drawer of his desk. He shuffled blindly around in the papers that littered its interior. I could hear something heavy scraping against the bottom of the drawer. He swore under his breath, coming up empty-handed, and slammed the drawer shut before reaching out to a bag of golf clubs that was leaning in the corner. He tugged on it until it toppled over.

He extracted one of the clubs. "I'll take a look," he said as he slid around the end of the desk. Then he flattened out on the floor and slithered like a reptile toward the doorway and the outer office.

While the sounds in the parking lot had not frightened me, Grant Carson's behavior seemed reason enough to be careful, so I moved slowly as I got up and walked to the doorway. My would-be employer was now crouched beneath his front window and was peering out between the lower slats in his blinds. He held his club's grip firmly in both hands and had the shaft resting on his shoulder.

"Four people are lying in the parking lot," he said without looking away from the window. "I think two of them are children."

Chapter Two

"Oh my god," I said as I rushed toward the window. "Are you sure?"

"They're getting up," Carson said. "They weren't hit. They're getting up." He stood too slowly to stop me as I sped across the outer office and opened the front door.

"Ellen, are you okay?" I shouted while sprinting headlong into the parking lot.

Highsmith, the son of a bitch, snapped, "She's fine!" before Ellen could answer me. He had already gotten up and was standing beside his disreputable van. A very good-looking white man in his fifties, he wore a dark suit which was now covered in red sand from the parking lot. Actually, I'm not being fair in saying that Willard Highsmith was merely good-looking. It would be more accurate to say that he was stunning. His dark, wavy hair, with just a touch of silver, was gathered into a foot-long braid that hung down his back. His teeth were so perfect that they would have been right at home in a slick magazine ad. His suntan was carefully maintained, and his dark brown eyes looked honest and sincere, if you didn't know him very well.

Ellen had also gotten quietly to her feet. She was a lot younger than Highsmith. In fact, Ellen and I had graduated from high school together. But today she was dressed like a much older woman, in a conservative gray dress buttoned to the collar. Her children, a boy and a girl in their early teens, stood a few feet away, swatting dust from their clothes. Strewn all around them were paper leaflets. Some had begun to blow away in the light breeze that moved across the parking lot.

I came to a stop in front of Ellen and asked her, "What happened?"

Highsmith again answered for her. "Firecrackers, I think, big ones," he said.

I ignored him and reached out to grip Ellen's shoulders, searching her face and repeating, "What happened?"

She just looked over at the kids, visibly relieved as they moved closer, unhurt but silent.

Grant Carson ambled into my field of vision still holding his golf club like an umbrella over his right shoulder. He seemed to be staring intently at Ellen. When he saw that I had caught him at it, he looked away.

Highsmith said, "No need for weapons, neighbor," gesturing toward the club. "We're not in any danger." Even when making nervous conversation like this, Highsmith's voice was remarkable—deep, resonant, and clear. If he weren't a shopkeeper, he'd have to be a radio announcer. In fact, he sort of was one because he did all of the talking on his own radio ads.

Carson looked down at the club in his hand almost as if he had not been aware that he was carrying it. "Sorry," he said as he let the shaft of the club slide downward and held it as if it were a walking cane. "I thought it was gunfire. When I saw all of you down on the pavement...I thought the worst."

Highsmith continued to try to knock the dust out of his suit. "I thought the same thing. But these were just kids trying to scare us. I guess they succeeded beyond their wildest dreams. I bet they're laughing their asses off somewhere right now."

I turned back to Ellen. Beyond the patches of dust that now covered much of her dress, I saw three distinct bruises along the left side of her face. They had been covered by makeup, but the shading was slightly wrong for her complexion and the bruises were still visible. I felt an anger that tightened my guts, and I looked momentarily toward the club in Carson's hand. My instinct was to reach for it and to bash Highsmith with it.

Ellen glanced at the club, too, and shook her head slightly. "I'm okay," she said. Then she gestured toward her children by lifting her chin in their direction and pursing her lips. Most anyone raised this far north in Arizona will point like that instead of rudely pointing with a finger, whites as well as Navajos, though the gesture is a Navajo tradition. "We're all okay," she added.

I glared at the man who stood facing Grant Carson and gripped my friend's shoulders tighter. "Come into the office with me, Ellen."

"I can't. I—we have to pick up these leaflets and get reorganized." She reached up and gently removed my hands from her shoulders and turned toward the children. "Pretty scary, huh?" she said, almost cheerfully. "Let's clean this mess up."

Grant Carson leaned over and pick up a leaflet that had blown against his leg. "What's all this?"

"It's part of our latest promotion. I'm Willard Highsmith—you probably know of me as Big Chief on account of the store." He nodded in the direction of the old mall's largest store over which a garish sign read Big Chief's Furniture and Appliances. "This is my family. Today we're trying to get ready for a big sale."

Carson smiled the kind of smile you paste on when you're not feeling friendly—that straight, tight smile that doesn't reach the eyes. "Yes, I've heard of you—heard your commercials," he answered.

Highsmith squinted at Carson's smile. "Is there something funny about them?"

"No," Carson answered. "Well, except that I assume you mean for them to be entertaining." Shifting the golf club / walking stick to his other side, he extended his hand and abruptly changed the subject. "I'm Grant Carson. My office is right over there. My, ah, assistant, Ms. Manymules, and I were startled by the noise."

Highsmith shook hands with Carson. "Thanks for coming to our rescue."

Carson shuffled his feet and put his right hand in his pocket. He looked skyward for a moment and seemed at a loss to know what to say. Finally, he looked at me and said, "We've got to be getting back to work. Naomi and I have a lot to do today."

But Highsmith wasn't finished with us. "If you're in the market for furniture, we've got a hell of a sale starting this weekend."

The children had begun to retrieve the leaflets that had blown farthest away. "These kids should be in school today, Willard," I said. Then I felt Ellen's gentle touch in the small of my back and stopped myself from saying more.

Highsmith ignored me and continued his pitch to Grant Carson. "We've made some special buys. The advertising won't come out until tomorrow. You ought to drop on down and get ahead of the crowds." He glanced toward the law office. "Some nice desks just came in. Walnut—you can't tell them from real wood."

I noticed with some satisfaction that Carson clenched his jaw and shook his head. "We've got to get back to work."

Just then a police cruiser pulled into the lot and drove right up to Highsmith's van. A uniformed cop with captain's bars pinned on his shirt collar got out, leaned against his car, and folded his arms across his chest. The name Miller was engraved on a black tag on his chest, but everyone here knew his name. Sage Landing was a small town, and Jack Miller was second-in-command on the town police force. "What's going on here, Highsmith? We got a report of gunshots."

"Firecrackers, Jack, but big ones," Highsmith said. "Kids."

The cop nodded. "Driving a supercharged pickup with oversized tires?"

"That's the one," Highsmith answered.

"Mark Banner's truck—the Ford Phallus?" I said.

Miller chuckled and turned to me. "His truck's a Dodge, actually."

"Yeah, I know, but I didn't want to make the alliteration with Dodge," I said. Miller and I had been in the same English classes in high school and were both just nerdy enough to still be making jokes about alliteration. And we both knew every truck in town.

"Too crude," he acknowledged, "but more people around here would understand it."

Carson looked at us and smiled. "Seems like high-performance cars always have low-performance drivers."

"That's the truth," Miller agreed. "But it wasn't the Banner kid. We already got the little jerks. They ran that short yellow light on their way north toward the lake. The patrolman smelled beer, so he's hauling them in. Just heard him make the call to dispatch." He made eye contact with Ellen, who was standing behind me. "You okay?"

She didn't say anything but must have nodded, because Miller looked at her skeptically before he turned toward Carson. "Did you see this happen, Mr. Carson?"

I realized that Carson's law practice must have brought him into contact with the police officers.

"No, we only heard it" Carson answered.

"Who's *we?*"

"Ms. Manymules and I were in the office when it happened."

Miller looked at me. "Naomi? You didn't see it?"

"No, like my boss said." I figured that calling him "boss" was a good opportunity to confirm my employment status in front of witnesses.

Miller raised an eyebrow and glanced at Carson before continuing. "We'll need a statement later, Highsmith," he said.

I stepped forward and poked Jack Miller in the ribs. When he looked at me, I nodded toward the teenagers. For a moment, he looked perplexed, but I mouthed a word, and he smiled and looked at Highsmith. "Why aren't these kids in school?"

Highsmith scowled. "They're *my* kids, Miller."

The cop shook his head. "They're Ellen's kids, but that isn't the point. The law says they have to be in school today unless they're sick. They don't look sick."

"*Or* on recognized family business," Highsmith answered. "They're on family business."

Miller leaned over and picked up a flier. After looking it over, he said, "Get them in school right after lunch, or I'll charge you. We've had this conversation before."

It was easy to tell that Jack Miller was getting angry, but, for a salesman, Highsmith was remarkably poor at reading people. He raised his voice and slapped his van's fender. "Stay out of my business, Captain! You don't have the right to interfere in family business."

Then Jack lost it. He spun on Highsmith and grabbed up a handful of his shirtfront, shoving the older man back against the van.

Grant Carson turned on his heel and started walking toward the office, saying loudly, "Naomi, we have to get moving if we're going to be ready for that meeting." I stared at him for a split second before my peripheral vision caught sight of Jack reaching for his nightstick, and I turned to watch.

Miller slid the end of his nightstick up under Highsmith's throat, and I don't know what he might have done next if Ellen hadn't reached out and put a hand his shoulder. That stopped him. He lowered the stick and stepped back. Everyone knew he'd gone over the line, but he didn't seem to care at the moment. I'd seen him go too far a couple of times in the past, and I knew that Highsmith had better watch his step.

But Highsmith just didn't know when to keep his mouth shut. "I'll file an assault complaint," he growled.

Well, by then *I'd* had enough so I stepped between the two men and tried to put my face against the Big Chief's. "If you don't shut up, you moron, I'm going to assault you myself." Now picture this. I'm about five-six and weigh about one-thirty. Willard stood about six-one and probably weighed in at around one-ninety. My nose was approximately at his collar bone.

Captain Miller pulled me back and started to smile. He nodded at Ellen, and for a moment I had a flashback memory of the two of them as our Homecoming king and queen together about half of my lifetime ago. They made just as handsome a pair now as they had then. Jack still had the build of an 18-year-old quarterback and his chiseled features had only improved with age. His hair was still boyish—not very long, but tousled and sunbleached—and his blue eyes were as intense as they'd been when he moved to Sage Landing as a kid.

His eyes stayed on Ellen as he said, "Do whatever you want about the complaint, Highsmith, but get those children back in school." Then he got back in his car and drove away slowly.

~ ~ ~

"What was that all about?" Carson asked once he and I had returned to the office and closed the door.

I tried to sound calm and professional, but I felt like screaming. "Willard Highsmith is a crooked son of a bitch with lots of enemies."

"I don't think people take Highsmith seriously enough to try to do him any harm, Naomi. Anyway, didn't he say it was just kids who threw the firecrackers?"

I nodded. "Some of what are called kids around here can be pretty rough little idiots."

"You mentioned Mark Banner. I know that name—where from?"

"His dad's a doctor at the clinic. Both of his parents are big shots. The kid's a wild brat with a mean streak, a fifth-year senior who is out of control sometimes."

Carson walked into his office and motioned for me to take a seat. Instead, I detoured back out to the front office where I rummaged around in the desk and found a legal pad and pen. Then I joined him in his office and sat down.

"So you don't like Big Chief Highsmith much." He picked up his golf bag and replaced the club before he sat down.

I scowled. "His wife is an old friend of mine." I paused and then added, "You must be aware that he isn't a Navajo."

"I don't think anyone thinks he is. It's funny, though, that he'd use that business name—Chief. Navajos never had chiefs, did they?"

"No, not really. Outsiders would sometimes label someone as a chief, but that's different." I was actually a little surprised that Carson had learned that much, because it wasn't the sort of thing likely to come up in casual conversation or legal negotiation. "Highsmith is a Texan. Like a lot of Texans, he claims to be part Cherokee. He sells a lot of furniture to Navajos just because he's the only big furniture store out here." I wanted to add that he was a rat-bastard, but I showed some restraint.

Carson's expression darkened and he waited a while before asking, "Do you think he gave her those bruises?"

I was surprised at the question and started to answer but thought better of it. "It's not my place to talk about their business. Let's just say no, I don't like him."

Carson nodded. He let the silence settle for a bit, keeping his eyes on some papers spread across his desk before looking at me. "Is it true that Highsmith cheats on his wife?"

I was surprised again. I hadn't realized that he was in on the local rumor mill. "That's what they say."

"They?"

"It's a pretty consistent topic of conversation." He said nothing, and I saw that he expected more. "I trust the people who say it," I added.

Carson smiled and leaned back in his chair. "I thought for a second that you were going to grab my four-iron and whack him with it."

"You're very observant," I said. "But you were already out of reach by then, hot-footing it out of there—and taking the club with you."

The lawyer—sorry, attorney—grinned. "I wanted to be able to swear that I hadn't seen Jack Miller kill the Big Chief in broad daylight in front of his own stepchildren."

I laughed. "All Jack has to do is wait—someday, I'm going to do it for him." I paused for a moment and then decided to change the subject. "Do you want to tell me a little about the living trust we're doing?"

Carson sat forward and got down to business. This was an important moment for me because it meant that I was actually going to start *working* for the guy."

"Do you know a man named Frank Armstrong?" he asked.

"The trucking company?"

"The owner of the trucking company and other businesses, yes."

"Yes, I do." Then I realized that sounded like I was a personal friend or something. "No, I don't. I mean, everyone sees the trucks and the warehouse. I'd recognize him because he drives a Cadillac with the company name painted on the side." I realized that I may have been babbling again so I shut up.

"He has a daughter named Linda."

"Her I know."

He looked quizzical.

"By reputation," I added.

"She's his only heir."

"Seems pretty simple to me, then. What are the complications?"

Carson started to say something, but paused. Instead of answering me, he asked, "Naomi, in your three paralegal courses, what did you learn about confidentiality?"

The earlier events in the parking lot must have left a bunch of adrenalin still pumping through my system. Usually it takes a while for me to reach full-on fury, but now I immediately felt my face flush. I sat up very straight and dropped my voice barely above a whisper. More like a hiss, actually. "Mr. Carson, I did not need any textbook or professor to tell me that maintaining confidentiality is the most important thing in the practice of law. What? You're worried that I'd gossip about a client's private legal stuff? Discuss his family relationships? Is that what you're getting at? Because if it is …."

Carson had leaned forward, his face alarmed, trying to get a word in. When I finally ran out of breath and paused to inhale, he was saying, "No, no, no," and waving *stop, cancel, do-over* jazz hands through the air between us. I fell silent.

He said, "Of course, of course, I didn't mean to imply…sorry."

Neither of us said anything for a good long while. Then I nodded at him, accepting his apology and maybe making one of my own.

Finally, he cleared his throat and said, "Frank Armstrong has liver cancer. He's on a transplant list, and time is running out."

That sort of stunned me. The simple legal-clerical task in front of me suddenly felt personal and sad.

~ ~ ~

Two hours later, I'd made a good start on the basic provisions of a living trust when the office phone rang for the first time that day. The caller asked for Grant Carson and gave his name as Chuck Margolin. I'd never talked to Chuck before, but I knew him by reputation, because boat-owner friends of mine tended to shake a fist at the heavens when paying the bill he'd sent them for working on their watercraft. My hunch was that this call might make Carson unhappy. Reluctantly, I punched the hold button on my phone, got up to poke my head through the door to Carson's inner office and announce the call, and sat back down at my desk. A moment later, Carson closed his door, and right after that I learned that I could hear him just as well through the wall as I could sitting right in front of him. It occurred to me that this unexpected conduit for information would probably be useful in the future.

"How in the hell can it be six hundred dollars, Chuck?" Grant Carson asked as clearly as if he'd been sitting next to me. Actually, he *was* sitting next to me, except that there were two flimsy layers of very cheap paneling —maybe one step up from cardboard—between us.

Carson's remarks were punctuated with brief silences.

"What clutch is that?…Jesus!…That much?…When?…Fuck that! Three weeks?…You said…But you said…I can't afford that…just now. I was expecting a simple adjustment or something….I *know* it's a special engine….I know it's a big boat….I can't, Chuck."

Then there was a longer pause.

"Yeah, I guess we could trade like that…. Right, no money changes… not necessarily any taxes… in theory….I didn't know you needed legal… Okay, I'll probably see you at the Lunker Room tonight….Sure, that will be fine….Order the goddamn parts, Chuck."

I heard Carson's receiver hit the cradle as clearly as if it had been the phone on my own desk. The conversation reminded me that Mr. Carson and I had never concluded our discussion about salary. I'd been right about what kind of mood the call would put him in, so how was I going to bring my salary up again? And how was he going to be able to give me enough work to do if he didn't get enough paying business? Trading legal services for boat repairs didn't sound like the road to success, and I needed for him to be a successful employer.

～ ～ ～

Carson went out for lunch at about 2:30, so naturally the phone rang again. The man on the phone said he was Abe Bingham and he wanted to talk to Grant about getting a divorce. Maybe two divorces, he said. I told him that Mr. Carson was out of the office on business and that I would have him return the call as soon as possible. I asked if there were any details he wanted me to pass along to Mr. Carson. I was disappointed when he just answered, "Grant will know what I'm talking about."

I would have loved to know details about Abraham Bingham and his wives. Lots of white guys around here have multiple wives, but few of them are as powerful and successful as Abe Bingham. It occurred to me to wonder if Mr. Bingham would be a paying client or one who wanted to barter something for legal services. I couldn't see how my new employer was going to pay me by trading favors all over town. But Bingham could certainly afford to pay us. He was a building contractor with projects all over the region.

When Grant Carson returned at 3:30, he had the faint aroma of beer about him, but he had gone home and found sneakers and a clean short-sleeved shirt. He hadn't found any socks.

In my most crisp and professional voice, I started to give him Bingham's message. "Mr. Carson, there was…"

He interrupted me. "Grant," he said.

"Most people call you Carson. You prefer Grant?" Up till now, I had avoided the whole issue of how to address my employer by not saying his name at all when talking to him.

"Carson, then. I don't care, just not *Mister* Carson."

"Okay. Got it. Anyway, there was a business call while you were out."

"Someone called here about a legal case?" he asked as if that never happened in a law office.

"Abraham Bingham."

"That would be about fishing."

"He said he wanted a divorce, or maybe two divorces."

Carson sat down in one of the front office chairs. He appeared to be pondering the information for a moment. "Abe doesn't talk about, uh, domestic things with me."

"He sounded serious, like maybe he really wants a law…an attorney," I said. "He said you should call him back." I hesitated and then plunged ahead. "Maybe we're bringing in some new business."

Carson shook his head. "Abe may *think* he wants a divorce, but he can't have one. Besides, I couldn't help him anyway." He looked up at me, probably enjoying my confusion.

"I thought anyone could get a divorce."

"Only married people," Carson said. "No, actually, people who aren't married *can* get a legal divorce, at least here in Arizona, if there is a presumption of marriage and property or children to be disposed of."

"Dispose of children?" I tried to make a joke and look shocked and disapproving.

He got it. "Right, no, I should have said property or custody issues to be decided." He got up and walked to his office door. "In this case there are no children, but there is a lot of property. In any case, all I can do is refer Abe to someone else because he doesn't live in Arizona."

"And we're not licensed in Utah?"

"Admitted to the Bar," he corrected. "*I'm* not admitted to the Utah Bar. Another way to say it is that I'm not an officer of the court in Utah."

I nodded. "I thought Bingham lived in Sage Landing," I said. "I see his trucks all the time."

"Oh, I guess at least ninety percent of his contracting business is here because we have the larger population, such as it is. Actually, Abe often stays for days at a time on his boat. The marina *is* in Arizona. Maybe I could argue that he's an Arizona citizen. I wonder what residence he declares on his taxes."

I interrupted. "But he's not married? Did you say that?"

"Not in a sense that's recognized by the court."

"Of course he's a *plig* and all, but don't they have some kind of legal standing?" Pligs—short for polygamists—are just another minority around here, especially just across the state line.

Carson raised one eyebrow. "Polygamy is against the law in both Arizona and Utah, so I guess that's more like an *illegal* standing…if it's true."

"It is, isn't it?" I asked, backtracking. I didn't know how well Carson knew Bingham.

"Well, obviously, Naomi, Abe's a plig. But I think the, um, members of the polygamous community consider the word 'plig' to be something like an ethnic slur. I believe the preferred term is 'plurally married.' So let's be a little more circumspect with the language, okay?" He smiled broadly.

CHAPTER THREE

MONDAY nights are knitting-group nights for me. We call it "Stitch and Bitch" because we often put as much energy into catching each other up about our lives as we do into actual knitting. Personally, I enjoy knitting and take it seriously, but I do my share of bitching as well. The two activities go pretty well together.

During periods of time when I've had an office job, my fourteen-year-old daughter knew that she had to fix dinner for her brother and herself on Mondays, because I'd be in a rush after work to head off to my group. When I walked into my house after leaving Grant Carson's office at about 5:30, she was already in the middle of cooking. That surprised me since I did not, as far as she knew, currently have a job for sure. She *had* known about this morning's interview, and I guessed that she had figured it out when she got home and I wasn't there.

We ate a lot better when Kai was doing the cooking. The preparations that evening were a good case in point. The air held the sharp bite of diced onion. A pile of chopped fresh celery rested on the cutting board. Chunks of sausage were sizzling in olive oil. In contrast, when I made spaghetti, only one pot of water and one large can were involved.

I leaned against the door jamb at the entry to the kitchen and admired my daughter. She was wearing a clean apron—a precaution I seldom took. The ingredients were organized neatly before her on the counter, and she was about to fill the big pasta pot at the sink when she looked up and saw me in the doorway. The ponytail sticking out of the side of her head flicked over her shoulder as she turned to face me directly, and that silly hairstyle struck me again as seriously out of place next to her beautiful, serious, intelligent face. I knew better than to say anything, though. At fourteen, she was navigating the challenges of teenhood in the 1980's pretty well. There were worse ways for a brainy girl to try to fit in with the other kids. She flicked the thick ponytail back and began to fire questions at me before I could even sit down. "Are you going to work for that man Carson, that lawyer?"

"Attorney. Where did you hear that?"

"My friends said you were typing at a desk in his office after school."

I wasn't surprised that in a town this small I might have been noticed as I worked in front of a large window. I didn't see anything wrong with my going to work for a lawyer, so I was curious about her reaction. "I think so. I'm doing some temporary work for him right now, and I hope it will work into something full time. We need a steady income. Is there a problem?"

"We have a steady income," Kai said, referring to child-support payments from her father. My ex-husband had been living in Texas and Oklahoma for years.

"It's not always enough, honey."

She allowed herself a brief roll of the eyes as she reached out to turn off the burner. Clearly, the challenge of explaining the situation to her dimwitted mother was going to take her full attention.

"Mom, why can't you go to work for some other lawyer?"

"Well, he's the one who's hiring. What's wrong with Mr. Carson?"

Kai folded her arms and spoke slowly and patiently. "People talk about him. I mean they say things about his, uh, life—how he...With women, you know."

I *did* know, but I wasn't happy that my daughter did. "Who do you know who talks about things like that?"

Kai sighed dramatically, "Oh, Mom."

I walked over and gave her a hug. "Everybody gossips in a small town. Whatever Mr. Grant does on his own time is none of our business. I work for him in a law office, and all we do there is practice law." I decided I wouldn't tell her the part about crawling around on the floor.

She looked at me for a couple of beats and then turned the burner back on. "What kinds of cases do you handle? Criminals?"

"It's not that exciting, I'm afraid. Right now, I'm working on a will."

"Whose will?"

"I can't tell you that. I have to keep most of my work confidential."

"You're going to Stitch and Bitch tonight, aren't you? I bet if I were there I'd hear more about it."

I laughed, because she'd been keen to join Stitch and Bitch since she was four, when she begged me to teach her to knit. I'd been so pleased that she wanted to share a craft that meant so much to me, but as soon as she'd finished two uneven ridges of basic garter stitch, she said, "Okay, now I can go with you to Stitch and Bitch." Her interest in knitting came to an abrupt end when I told her that Monday nights were for grown-ups only (I was proud of myself for not adding "thank god" when I broke the news). Now I just put my arm around her shoulders again and said, "If you were there, you'd hear about the cardigan that I've ripped out and started over three times."

Throughout this brief exchange, my son, Len, sat quietly at the kitchen table pretending to be absorbed in homework. I knew better. First, because long experience had taught me that this quiet twelve-year-old never missed anything that was going on around him. Second, because his chin had lifted slightly when his sister had used the words "with women." I wondered how much Len had heard in his pubescent-boy circles about nightlife aboard Carson's *Deep Inn*.

A knock at the door interrupted us, and Len went to answer it.

"Mom," he sang out in a voice that could have been heard three houses down. "There is a man here to see you."

That was a sentence that I hadn't heard for a couple of years. Well, maybe it hadn't been that long, but it felt that long. I turned to go to the front room, and Kai quickly turned off the burner again to follow me, overriding any sense of propriety that I spent years trying to teach her. She was rewarded by seeing Grant Carson at our front door.

The last thing Carson had said to me was that he might call me in the morning if he needed me. I figured that he wouldn't actually realize that he needed me until about noon, by which time he would be way behind on his work. He was already way behind on his work, but I figured it would take him until noon each day to realize it until I got him trained. I estimated that it would be a week before he'd see the light.

So I was surprised to see him at the door and even more surprised to see how he was dressed. When I'd left the office, he was sporting denims and a camp shirt. Now he was wearing khaki slacks. His still-sockless feet had been shoved into clean tassel loafers, and he had changed to a white T-shirt under a freshly pressed long-sleeved blue shirt. He had tucked the shirt in and secured the pants with an actual belt. His hair was still damp, and he smelled of aftershave.

"Children, this is my employer, Mr. Carson," I said, setting an example of formality that I hoped they would follow.

Carson stood silently, his gaze alternating between my two children. I began to wonder if he had ever seen teenagers before. Their presence seemed to strike him dumb.

Now it was Kai's turn to surprise me by stepping forward firmly and extending her hand. "How do you do, Mr. Carson. I'm Kai," she said. "It means 'willow tree.'"

Carson shook her hand briefly and said, "Hello, Kai. Call me Grant."

I just stood there observing everybody's civility while my son found his voice. Raising his right hand in what I guessed was a gesture of greeting, he said, "I'm Len."

"Glad to meet you, Leonard," Carson said.

Len glared at me. My son and I had had conversations about this countless times. I'd wanted to give him a Native American name, and Len is a Hopi name meaning "flute." I'd also wanted to pick a name for him that was easy for white people to pronounce and was familiar to them. It hadn't occurred to me at the time that Len was also short for Leonard.

Naming kids is a funny business. You try to find something unique, something nice, something easy to say, and maybe even something that expresses a bit of your family heritage. Then you also want something that can't be mocked, or somehow twisted into a stupid nickname. You want something that isn't trendy but also isn't hopelessly old-fashioned. Even if you accomplish all of that, what's to keep some asshole from having the same name and becoming famous with it? Then you've given your kid an asshole name.

My efforts had paid off pretty well with my daughter. Kai had always liked her name. But poor Len's feelings about being a "Len" were mixed.

"It's just Len, not Leonard," I said simply. Grant Carson seemed satisfied, even if Len never would be.

He surprised me by speaking up. "Mr. Carson," he said, "is it legal to change your name?"

Carson smiled at him—not a condescending smile, but one that showed that he was paying attention and considered the question to be a good one. "Yes. Are you thinking of doing it?"

"How old do you have to be?"

The attorney smiled and looked at me. "Actually, Len, you don't have to go to court or anything."

"You don't?"

"Not in Arizona anyway."

"No judge or anything?" Len asked with a slightly higher pitch to his voice, though lately he had been cultivating as deep a voice as he could manage.

"Right. No judge or anything. As long as you're not using a different name for purposes that are illegal or fraudulent, you can use any name you want in the state of Arizona without any legal proceedings at all. Actually, you can do that in most states. Your name belongs to you, and it's pretty much your business what you do with it."

Len didn't seem to know what to say. When he stayed silent, Carson continued. "My own mother, for instance, never used her birth name in her adult life. Even at her funeral, they used the name that she had given herself as a teenager—the name of a movie star of the 1940's. I doubt if ten people who knew her as an adult ever knew what her real name was."

Len looked over at me and smiled broadly. I knew better than to say anything at that moment. I turned to Carson. "What can I do for you?"

"I need you."

At that, my daughter's mouth actually fell open. She put her hands on her hips and looked from his face to mine.

Her expression wasn't lost on Carson. He hastily explained further. "At the office tomorrow morning...I'm going to need your help. I realized after you left that there were quite a few unfinished matters on my desk. I think I left you with the impression that you might not be needed at work tomorrow, and I wanted to come by and make sure that you could be there. In fact, I'm sure you'll be needed for the rest of the week." While his words were addressed to me, he said all this while looking directly at Kai.

Len had already disappeared down the hall toward his room, and Kai said, "It was nice to meet you, Mr. Carson, but I've got to get back to fixing dinner." She turned and walked away toward the kitchen.

Carson called after her, "It smells really good, Kai," and then looked at me to ask "Spaghetti?"

I raised one eyebrow. "You were expecting maybe frybread and mutton stew?"

"Just making conversation, Naomi," he said, rolling his eyes. "Speaking of which, we never finished our conversation about pay. Would twenty dollars an hour be okay?"

"I only asked for fifteen," I said.

He shrugged. "I'm not very good at salary negotiations. What happened was I made some phone calls at lunch and asked about pay for good paralegals. What I found out was that if I started you at fifteen, I'd have to negotiate with you again soon. I figured I'd save myself some grief and just pay the rate to begin with—and there aren't any benefits. I don't have any health care plans or pension plans or any of that—and it probably won't be full time."

"Twenty is a bit high for here."

"I think you'll find that you'll be working pretty hard."

"I'm not very experienced." I couldn't believe that I found myself arguing against higher pay, but I didn't think that Grant Carson really knew what he was doing when it came to paying people. I wasn't sure that he really knew what he was doing about anything.

He seemed to consider my point. Then he shrugged. "If I find that I've made a mistake, I guess I can fire you."

"Okay. We can discuss this again later after we see how it goes. Thank you."

Carson nodded, then turned away and walked toward his little truck without further comment.

~ ~ ~

At 6:45, I was the last to arrive at my knitters' group. That meant I had to sit in the middle of the couch with my yarn on the floor in front of me while I counted stitches and eased my way into the conversation. Most members of our loosely organized group were there. The hostess for the evening was the high school assistant principal, Maggie Thornton. Sitting on the couch with me were Peggy Thomas, a Sage Landing police officer, and Sue Gallo, the town's busiest hairdresser. Laura Dumfrees, an accounting clerk at the plant, was there. We also had Alice Yazzie who was the part-time parish secretary at Saint Gerome's. Beside her was Mary Hogarth, a dental assistant who was the sister of the local Methodist minister.

That's more detail than you wanted, but there's a point to my telling it: on any given Monday night there was gathering of women who, taken as a whole, knew just about anything that was going on in town. The group also included a manager from the Bureau of Reclamation, a park ranger, and a medical file clerk, though Bobbie, Wanda, and Lucille weren't with us that night. None of us attended every Monday—life occasionally got in the way, and it was rare to see all of the participants together at one time. No matter who was there and who wasn't, though, once the wine was opened and a little time passed, information would begin to emerge—sometimes accompanied by the disclaimer "this goes no further." In extreme cases, someone would invoke the "cone of silence." Even though only some members of the group weren't old enough to remember what that was from watching the old "Get Smart" TV series from back in the 60's, everyone understood the request.

The funny thing was that saying something like that wasn't really necessary, because it was very rare for anything shared on a Monday night to see light of day beyond the group. We didn't take information that we gained here to the outside world. Monday nights made each of us much better informed about what was going on in town, but we didn't spread things outside the circle. As things had evolved, anybody who did was sort of eased out. This was something we understood rather than decided; it had developed, unspoken, over time.

On this particular Monday night, I was already the subject of conversation before I arrived. I don't mean that everyone got quiet when I walked into the room. Quite the contrary, I was immediately besieged with questions.

"Has Carson invited you out to his boat yet?" Laura asked me point blank.

After I said no, Sue Gallo asked me if Carson's inner office had a couch.

"No," Peggy answered for me. Everyone looked pointedly at her. "I've been there on police business," she said, looking down at the big red fuzzy slab of knitting that had sprouted unevenly from her needles. She worked at it on Monday nights only, so she'd never really gotten the hang of knitting or even decided what this large flat piece was supposed to be. With apologies to Elvis, we called it her "hunka hunka burnin' red."

Since I could offer no salacious details about Grant Carson or his office, the conversation turned elsewhere.

"Hey, I heard that Jack Miller beat up Willard Highsmith in the old mall parking lot this morning," Maggie said. She turned to me and asked, "Did you see?"

Good lord. "I was there, but that didn't happen," I said. "Jack just grabbed Highsmith and warned him about keeping Ellen's kids out of school."

"But Grant whacked him with a golf club," Alice said confidently.

"No, he didn't!" I said, realizing that I was being no fun at all. I added, "But I thought he was going to for a minute."

There was no sense in wondering where they had gotten their information. Sage Landing is the kind of place where someone is sure to see anything that happens and always tells someone else pretty fast. Stories change on the fly, so everything gets a little twisted by nightfall.

"Okay, so tell me this, Naomi," Alice Yazzie persisted. "Did you get a good look at Ellen this morning?"

I nodded and looked down, suddenly getting very absorbed in the ribbing pattern on my needles.

"And had that bastard been slapping her around again?"

Still looking down, I shrugged slowly. That was as good as a "hell, yes!" to Alice, who again made no secret of her opinion that Ellen should take her kids and leave the bastard.

Then someone asked if anyone knew if it were true that Willard Highsmith was getting it on with the high school principal, Gail Banner. Remember that we were sitting in the home of the *assistant* principal, who was lounging on the floor next to the coffee table, dipping a chip into the peach salsa that she had made.

I'd better explain more of the unspoken rules of discussion that had evolved in the group. Long-standing Stitch and Bitch custom involved our tacit agreement that, in circumstances like these, Maggie was silently acknowledged as being in a tight spot because we were talking about her boss. Whenever someone in the group was in a position to have inside information that might compromise her professionally or ethically, the expectation was that she would sit silently and keep her eyes on whatever she'd brought to work on, or get up and refresh her drink in the other room, or otherwise take herself out of the discussion. We might hope that she would smirk or smile as appropriate, kind of like the Cheshire Cat, but she was never pressured to divulge anything.

In this case, though, Maggie Thornton joined right in because she didn't have any information and was just as interested as the rest of us. Both Willard Highsmith and Gail Banner were sometimes items on the infidelity radar screen in Sage Landing. This recent pairing, if true, was especially interesting since Highsmith was a well-known store owner, and Ms. Banner was not only a public figure but also the wife of one of Sage Landing's better-looking physicians. On top of all that, the Banners' son Mark was a senior at the high school. All in all, knitting needles were moving pretty fast before we had even opened the second bottle of wine.

~ ~ ~

When the meeting broke up, it was still early. I didn't feel like going home to face further interrogation from my daughter yet, so I drove out to the north edge of town and walked out to the cliffs along the lake. I watched the moon begin to rise from behind Navajo Mountain to the east. I let the warm October night air and the beautiful surroundings wash away some of my worries, at least for the moment.

Turning to face north so that the lights were at my back and the lake stretched out in front of me, I did a mental review of recent developments and counted my blessings. It looked like I might have landed a job, and a good one at that. I was up to date on my house payments, and there was a small cushion in my checking account. My kids weren't in any trouble. They never had been, but I didn't intend to take that for granted.

After a few minutes my sense of peace was broken by a loud pop echoing through the canyons, followed by at least one more. At least I thought I heard two, a few seconds apart. The echoes made it difficult to be certain.

I thought of the firecrackers that had gone off in the parking lot that morning and wondered if the same kids were at it again. If so, they had managed to get their hands on something bigger this time—big cherry bombs maybe. It sounded as if they had thrown them down into a canyon to the east of me, between where I stood and the moon which was still climbing above Navajo Mountain.

The thought of reckless teenagers hanging around the cliffs where I couldn't see them made me nervous. I ducked down into a large crack in the top of the cliff right in front of me to wait and see if any bad guys were around—no sense in moving conspicuously through the moonlight to get back to my car. Once I'd eased myself down into the cleft, I was shrouded in total darkness. Since I'm dark myself, I figured I'd be pretty secure until the moon got a lot higher. I felt around until I had a firm grip on a ridge of rock. The term *cliffhanger* came to mind, but I wasn't exactly hanging off the edge of a cliff—just clinging to the top of one.

I wasn't relaxed any more, though. I was alert, straining to catch any sounds at all. Within a minute or so, I heard the rhythmic sounds of a swimmer far below me in the lake, too close to the cliff's wall for me to see without leaning out to peer straight down. The sounds told me that the swimmer wasn't heading across the channel to the low, sandy island that lay a few hundred yards out from the cliff. Instead, whoever it was seemed to be swimming westward along the base of the cliffs. Had the swimmer thrown the cherry bombs, somewhere near the canyon to the east? Maybe so, and what I was hearing now was the culprit putting as much distance as possible between himself and the canyon where he'd done the deed by swimming in the opposite direction. But it would be a very long swim before getting to a place to climb out of the water, because there wasn't any beach for more than a mile along that way. The sheer cliff wall dropped directly into the lake.

Then a boat drifted out away from the cliffs and into my line of vision about three hundred feet below me and maybe two hundred feet out in the lake. I relaxed a little. Whoever was swimming was no doubt from the boat and had a safe place to return to.

But the sounds of the swimmer continued steadily westward, now hundreds of feet from the boat. I looked back at the white runabout and wondered if the invisible athlete below me was skilled enough to make it back there.

Then I saw the butt. Well, that's what caught my eye first. It looked like someone's butt was shining up at me from the far side of the boat. A distance of hundreds of feet in the dim light of a rising three-quarter moon can play tricks on you, and maybe I just had butts on the brain.

Anyway, this butt seemed to be mooning me from the edge of the drifting boat. The low-angled moonlight wasn't yet making it into the boat so I couldn't see what part of the person was in the boat. Whoever it was, if it was anybody, was either climbing into the boat from the side away from me or was leaning way over toward the water. Or it was something else altogether. Some towels, maybe? The thought that I might need some professional help crossed my mind.

I figured that two people were swimming, at least one of them naked. Swimming naked, though technically illegal on the lake, was very common both day and night. Some people blamed it on the French tourists who came here in large numbers every year, but I knew, first hand, that lots of us locals swam naked whenever we got the chance. October was a perfect time for it because the heat was out of the air, but the water was at its warmest. So two people were swimming—one had made it back to the boat or hadn't left yet. Or one person was swimming, having left some towels conveniently draped over the side of the boat.

The sound of the swimmer faded away far to the west. All was quiet again, and it was time to get home.

CHAPTER FOUR

At ten o'clock the next morning, Frank Armstrong and his daughter Linda arrived at the office to meet with Carson. Linda was wearing net gloves, an artfully draped T-shirt that bared one shoulder, and a really short skirt. Her bangs were feathered straight up from her forehead and cemented with a whole lot of hairspray that I could smell as she walked in. The rest of her blond hair was a frizzy mop sticking out toward her sunburned shoulders. Just to complete the impression, heavy dark lines and shiny blue glitter surrounded the sullen eyes in what would have otherwise been a pretty face. She looked like an MTV wanna-be. *Her poor father*, I thought.

I felt really uneasy as I ushered them in because of what I now knew about the man. Not only was he dealing with a daughter who was way more than a handful, but Armstrong was also probably dying and would soon be *ad'en*, the Navajo word meaning simply "gone." I had rarely been in the room with a dying person, maybe never.

Neither of them knew me, and they paid little attention to me as I announced their arrival to my boss. Armstrong closed the door to Carson's office behind them. That prevented me from watching them had I wanted to, but of course it didn't have the slightest effect on my ability to hear them. Which was good because I wanted to find out if my hunch that Linda would behave badly was correct.

Since the death of her mother almost four years earlier, Linda had been about as self-destructive as a girl in her mid teens can be. Unfortunately, Mr. Armstrong had not shared that fact with Carson. Consequently, the trust was set up as if she were a responsible adult, because all Carson knew was that she had just turned eighteen. I'd refrained from passing along my own opinion.

I listened through the wall while Carson explained to Armstrong that, under the terms of the trust, his heir would have access to the estate almost as soon as he—well, without the delay and expense of probate.

"Would it be possible to protect... the assets... until she's a lot older?"

Linda's angry voice interrupted the men. "This is morbid, Daddy. And it's insulting."

Yep, that's the reaction I was expecting. A lot of entitlement, no compassion. Trying hard to be fair, I told myself that maybe her father hadn't shared the seriousness of his illness with her.

Mr. Armstrong continued as if Linda hadn't spoken. "What if I do nothing and then I happen to die?" Happen to die, huh? So I'd been right—he was pretending that this was just a routine legal appointment. She probably thought it was because of her recent eighteenth birthday.

In the pause that followed, I could imagine Carson wondering how to respond as if this were, in fact, a hypothetical, what-if kind of a question instead of a genuine worry. "If you do nothing and then die without a will, your assets will be frozen. Then the state will decide how—and when —to disburse them. At that point, Ms. Armstrong would be free to do what she wanted with whatever they directed her way. But the costs can be considerable, so the amount that would pass to her would be substantially reduced."

"I'm in the room, you know?" Linda burst out.

Her father said calmly, "Yes, you are. I am not making these arrangements behind your back. You are included in the meeting so that you can have some understanding of your assets."

Linda didn't say anything, so Carson was able to make a suggestion. "Frank, depending on whom you choose as trustee, we could add language protecting the principal against encroachment by creditors." My ears perked up, because I realized that he was suggesting a spendthrift trust—a descriptive but rather unflattering name for an arrangement that did more than protect the principal; it could also dole out funds gradually, over time, like a kid's allowance. Accordingly, Carson chose his words carefully as he went on to explain, "The trust could also specify the rate of access to the inheritance."

Linda Armstrong might lack self-control, but she didn't lack smarts. She understood exactly what Carson was saying. "This is embarrassing as hell!" she shouted. "My dad is sitting here trying to make sure that I don't do anything that he considers stupid with his money once he's dead. You're both talking about me as if I were invisible."

"No, we are not," Mr. Armstrong said in a low voice that sounded like he was clenching his jaws as he spoke.

"And you are talking about me as if I were stupid or slow or something—both of you. I'm right here and I'm an adult and I know what I'm doing."

In the silence that followed this outburst, I watched an elderly woman push a walker slowly past the front window. She made it all the way across, and there was still no sound coming through the wall. That's how long it was. The air must have crackled with tension in Carson's office.

Finally, Armstrong said, "That hasn't always been the case."

When I thought of some of the things that I knew about Linda's teenage years, I found it almost frightening to think of her being alone and wealthy. I realized that everything I thought about her was based on rumors and second-hand stories, but they all carried a common theme of self destruction: an impressive array of using drugs, alcohol, promiscuity, starting fist fights, and running away from home. Frank Armstrong no doubt knew a lot of additional stuff that I didn't know. That all had to be worrying him, and there didn't seem to be much that Carson could do to ease his mind. On the other hand, all of his worries were probably about to be over.

I couldn't help trying to imagine what I'd be thinking if I were in his shoes. If I knew I was going to die soon, I'd be worried that my children wouldn't have enough money to get them through to adulthood. I certainly wouldn't be worried that they would have *too much* money to get them there. Besides, by one measure Linda was already an adult. I have to admit, though, that to me eighteen never seemed old enough for what came with it. Poor Frank clearly felt the same way.

After another uncomfortable pause, Carson cleared his throat and suggested that a good next step might be an open discussion between the two of them with him sitting in as adviser. Armstrong asked how much it would cost to do that and was told that Carson would charge his full legal rate of a hundred and seventy-five dollars an hour. All things considered, Armstrong seemed surprisingly whiny about the money, but Carson reminded him that a workable legal agreement might save a considerable amount for the estate. As a final touch of salesmanship, he added that legal fees down in Phoenix were a lot higher.

For my part, I was just glad to hear that the office was going to be bringing in some legal fees. I didn't know particulars about Grant Carson's financial situation, but he seemed to be worried about the cost of his boat repairs and he drove an old truck and he didn't dress very well. If he was going to be able to pay me, especially now that I had a raise, we needed more business.

The door to Carson's office opened, and he brought the Armstrongs through. Frank's face looked gray and exhausted, while Linda's looked surly and peeved.

As they said their goodbyes and left, Jack Miller walked in. He didn't look all that great, either, in marked contrast to his usual energetic, put-together, official appearance. Today he was baggy-eyed and unshaven, and his uniform was rumpled. He nodded at me and asked Carson if he had a few minutes. The two of them retreated into the inner office and Jack closed the door—as if that were going to make any difference.

"Do you mind if I ask where you were last night, Mr. Carson?" Miller asked in a very cop-like voice.

Carson was silent for a moment and then answered, "Yes, I do mind. I'm not just playing attorney here, Captain. The information you ask for is personal and I wasn't alone. Unless it's necessary, I don't want to go into that."

Sounding even more official, Miller said. "It was just a preliminary question, counselor."

"Captain Miller, it sounds to me like the kind of question you ask when something bad has happened."

There was a moment of silence, and I sort of leaned closer to the wall. When Miller spoke again, it was clear that I needn't have bothered. He was kind of loud.

"Funny you should say that. Something bad *has* happened. The way things go around here, everyone in town will know what it is by this afternoon, so I might as well say it now. Willard Highsmith is dead."

I suppressed a yelp of surprise.

After a moment, Carson said, "And it wasn't an accident?"

"No."

Through the wall, I heard Carson's chair squeak as he shifted his weight. "Captain Miller, I barely knew Highsmith."

"We heard that you might have had a run-in with him yesterday before I arrived," Miller said.

"No, I didn't—that is to say it wasn't a run-in. Yesterday was the first time I'd met the man, although I'd heard of him." Carson paused and then said, "Now, what happened between *you* and Highsmith—that was a run-in, I'd say."

Sounding less official now, Miller shot back, "It sure as hell was, and I got grilled as soon as I got back in town this morning—even before I knew the guy was dead. Luckily for me, I escorted a prisoner to Phoenix yesterday afternoon. Frankly, I'd be a prime suspect otherwise."

"Are you letting out information about how he died?" Carson asked.

I could hear Jack turn a page in his notebook. "He was shot to death."

"Is his family all right? Was it in his home?"

"No. I mean it didn't happen at home. Ellen and her kids are fine." Even through the wall, I could hear the relief in his voice, and I exhaled the breath that I hadn't realized I'd been holding.

"Well, where?" Carson asked. There was silence for a moment.

I heard Miller close his notebook. "I don't know how many details will come out this afternoon, so I don't know how much to try to withhold right now. You understand."

"I was a prosecutor for a few years," Carson said. "I know exactly what you mean. Is there any question about it being murder?"

"Not as far as I'm concerned, no," Miller answered.

Then he spoke directly to me even though the door was closed and there was a wall between us. He didn't even raise his voice to say, "Naomi, I would appreciate it if you didn't say anything to anybody about this conversation," and it was obvious that he knew that our office wall acted more as a sounding board than as a privacy barrier.

I sat in shocked and embarrassed silence. The other side of the wall was just as quiet for a long moment. I dropped my pencil. It clattered across my desk and clanked into the steel waste can.

"Naomi?" Carson said in his normal tone of voice.

"Yes," I answered very quietly.

"Naomi?" Carson said again. "I can hear you just as well as if you were sitting right beside me."

"She is," Miller said.

"Jesus," Carson said.

"Mary and Joseph," I said in my regular voice.

"Holy shit," Carson said. "We've got to do something about this."

"It won't be easy," Miller said. "Insulation in the wall and a couple of layers of drywall would be pretty cheap, but it wouldn't help much. That and insulation overhead plus soft wall coverings in here would probably be a lot better. That's what we do down at the station." He opened the door and stood looking at me. "I've known Naomi long time. I doubt if you have to bother with all of that."

Carson joined him at the door and looked at me. "But what if some client found out that they didn't have any privacy in my office?"

"I can see where that could be a problem," Miller said.

I looked from one to the other. "Hey, I can still hear you guys, you know?"

Carson continued, "I mean if the phone rang or anything…"

"Yeah," Miller said, "that would do it."

Carson just smiled and shook his head.

When we were alone again, Carson didn't say anything about the wall. He just stood around my office looking at the ceiling and tapping the partition.

"A murder case," I said.

"Not for us. This is a murder case, all right, as far as the police are concerned, but not as far as we are concerned. At the moment, you and I are actually suspects, though I doubt anyone takes that seriously."

I was reluctant to pry into my new boss's private life, but I asked anyway. "Can you answer his question about your whereabouts if you need to?"

Carson shrugged. "Sure. It might embarrass someone, but she's single. What about you?"

I busied myself with retrieving the pencil from the waste can and putting it on the desk. "Me? He's never going to ask me where I was."

Carson walked over and looked out the front window toward where our little parking-lot scene had taken place the day before.

"Yesterday morning it didn't look to me like you liked Willard Highsmith very much. I wonder how it looked to the Captain." He walked back to his office door and leaned against the door jamb. "How much did you dislike him? And, more to the point, how much does Miller know about that?"

A chill ran through me. Quite a few people knew that I pretty much hated Willard Highsmith. Jack Miller was one of those people. Luckily for me, I was low on a long list of people who pretty much hated Willard Highsmith. "I wonder when he died," I said.

"So do I," Carson said. Then he turned and looked at me with widened eyes, like he'd just remembered something. "You said you were going to kill him."

"I did not!" I may have stamped my foot.

Grant Carson smiled and managed to be appealing even while being irritating, but then he pointed his finger directly at me. Very rude. "You said that if Miller waited long enough, you'd kill Highsmith for him."

"Not seriously! It was a figure of speech." This conversation was going way off in the wrong direction, and I wanted to turn it around. "When you came by my house at dinner time, you had dressed up a little. That wasn't for me, was it?"

"Uh, no. Well, not entirely."

"You were on your way to meet somebody."

"Not right then. For a late dinner after I had a few beers—in public—at the Lunker Room. My date had something she had to do earlier."

"Jack asked where you were 'last night.' Since he didn't say when last night...well.... was this a dinner that lasted long enough to cover you no matter how late Highsmith might have died?"

"Absolutely. How about you?"

"All of my time is accounted for, not that anyone would ever think I could kill anybody."

Carson tilted his head to one side, looking rather skeptical. "Well, I've come to the conclusion that anybody could kill somebody else, given the right circumstances. The list of reasons seems to be almost endless." He looked absently over my shoulder at the paneling behind me. "We're going to have to do something about this wall eventually. In the meantime...."

I interrupted him. "Go in your office and see if you can hear me on the keyboard."

He did and he couldn't. When he walked back into the front room, I said, "We can fix this phone out here so that it doesn't ring. Then, when someone calls, you can just ignore it, and I'll answer it."

He shook his head. "Or we could just disable the ring in my office," he said.

"Think about it," I said.

"Oh, yeah, it's *your* phone we don't want clients to hear through the wall."

I stuck both of my thumbs up.

"But, seriously, we'll have to do something about this eventually." He tapped the wall. "Before too long. Because even if they don't hear your phone ring, they'll hear you answering."

"I know. I meant that the phone thing would help temporarily. Just be sure there's no gap in your conversation when I answer, so the clients are listening to you instead of noticing that they can hear every word I say. We can do the rest later when we've got enough business," I said. "Like, for instance, this murder case."

"I already told you...."

"This happened in town, right?" I said. "And whoever did it is probably from around here. Anyway, they did it here, so it's a local case. It will have a defendant. Defendants *pay* their lawyers."

"Sometimes they're broke."

"Then the state pays. And these cases can take a lot of time," I continued, as a vision of long lists of billable hours filled my head.

"I hate to tell you this, but the state pays an insanely reduced rate in those cases. Besides, this isn't my kind of case." He backed up to one of the side chairs and sat down.

"At the moment, hardly anything is your kind of case, right? I mean it's not like you don't have time. And you've done criminal law before—in Phoenix, you said."

"Calm down, Naomi. You're way ahead of yourself. Besides, I'm not the only attorney in town."

I lowered my head and my voice. "I think the others are pretty busy," I said. "Isn't there something you want to buy for your boat?"

Our discussion was terminated by the sound of tires sliding to a halt just outside our door where there aren't any parking spaces.

Police Captain Jack Miller opened the door and glared at me, looking very police-like and not at all old-friend-like. "Naomi Manymules, were you parked on the north edge of town last night? And were you walking out by the cliffs in the dark at about ten o'clock?"

CHAPTER FIVE

My boss stood and put his hand up with his palm facing toward me. He looked a little like a traffic cop—one who didn't have a uniform or a pair of shoes. More like I imagined a traffic cop might look in a third-world country. "Don't answer that."

Miller looked surprised. "Since when are you a criminal lawyer, Mr. Carson?"

Carson pointed emphatically at Miller. I made a mental note that I needed to coach him about not using his finger to point if he was going to continue to live around here. "Since it became evident that *you* think my assistant is a suspect in a murder case."

I remained seated, smiled at Carson, and shook my head in a way that I thought might be reassuring. "Now, now. Jack didn't say that I was a suspect," I said, looking from him to Jack and back again. "He doesn't think that I'm a suspect."

Carson stepped in front of me, placing himself as a sort of shield between Jack and me. "Trust me, Naomi, he thinks you're a suspect. I've been in this business for a while, you know?"

Suddenly my well-armed friend in his police uniform looked different to me than he ever had before.

Miller smiled, "Calm down."

"Tell her her rights, Captain."

"I'm not making an arrest, Carson. What's got into you?"

"Yes," I said, getting back to Miller's question. "I parked out by the lake for a little while last night after stitch…my meeting. I guess it was about ten o'clock when I walked back to the car."

"Damn it," Carson said, turning his head toward me, "this is a murder investigation, Naomi. Please be quiet and learn something about how lawyers do this."

I couldn't help noticing that he said "lawyers" instead of "attorneys," proving my point, but for once I was able to keep the thought to myself.

"And later," Miller continued. "This is going to sound strange to you, Carson, but I have to ask." He turned to me and took a deep breath. "Naomi, later, around midnight, were you running…uh… sort of streaking …uh… naked. Naked…" Here he barely suppressed a smile. He began again, "running without clothes on, through the Long Vista neighborhood?"

At that, Grant Carson turned to face me and lowered his traffic-signal hand. He seemed to be speechless. The prospect of having an office manager who ran through the town naked seemed to give him pause.

The two of them stood there gawking at me, and I could see myself running naked through their imaginations. "Good Lord, guys. What are you, thirteen?" Neither of them answered so I looked pointedly at Jack and said, "As I recall, *I'm* not the person in this room who once ran across the bridge naked on a dumb football-team dare."

Jack flushed bright red from the rumpled collar of his police uniform to his boyish blonde hairline. The poor guy had marched himself straight into the main drawback of staying in the small town where you grew up: the stupid things you did as a stupid kid stuck to you forever.

Then things popped up at the worst possible times, like now!

"Naomi," he started, but I turned to Carson and barked, "As for you, *counselor*, …" and I paused to let him grow up a bit, "do you want me to dignify Captain Miller's question with a response?"

He put his hands on his hips. "What difference does it make what I want? You seem to be ignoring my advice so far."

I turned back to Jack, who wisely kept his mouth shut.

"No. At midnight I was sound asleep. Ask my kids."

Carson was all business now. "He probably will, Naomi, and he'll talk to everyone who was at your meeting. I'm trying to tell you, seriously, that you are a suspect at the moment. Jack ought to tell you that himself."

Miller, too, had recovered his professional persona. He sat down and leaned forward, forearms on thighs, clasping his hands in front of him. "He's sort of right, Naomi," he said. "Someone recognized you as you walked across the mesa away from the lake last night at about ten o'clock. The witnesses were sure it was you."

"Obviously, that time fits in with the time of the murder," Carson said. "It is also obvious, Naomi, that *where* you were seen fits in with some aspect of the murder. Do you see what I'm telling you? Jack isn't here on a casual visit."

I looked over at Jack Miller. The teenaged streaker had disappeared, and I saw a policeman. "I sure as hell wasn't streaking naked through Long Vista at midnight."

Miller nodded. "Okay," he said, "but somebody was."

Carson paced back and forth in the front office for a moment and then said, "And that has something to do with the murder as well. Different witness, I presume. Are they sure it was a woman?"

Jack was silent for a moment and then decided to answer. "Very sure... an adult woman."

I said. "Naked?"

"Absolutely naked, the witness said."

"A reliable witness?" Carson asked.

"Not entirely. The witnesses are two teenage boys who were out way after they should have been and were picked up last night with the remains of a twelve-pack. They didn't tell us about the naked woman until this morning when they overheard talk about the murder. They could see that they might be suspects themselves, I guess, and they started telling us everything they had done and seen the night before. We questioned them separately and are convinced that they saw a woman at about midnight. It was at a distance, and they only saw her briefly."

"But I'm guessing that the murder was closer to ten o'clock and that it wasn't in the Long Vista neighborhood, am I right?" Carson asked.

Jack nodded.

"So Naomi isn't off the hook?"

"No. The naked-woman thing may be unrelated."

I guess Jack meant that although I wasn't a streaker, I still might be a murderer. I was just relieved that my kids wouldn't hear that I was suspected of public nudity.

Carson just looked at me, and I nodded my understanding. It occurred to me that a few minutes earlier I had been trying to convince Grant Carson that we should represent the defendant in this case. I hadn't meant to be the defendant myself. Even the slight suggestion that I might be had sort of cooled my enthusiasm for the whole thing. Criminal law didn't look like so much fun anymore.

~ ~ ~

After Jack Miller left, Carson asked me if I was sure I hadn't been running naked through the neighborhood the night before. He seemed to think that the question was funny. I didn't, but I wasn't in the mood to scold him further.

"Dead sure," I said. "Long Vista is quite a ways from my street." I paused before asking, " Speaking of dead, do you really think I'm a suspect?"

Carson resumed his pacing in front of the window. "Technically yes, but you won't be one for long. The police will be working furiously right now, following every lead that pops up. These first few hours are crucial for them. Naturally, they had to ask you about being out on the mesa."

"Oh!" I squeaked, suddenly realizing that I might have heard Highsmith's murder. I gulped and then took a deep breath to get my voice off the ceiling. Then I continued a bit more calmly, "He was shot near the edge of town."

Carson dropped down into a chair, his face concerned now. "How... how did you get involved?"

"I didn't mean that. I meant that I heard something when I was out on the cliffs. I'm still not sure what it was. Those firecrackers yesterday, you know? I thought I was hearing more of that."

He leaned forward. "Were you close to it, you think?"

"Pretty close. I was out at the edge, pretty much straight north of where High Street ends. The sounds were coming from my right as I looked at the island, so they would have been coming from east of me, not far."

"Is there anything else? Did you see anyone?"

I spread my hands on top of the desk and concentrated. "I heard someone swimming. I never saw them. Whoever it was swam along the base of the cliffs away from the boat. They were still swimming when I decided to go home."

"The boat?" He frowned. "What boat?"

I cleared my throat and took a deep breath. "There was a boat that seemed like it was drifting away from shore."

"Well, did there *seem* to be anyone on that boat?" Carson was clearly forcing himself to speak calmly and patiently.

I nodded. "Seemed is the right word. I can't be sure, because there wasn't much light out yet, but it seemed like someone was either climbing or leaning over the far rail…maybe without clothes on."

"Man or woman? It should have been easy to tell under those circumstances."

I shook my head. "Not so easy, no. All I saw—or thought maybe I saw —was a butt. And that's all I'm going to say about that."

After a moment my boss stood up. "Unfortunately, now you're going to say it all again, officially, because we have to go over to the police station and get Jack and make a statement."

"But you said…"

"That was before I realized that you might be a material witness. You weren't arrested and haven't been charged. Therefore, you don't have the right to remain silent if you may have evidence to offer. It's a crime to withhold evidence."

Carson drove us directly over to the police station, though we could have walked the distance in a few minutes. When we got there, I noticed that the Highsmith family van was parked in the lot and wondered if it had been towed in from the murder scene. I didn't want to walk too close to it in case there was blood, or worse, visible from outside. I made a wide path around the old car as I walked toward the front door of the station, but Carson walked right up to it and stuck his head in through the open window on the driver's side. I noticed that he held his hands behind his back while he did that.

"He wasn't shot in here," he called out. "You didn't see this thing parked out there on the mesa anywhere, did you?"

"No, but that's gross," I said.

"What?"

"The way you stuck your head right in there to look for the gore. How do you act at a highway accident?"

Carson looked a little insulted, and I had to remind myself that I didn't need to say every critical thing that popped into my head. My job wasn't all that secure, and I had lost jobs in just this way before.

He started walking toward me. "You want me to be a defense attorney, right? One thing that defense attorneys do is try to gather information about the crime scene. You never know what might help, and you never know where or when you might get the information. I should take an especially strong interest in the murder scene and the murder weapon."

"Right, I'm sorry."

"And if we ever do get a serious automobile accident case, I'm going to do the same thing. So, as to your other question, at a highway accident I would look inside the car, and I have done so too many times."

When he walked up to me, I said quietly, "So you'd rather write wills and do divorces."

"I don't much like divorces, either," he said.

Inside the small lobby of the station, we were greeted by the sight of Peggy Thomas sitting behind the counter. It was clear that she was surprised to see both of us. There was a split second of eye contact between Peggy and Grant

Carson, and I spotted a microscopic smile on his lips. That's all it took for me to see what was up with them. I admit to being a little surprised.

As we stepped up to the counter, Peggy spoke before Carson could explain why we were there. "They've got Ellen Highsmith back there," she said in a voice so low that we could barely hear her. Then she returned to normal volume and said, "Mr. Carson, Naomi, what can we do for you?"

I made eye contact with her and threw all the questions I could into my expression without saying a word. She gave a little grimace that said everything: Ellen Highsmith was a suspect. Carson caught on to the exchange of information and held his hands out in front of him briefly, holding his wrists together as he raised an eyebrow. Peggy whispered, "Not yet." If I understood the pantomime correctly, this all meant that, while Ellen was clearly a prime suspect, she hadn't yet been arrested.

I felt a knot in my stomach.

Before we could exchange any further silent information, Captain Miller came down the hall towards us. "What's up, counselor?"

"After you left, Naomi realized that she may have information pertinent to the case."

Jack frowned at me.

"Maybe not," I said. "You're busy. We'll come back later, maybe."

Carson took hold of my arm in a way that was sort of half reassuring, half restraining. "Have you got a minute, Jack?"

"Sure, go on back to the last office on the right. I'll be there in a minute."

As Carson ushered me down the hall, we passed a room with a small window in its door. I couldn't resist looking as we passed. Ellen Highsmith was sitting at a small table in the barren room. She looked up and saw me. Carson looked too, and he nodded grimly at me as we entered Jack's office.

"Motive, for sure."

"What?"

"Come on, Naomi, I saw the bruises yesterday, you've obviously seen it many times. I'm sure that Miller has too. Motive is not a question. The question is opportunity. Believe me, the first question that Jack is going to ask you when he gets in here will be about the whereabouts of Ellen Highsmith at around ten o'clock last night."

Jack must have heard the remark as he walked down the hall. The first thing he said when he walked into the room was, "That's right." He gestured and said, "Let's all get comfortable." He remained standing, but when we were seated, he said, "When was the last time you saw Ellen?"

"Before noon yesterday. You were there."

He made a note. "Not out on the mesa last night?"

"No, and I didn't see her car out there either."

He looked up from his notepad. "What *did* you see out there?"

Carson answered before I could open my mouth. "That's what we came in to talk to you about, Jack." He nodded at me—his permission to speak.

"Actually, I heard something, and now I realize that it might have been gunshots."

Miller sat on the edge of his desk. He was a tall, muscular guy to begin with, and his sitting above us like that was quite intimidating. "What time?" he said.

"A few minutes after I got there, maybe 9:45 or so."

He jotted something in the notebook he was holding. "Naomi, what were you doing out there at that time of night?"

I wasn't exactly sure how to explain it. "Jack, you weren't in Sage Landing last night, but you know how sometimes, in October, the night air is so sweet, with just a whiff of smoke from fireplaces or bonfires? Just the right temperature and no wind, and just enough moonlight to make the water shimmer? It was like that last night. I went out to look at the lake for a few minutes, to relax before going home to the kids and the laundry."

He gave me a long look. He did know, but he didn't want to say so. "And then?"

"I heard the noise, but I thought it was firecrackers, like yesterday morning. I waited till it had been quiet for a few minutes, because I didn't want to risk running into whoever was tossing big cherry bombs around. Then I walked back to my car and drove home. I don't know the exact time, but it would've been around ten o'clock."

"We know the time that you were walking back to your car because a High Street resident took down your license number and called it in. He had heard the noises, too, while he was out walking his dog. He thought they sounded like gunshots. He'd noticed your empty car and copied down the number. Shortly after he called it in, he saw you drive by. He said he didn't know you—we got your name from the plate number. The deputy who took the call last night ignored the information because *he* knew you. This morning, the witness identified you from a news clipping he brought in."

News clipping? That stumped me. I'm not a very newsworthy sort of woman. I guess my confusion showed in my expression.

"When Len won that award at the science fair last week, you were with him in the picture next to the story that the *Gazette* ran about the fair. The witness brought it in this morning."

I nodded and felt a little sick. The *Sage Landing Gazette* came out weekly, and it was just my luck that there hadn't been much other news for them to include. Now people were coming to the police and pointing at pictures of me because they thought I'd killed Highsmith. For a moment, I felt as naked as the streaker we'd been told about.

"There was something else," Carson said. "Naomi heard someone swimming."

Miller's eyebrows went up a notch. "Swimming? Where?"

"Along the base of the cliff. Swimming west away from a boat."

"You saw a boat?" Miller said.

"A minute or two after I noticed the swimming. It was drifting in the darkness, and it's a long way down to the water there. I must have been looking at it from over a hundred yards away, but I could tell that it was an open-bow runabout."

"How big?"

"Pretty big, but usually if they're much bigger than seventeen feet, they've got a cabin."

"And this one didn't have a cabin?"

"No."

"You're sure?"

"It was an open-bow runabout. I'd guess less than a twenty-footer. No cabin. It was an outboard, now that I think about it."

He nodded and scribbled again in the notebook. "Was anybody on board?"

I wasn't sure that I wanted to talk about thinking that I saw someone's butt. "Maybe."

"Maybe you saw somebody on board?" Miller asked, making more notes.

"I had the impression that maybe I saw somebody's butt. I know that sounds silly, just the butt."

Jack didn't look surprised. He just continued making notes with an impassive expression. "Man's butt, or woman's butt, do you think?"

"Maybe not even a butt, maybe something else. It kind of looked like someone was either climbing into the boat or leaning way over out of the boat. The part of them that was inside the boat was in shadow, completely black. The part of them that would have been outside the boat was on the other side of the boat, out toward the island. The only thing that was visible was their butt, or it might not have been a person at all. I don't know. It could have been a folded up towel or something else. It was a long ways away. It just struck me for a moment that it looked like somebody's butt."

While Carson's face stayed neutral, Miller was now looking grim. "Tell me about the swimmer," he said. "Did you see the swimmer at all?"

"No. I just heard someone swimming. The sound was coming right up the cliff wall, amplified off of the water right below me. There wasn't any wind. The sound was quite clear. Someone was swimming along the base of the cliffs toward the west."

"Away from the boat? For how long?"

"Until I left. Actually, they'd gone so far to the west that I'd lost track of the sound. Or maybe they'd stopped and were treading water or gripping the cliff's rock face somehow. Anyway, I couldn't hear any swimming by the time I left. Maybe five minutes."

"There's not much to hold on to along there," Carson said. "Must've been a hell of a swimmer."

"Oh ick," I said suddenly. "That was Highsmith's butt, wasn't it?"

Jack permitted his face to relax for just a moment. "Yeah, that's what you saw, Naomi. Sorry."

"Okay, then, who was doing the swimming?" Carson asked.

"That, counselor, is the prize-winning question." Miller looked over at me again. "Do you know anything about how well Ellen Highsmith can swim?" Then he added, "Not very well as I remember." He made a note.

Carson looked at him as if he had just committed some breach of police protocol—kind of a disapproving, inquisitive look. I had this strange feeling that Carson was on the verge of saying, "Your Honor, I object," but he just continued to stare silently at the policeman. Jack repeated the question to me.

"I don't know. I don't think I've ever been swimming with her," I lied. "Didn't you guys used to swim... you know, back when... back in high school?"

Miller looked up at Carson and then back over at me. "You don't remember her swimming very well?"

The fact that he'd ignored my question bothered me. Jack and Ellen used to go to the beach a lot. If I was correctly remembering her stories about their dates, they swam together—might've been mistaken for French tourists. Clearly, he didn't want me to say that, and it was just hearsay, technically, anyway.

"That's correct." I said.

"You don't remember that she could swim at all?" He made some more notes.

Carson's frown had deepened as Jack pursued the topic of Ellen's swimming, but he made no comment about it. Then he asked a question. "What about clothes? If Highsmith was nude, maybe the other person, the swimmer Naomi heard, was skinny dipping as well. You must've found the clothes they'd been wearing on the boat."

Miller hesitated, but then decided to answer. "There were lots of clothes —that's the problem. The boat has storage spaces all along both sides. All the clothes were stuffed in those. There were several swim suits, lots of sandals, and towels. There were also several T-shirts, some halter tops, and various sizes of shorts and shirts, both men's and women's. Some of the stuff was clean, some was muddy. Pretty typical for a family boat that gets a lot of use."

Peggy Thomas appeared in the doorway. "Ellen's saying that she wants an attorney. She says she wants Carson and Naomi."

CHAPTER SIX

A N hour later, Grant Carson, Ellen Highsmith, and I were seated in Carson's office. No charges had been filed against Ellen, and she had driven her own van over to our office. Carson and I stopped on the way back and picked up some sandwiches at the grocery store. While I spread things out for lunch, Ellen wrote a modest check that officially retained Carson as her attorney.

She looked so tired. It had been less than twenty-four hours since I'd seen her in the parking lot outside Carson's office, brushing off the dust and quietly trying to keep things on an even keel. She'd seemed tired then, too, but now she was even more subdued. I noticed that she wore no makeup except the foundation that covered the bruises on her face. The corduroy dress she was wearing looked like the one she'd been wearing the day before, except it was navy blue instead of gray. Her long, black hair was loose around her face, hiding her expression as she looked down at the checkbook on her lap.

Carson asked her gently about financial arrangements for her and her children. She told him that there was probably enough money in a joint checking account for two or three months of usual expenses. She added that there was a mortgage-life policy that would pay off the house. I was a little embarrassed to be talking about how my friend was going to pay us. I guessed that I would have to get used to that part of practicing law in a small town.

"And the business?" Carson asked. "Is the furniture store solvent?"

"As far as I know," she said. "My... husband..." she stopped and cleared her throat before going on, "My husband preferred to keep business details to himself."

"Where are the kids?" I asked, handing her a sandwich and a paper napkin.

She opened the folded napkin and spread it over her lap but set the sandwich aside. "In Kayenta with my mother. I took them out there yesterday after school."

Carson unwrapped his sandwich and shoved a straw down into his soda. "Why don't you start with that, Ellen? List your activities for us from the time we saw you yesterday until now," he said.

She looked at me. "You may have to translate a few things," she said.

I didn't know what to make of that. Ellen spoke English as well as I did, and I probably spoke Navajo better than she did. I couldn't remember having many conversations with her in Navajo in recent years.

She began in English. "Right after we left you in the parking lot, I took the kids to school. I got them there in time for lunch. Willard was very angry when I got home after that. He said that Jack had insulted him in public and that taking the kids to school was the same as siding with Jack."

She saw me glance at the obvious cut on her lip that had not been there the day before.

"He got a little out of hand," she said, "and I decided it would be a good time to get the kids out of the house. So when school was out, I picked them up and drove them out to Kayenta." Then she unexpectedly switched to speaking Navajo. "I took them to my mother's."

"What did she say?" Carson asked quietly.

"To her mother's house," I said haltingly, aware that my voice sounded puzzled.

Carson paused while he looked at me for a moment. "Do you understand Navajo?"

I understood Navajo, of course, but it surprised me that she was speaking it. I simply nodded and repeated, "She said she took the kids to her mother's house."

"How far is that?"

"A little over two hours' drive," I answered for her.

She started again in English, but now her voice was faintly clipped, as if she had a Navajo accent on her English, which she did not. It sounded like she was reaching back, explaining something from deep in her past, instead of something that had happened just yesterday. "I stay... stayed for dinner. Until past six o'clock. Then I... go home, but I didn't get there."

"What do you mean you didn't get there?" Carson asked.

"I had to turn around."

"You went back to Kayenta," he said.

Ellen again switched languages and spoke to me in Navajo. "I'm going to tell you about the coyote. Does this *bilagáana* understand anything about the Navajo way?"

Bilagáana is one common Navajo word for white folks. By *bilagáana* she meant Carson as a white man, not as a lawyer, and by the Navajo way she could have meant any number of traditions. I had no idea where she could be going with this.

"I don't know," I answered in English.

She continued, haltingly, in better Navajo than I remembered her speaking. "I was driving east, but a coyote crossed the road in front of me. It was just before dark, pretty close to Sage Landing."

I sat silently for a moment contemplating what she had said. According to Navajo tradition, if a coyote crossed in front of someone, especially if it was to the east, it was like a roadblock. The traveler should not continue until at least sunrise the next day. Knowing Ellen, I was a little surprised to hear *her* say this, but it hadn't actually come up before.

"She's telling me about a coyote," I said to Carson.

"What? She hit a coyote on the road?" he asked, looking from my face to hers and back again.

"No, she didn't hit it. Be patient—I'll explain in a minute." I turned to Ellen and said in English, "There's more?"

Ellen nodded and continued in Navajo. "He ran right across the road in front of me. I was barely able to stop the car before it got to the place where he had crossed. Then he looked at me, right at me. And I sat there thinking about it."

She looked over at Carson and switched back to English. "I was almost home. It didn't make any sense to stop, but it was such an obvious sign. I couldn't ignore it." Then she added, looking at me, "I didn't have any corn pollen."

I stared at her, again surprised. I didn't remember hearing her mention specifics about prayer ceremonies before. It was true, though, that if she could have used corn pollen to pray over the coyote's footprints on the road, she could have crossed its path last night.

"Explain now, Naomi," Carson said.

"She says that a coyote crossed her path in the twilight. Then it walked east of her and looked right at her."

Carson's expression said that I had more explaining to do.

"Traditional beliefs about coyotes are complicated. Some say that a coyote crossing your path is always bad luck, but some say it's only bad luck if the coyote crosses to the east. If it's to the east, it's supposed to be very bad, no matter whose version you're listening to. I'm talking about tragedy here, death maybe. Anyway, under the circumstances she's describing, a lot of Navajos would at least stop and think about it before they proceeded. Many people wouldn't go on."

"What about you?"

I thought a moment and answered honestly. "I might go on about my business and ignore the coyote. But I probably would've slowed down, maybe even stopped. It would depend on my mood, maybe, and whether anything bad had already happened that day." And, I thought but didn't say out loud, it would also depend on how much I was willing to tempt fate. Not that I'm superstitious, but come on. Those yellow eyes in the gloom? Who wouldn't be a little spooked?

Carson looked unconvinced but wanted to continue. "So a coyote crossed her path?"

"And looked at her. That's important. And the coyote came close to her on her east side. Even *I* might have turned around if I'd had the awful day that she'd had. What she's describing is a big deal—very dark. Dark enough to make you think long and hard, even if you're not very traditional. Even if you don't think you're superstitious. Why take chances, right?"

"But corn pollen would've made it okay? Is it like *magic dust* or something?"

I didn't think he meant to be disrespectful, and he was my boss, but this flippancy was not acceptable. I chose my words carefully, saying, "People's traditions can seem odd to outsiders, I know, but that is no reason to make fun of them. Please do not do that."

He had the grace to look embarrassed. "I apologize, Naomi. You're right. Please forgive me, Mrs. Highsmith, and help me understand why it was important that you didn't have corn pollen with you last night."

Ellen and I looked at each other, then at him. It was as hard to explain as turning wine into blood or bread into body. Ellen said, "Corn pollen is ... sacred. It's prayer. It restores, brings safety. And health and balance."

Grant Carson nodded. "Thank you. Now, please go on. Then what did you do?"

Ellen continued in English. "There was already trouble in my household. I feared that crossing the coyote's path would bring worse trouble to us. I turned around—I hated to do it, because it felt silly in a way, you know."

I shook my head and reached out to take her hand. No matter what I thought about the coyote and its path, she shouldn't feel silly about doing whatever she could to avoid adding to the trouble in her home. "And you drove back to Kayenta?" I said.

Ellen squeezed my hand briefly before letting go of it. "No, I had to work things out with Willard. Things couldn't go on the way they were. And encountering the coyote that way felt like a terrible warning. So I had to get home."

"Home to Sage Landing?" Carson asked. "But you were already... what did you say...almost home?"

"I drove back down past Kaibito all the way to the junction and turned west past Tuba City and went to the main highway. Then I turned north and came on home."

Carson shook his head and we waited while he did the mental math. "If you turned around up here close to town, anywhere north of Kaibito, and drove all the way around by Tuba City, it would have taken you at least three hours."

"Way more than three hours," I said.

"At least three hours, even if you were speeding." He sat quietly for several minutes. So did Ellen. I glanced at my unfinished sandwich, but I was too tense to continue eating, and I'd wrapped it up and tossed it in the wastebasket by the time Carson started talking again. "But if you drove straight from Kayenta to Sage Landing, you would have been here by, what? Maybe eight or eight-thirty. That's what the police are going to say. What's going to convince them that you went the long way around?"

"I stopped at McDonald's in Tuba City. Maybe they will remember me."

"About what time?" I asked.

"Probably nine-thirty or so."

"On a Monday that late at night, there couldn't have been too many people there," Carson said.

"A couple of people were sitting around. I just got a milkshake. Maybe the clerk will remember me."

"What flavor?"

Ellen answered immediately, "Chocolate."

"Man or woman?"

She just stared blankly at Carson.

"The clerk."

After a moment's hesitation, Ellen answered, "Young man, I think."

"You think?" I said.

"Honestly, I can't always tell with kids these days. Maybe I'm getting too old. I wasn't paying attention to that." Her voice was weary.

Carson went on. "We need something better, Ellen. I don't think this is going to work. We don't know yet whether or not you will be charged, but if you are, you need a better alibi."

She frowned. "Mr. Carson, it had been a terrible day. I didn't want to talk to anyone. I could hardly even talk to my mother when I took my children to her home. Crossing paths with the coyote after that felt like the last straw. It made me feel like... it made me dread what might happen. Turning around was the only thing I could do. By the time I got home, I was so tired that I hit my garage door with the car."

"And what time was that?"

Ellen shrugged. "Sometime past midnight."

"Anybody see it?" He was making an effort to sound encouraging rather than skeptical, I could tell. He was almost succeeding.

"My next door neighbor. He heard it and came out of the house. I was dog tired. I was afraid Willard would be very angry. I asked my neighbor to stay until I could talk to Willard, but Willard wasn't home."

"After midnight your neighbor talked to you?" Carson didn't seem as impressed by finding a new witness as I thought he should be.

"Yes, and the authorities can look at the garage door and the front of the van."

"That's good, Ellen," I said, relieved.

But Carson shook his head, and when he spoke, his tone was gentle. "It only proves when you got home, not which route you took to get there,"

Ellen took a deep breath and spoke to me instead of to Carson. "I told my neighbor about the coyote, because I was still very upset. He said that maybe nothing bad would happen, even though the coyote looked right at me, because I'd turned around." She glanced at Carson and then turned again to me. "I guess he was wrong."

I managed to restrain myself from blurting my considered opinion that the world was better off without her rat-bastard husband. And there wasn't anything else to say, really.

But Carson still had one more question. "Ellen, did you have any kind of weapon with you that night?"

She looked over at me again, like maybe she didn't quite believe that he was asking her something like this. I just shrugged, and she glared at Carson. "You mean a gun? No. Nothing like that. I picked up my children at school, and I took them to my mother's home. Why would you think I'd have a gun while I was doing that?"

Carson looked at her steadily for a moment before answering. "It's a reasonable question, Ellen, and I won't be the last person to ask it."

"Then you won't be the last person to hear this: I don't allow guns near my children. Ever. No way would I have one in the van when I picked them up and took them to Kayenta. And my mother doesn't have guns so I didn't get one there. McDonald's doesn't have guns, so I didn't get one there, either. There was no weapon in my van that night."

She picked up her purse from the floor beside the chair and said, "Anyway, I don't think they're going to charge me. I just thought that I would ask for a lawyer because it seemed like a good idea."

My boss looked grim. "Yes, it was a good idea, because I think that they *are* going to charge you. Let's look at it their way for a minute. You had a motive—the most common motive in homicide, a family fight. Until we can show otherwise, you had the opportunity. If we can get a positive identification from someone in Tuba City, we'll be okay. Otherwise, you had motive and opportunity in the eyes of an investigator."

Ellen looked down at the purse in her lap. "The investigator is Jack Miller. That's why I don't think they're going to arrest me."

Carson paused and frowned slightly. "Are you presuming on the strength of a friendship that Captain Miller won't do his job?"

"No," she said. "But I believed him when he told me not to worry."

He leaned forward across the desk and rested his hands on the surface in front of him. "Told you? Explain that."

"I don't want to get Jack in trouble. He just said not to worry—that everyone knows I couldn't have done it." She looked Carson directly in the eye and added, "Because I didn't."

Carson just nodded. Clearly he thought Ellen was being naïve. "What's your relationship with Captain Miller?"

Ellen didn't answer. Carson watched her face as he waited.

I decided to break the stalemate myself. Whether she realized it or not, Ellen was in serious trouble, and she couldn't afford to clam up on her attorney. "They were lov…very close in high school. I don't think Jack ever got over it," I said. "I'm sorry to speak out of turn, Ellen, but everything counts here. This could be death penalty stuff for whoever killed Willard."

Carson resumed his questioning. "What, exactly, did Jack say?"

Again

Ellen didn't answer, and the silence was almost like another person in the room—someone I know well. Of course Navajos aren't any quieter than anybody else, but we can be quiet for a long time. It doesn't bother us a bit. And when we're being pressured by a *bilagáana*, the more pressure, the longer the silence. *Bilagáana* don't deal well with silence.

After a couple of minutes, Ellen simply rose, nodded at Carson and then at me, and walked out of the office. We heard her start her van and drive away.

"Time for a drink," Carson said. "Let's lock up and go to the Lunker Room."

That seemed like a peculiar way to run a law office, but it's exactly what we did.

~ ~ ~

An hour later, we had driven out to the edge of the lake, secured a quiet booth toward the back of the Lunker Room, and ordered a pitcher. I was halfway through my first and only glass, and Carson was halfway through the rest of the pitcher.

On our way in, we had passed a table where Abraham Bingham was sitting. Neither of his wives seemed to be around, but he was with some woman I didn't recognize. She was probably from over the state line. I guessed that she was over forty, maybe even late forties. Her elaborately-braided strawberry blonde hair showed a few strands of gray. She was tastefully made up and dressed, warm smile, very nice-looking.

Now Carson slid out of the booth and wandered over to talk to them. The woman kept a hand on Bingham's shoulder the whole time. Finally, Carson came back to me and sat down. He resumed our conversation as if there had been no interruption.

"Her English sounded pretty good to me," he said, at last returning to the topic of our law practice. Assuming, that is, that he was talking about Ellen and not the white woman who was with Abe Bingham. "Does she usually speak Navajo with you?"

Now I was in something of a spot, but I'd had some time to think about it. Today Ellen had wanted to talk to me in Navajo, and I was beginning to understand why. I shrugged. "She talks Navajo sometimes. Her English is fine."

"What about the Navajo way? Is she that traditional?"

Again I was in a tight spot. I knew she had a cousin who followed Navajo spiritual practices, and Ellen's mother observed Navajo traditions, mostly. Ellen, on the other hand, had tried on a few other things that I knew of. She had been a Mormon for a while. Her current husband, or rather her deceased husband, attended the largest Evangelical church in town. I knew that Ellen attended church with him and made her children attend. But none of that meant that she hadn't quietly returned to traditional Navajo beliefs. I just hadn't known about it.

I knew that people who are not particularly religious when they're young and single sometimes return to their religious roots when their own children are teenagers. Maybe that's what was going on with Ellen. And here sat my boss asking what I knew about Ellen's practices. If she needed a defense attorney, Grant Carson was going to be it, so I wanted to give him the answers that would do the most good for her case.

"She has a cousin who is well-known as a traditional healer," I said. I couldn't tell if Carson spotted the evasion. "I've been to sing ceremonies with her." That, too, was true. When we were teenagers, our whole crowd used to go out to ceremonial sings once in a while. In Navajo tradition, a sing is a purposeful religious ceremony, but to us teenagers it was mostly an excuse to get together at night and hang out.

"If she gets charged, we are going to have to do better than a coyote story."

I knew he was probably right, but it frightened me. And it irritated me, too. "Calling it a 'coyote story' like that makes it sound like a Roadrunner cartoon. It isn't just a story. Ask around—almost anyone can tell you about somebody whose truck broke an axle, or whose child got sick, or who had something else really bad happen after they crossed a coyote's path."

I could feel my face getting red, and Carson looked uncomfortable as he tried to interrupt my righteous tirade. "Naomi, I didn't... I don't..."

"I'm just—she has great kids," I said, suddenly feeling as tired as Ellen had looked. "Her daughter and Kai are good friends. Her first husband died in an accident several years ago. No insurance that time—on him, I mean. No life insurance. Ellen has a high school diploma and two kids. It's been rough, but she's done a great job."

Carson studied my face. He looked like he wanted to say something but poured himself another glass of beer instead. "Where does Willard Highsmith fit into this?"

"Highsmith came along—he's a real son of a bitch by the way—and he wanted a Navajo wife. I'm sorry to say that, but it's what I think. It's what a lot of people think. He was establishing himself up here on the edge of the reservation and wanted to build up an Indian image."

"Why would that make him want a Navajo wife, specifically?"

"There are a lot more Navajo customers than white ones up here. He acted like marrying a Navajo and driving her kids around town made him a Navajo, too." I paused for a breath. "The worst thing that I can imagine is if Ellen gets taken away from those kids."

After taking a moment to digest what I had said, Carson shook his head. "Highsmith is dead. Maybe you're glad he's dead. Maybe half the town is glad he's dead. But there's going to be an investigation, and there's a high likelihood that there will be a trial and a conviction. If Ellen Highsmith killed her husband, those kids will lose their mother. If she gets arrested, our job is to minimize the consequences."

"Oh? If she gets arrested, I thought our job would be to prove she didn't do it."

"Not exactly. It's our job to prove she didn't do it if she didn't do it. We don't get to make things up."

That was a bad choice of words on his part, and he knew it as soon as they left his lips. But before I could get wound up again about how clear it was that Ellen was innocent, he changed direction and asked, "What's this business about her and Jack Miller? What do you think she meant?"

Another tight spot. I knew that Jack Miller had never gotten over Ellen, so it wasn't impossible that he might stretch the rules a bit to protect her. At least that's what I guessed. In this case, it didn't seem like such a bad thing, but Carson was sitting here sounding all straight-laced and by-the-book. So I had to be careful about how I phrased this particular piece of history.

"Well, you already gathered that they were a big item in high school. I already said that. Then Ellen met a nice guy over in Kayenta. Jack was away at college. Ellen married the new boyfriend and had two kids."

"How did Jack take that?"

I remembered a succession of sad and complicated events, not all that long ago. "He took it pretty hard. He quit school, joined the Marines. By the time he got out, Ellen's first husband had died in an automobile accident. Jack tried to pick up where they'd left off before he went away to college, but it didn't work. Maybe he just moved too soon, I don't know. She came back over here to Sage Landing to take a job as a classroom aide."

Carson started fidgeting with his glass and looking at the pitcher. I put my hand over the top of my glass.

"And Miller started trying for her again?"

"No. He was down in Tucson—his first police job. In the meantime, along came Willard Highsmith. I'll never know what she saw in him."

He raised an eyebrow. "Probably the same thing a lot of women saw in him, from what I hear."

"Maybe. He makes my skin crawl and always has, but he is…was a good-looking son of a bitch," I acknowledged.

Carson poured the last of the beer into his glass. "I imagine that the stability had some attraction, too. Like you said, it's hard raising two kids alone, working a job that doesn't pay very much."

I had to admit it—that was true, too. Ellen wanted her kids to have everything they needed. Security, a bright future, a good family life. I shuddered, thinking about that last part. It hadn't turned out so well.

Carson was watching my face, which tends to broadcast my every thought and feeling. "Did she kill him, Naomi?"

"She couldn't have," I said. "She was in Tuba City at the time."

"Did Jack Miller kill him?"

"The swimmer killed him," I said.

Chapter Seven

I walked to the office on Wednesday morning, detouring on the way to pick up a few things at the grocery store. In the snack aisle I ran into Wanda Polacca, who was putting a lot more in her basket than I was in mine. "Looks like you're getting ready for a siege," I said.

"Long boat trip ahead," she said. "I've got to go all the way uplake to Bull Banks Bay to meet with some FBI guys who have flown in there already."

"FBI? I know the lake is federal, but the FBI? For a jerk like Willard Highsmith?"

Focused on the Doritos bags she was holding—I could see her wondering if two bags would be enough or three too many—Wanda glanced up at me like she didn't know what I was talking about.

Then it clicked. She shrugged, "I don't know if they'll be getting into that one. It was so close to town. They might, but that's not why they're coming. No, a couple of people have been found dead on a boat way uplake," Wanda said. She pushed her cart over to a display of soda and put a case of it in her cart.

"Was it a boating accident?"

Wanda was looking around, probably wondering if she'd forgotten anything. "Doesn't sound like it. I don't have details yet, but I'm handling the Park Service administration side of things. I was told that the FBI guys are some sort of forensics team."

I handed her some boxes of shortbread cookies to add to her provisions, since everyone wants something sweet when they have to spend all day on the water. In my vast experience, shortbread works best since it doesn't melt or fall apart. She'd thank me later. "The lake is becoming one big crime scene," I said. "Highsmith on Monday night, then this last night."

"Yeah, isn't it?" She nodded absently. "But this happened on Monday night, too, I gather. Speaking of Highsmith, how's Ellen?"

"Better off, I'd say." That just slipped out, but it got a laugh out of Wanda.

"I bet his case is on my desk, too, but it'll have to wait," she said before our shopping carts parted ways. As I checked out, I wondered if she'd end up arm-wrestling Jack Miller for it. Highsmith had for sure been on the lake when he was shot, but whoever shot him could have been standing inside the town limits, like I was when I heard it.

When I got to the office, I was rather shocked to discover Carson already there. He was reading a two-week-old copy of the New York Times with his feet up on his desk, battered loafers shedding sand on the blotter.

"Good morning," I said, looking pointedly at his bare ankles.

He was unfazed. "Hey there, Naomi. Did you get Oreos?"

"Breakfast of Champions," I said under my breath, handing them over before shoving the remaining junk food into his mostly-empty filing cabinet.

He tore open the package and held it out, happy to share, but I just went to my desk, dropped the change into the envelope where we kept our petty cash, and got the computer going on its start-up routine.

My desk was positioned so that I could look out the window and see down along the broad sidewalk that used to be busy with shoppers when this was the location of Sage Landing's only strip mall. Now, though, seeing anyone on that sidewalk was pretty rare, so it caught my attention when I noticed a woman slowly making her way toward our office. She stopped and looked into windows as if she were shopping, but really she couldn't have been looking at anything much. She seemed out of place wandering along the cracked sidewalk, wearing a trench coat, large sunglasses, and a colorful scarf that covered most of her blond hair. She had worked her way along the building to within about twenty feet of our door before I recognized her.

It was Gail Banner, the high school principal. Since it was about ten o'clock in the morning on a school day, I was a little surprised to see her. I was even more surprised when she walked in our door and asked if Mr. Carson was in. Of course, from the inner office he could hear her just as clearly as I could, but he had the good sense to remain silent. After I stuck my head through his door and raised my eyebrows at him to signal *what the heck?*, he came out to greet her.

That done, the two of them retreated to his inner office, and he closed the door. Now they had all the privacy they needed. I wondered for a moment whether she was a client or a girlfriend. With her whispered reputation she might have been either one. Even though she was a married woman in a small town, Gail had a sort of above-it-all attitude, and she seemed to get away with it—at least she had so far. From what I'd heard about Grant Carson, her being married wouldn't have stood in his way, either.

"I may need your services, Mr. Carson," she said. "What do you normally require as a retainer?" She was used to projecting her voice across noisy classrooms, so I hadn't even needed to lean toward the wall to hear her clearly.

I heard his chair creak as he shifted his weight. "That depends on the type of case, Ms. Banner."

"I'm afraid that if there is a case at all, it will be a criminal case," she said slowly with her voice lowered a little. "I hope, rather I expect, that I will never be involved and that my coming here will later seem ridiculous to both of us."

After what felt like a long silence, Carson answered, "But at the moment I assume that it seems…prudent."

"Quite, I'm afraid."

Carson cleared his throat and said, "Our firm requires a minimum retainer of a thousand dollars."

That was the first time that I'd heard we had a minimum retainer, but I didn't hear Gail Banner fall over or anything, so I guess she took that pretty well.

After a moment, Carson continued. "If charges are brought, that retainer will be used up pretty quickly. Criminal defense can become very expensive. What is the nature of the case?"

I could hear Gail rummaging around in her purse. "It's possible that I may become implicated in the murder of Willard Highsmith."

I caught my breath so quickly that I was afraid I was going to cough and reveal our office's little flaw. I held my breath and heard no reaction from the other room.

"I don't require that the retainer be in cash," Carson said.

"I don't want to write any checks. I'm hoping that this will all go away without anyone ever knowing anything about it."

I heard Carson drop something into his desk drawer and close it. "You said you might be implicated?"

"I was present when he was killed. I left the scene and didn't report it. That's a crime right there, I think. Is that correct?"

I had to bite my tongue to keep from saying something sarcastic right out loud.

Carson just continued in his calm-lawyer voice. "Perhaps. We're still within a reasonable time frame for you to come forward so I don't think there would be any charges on that matter. As far as I know, the police are still looking for suspects. A bigger worry is that they may include you on *that* list."

She took her time before answering. "This is a delicate matter. Willard was married; I'm married. He was a public figure as I certainly am. You can see why I had hoped, and still do, that no one would know that I was there."

I could hear the wheels on Carson's chair as he rolled back away from his desk. "In all honesty, the police aren't likely to charge you for withholding evidence under the circumstances, but they could if you don't come forward pretty soon. Beyond that, there is the very real possibility that you could help them solve this case."

This seemed to offend her. "You realize that I'm not the murderer."

Carson was silent for too long for our client's comfort. For the second time in two days, I was glad to have a wall—even a flimsy one—between me and someone weathering all that silence.

"A death isn't necessarily a homicide. There may be circumstances…" He halted and cleared his throat. "You mean to say that you were in no way…"

"Of course not, and I can't shed any light on who is. Willard and I were floating a little ways up a canyon near town."

"I know…the location was pointed out to me on a map," Carson lied.

"We were swimming. That is I was already swimming—he hadn't jumped in yet. He was standing in the boat and I had dived in and was treading water ten or fifteen feet away."

"And you saw him get shot?"

"No, I heard a shot and saw Willard look up. Then there was a second shot, and he dropped."

"Did you see anyone else?"

"No, but I didn't really look. I had no idea which direction the shots had come from, and I wasn't even sure he'd been shot. I mean, he could have just dropped down for safety, I thought at first."

"What did you do?"

"Nothing. At first I did nothing. I continued to tread water, but I was in a state of shock, I guess. Willard hung over the side of the boat, his arms in the water, his head hanging limp. I panicked. I didn't think for a moment that it was an accident. Someone had shot him and that someone could probably see me as well as they could see him. At that time I was only about ten yards from the wall of the cliff so I swam over to it and found a handhold so that I could rest."

"Again, you never saw anyone?"

"We weren't far off the main channel. The cliffs along there go almost straight up for a couple of hundred feet. I didn't see anyone on the island. Frankly, I didn't try to scan the cliffs looking for anyone. I just wanted to get the hell out of there. I was afraid to swim back to the boat. I was in shadow and the boat was in moonlight."

I could hear Carson's pencil scratching notes. "So you swam away. That's a long distance from the nearest place to climb out of the water."

"Tell me about it. I had no choice but to swim along the base of the cliff wall, stopping to find a handhold in the rock when I needed one. Finally, I could turn south toward the dam. A half mile later I could climb out."

He paused for more notes. "At that old construction road that runs down near the east side of the dam?"

"Yes."

"From there you were only a few hundred yards from the nearest restaurant. You could have called the police."

In a voice filled with exaggerated patience, Gail Banner answered, "No, I couldn't have. In the first place, it was past eleven by then and everything was closed. In the second place, I was without any bathing suit... we were ... skinny dipping."

I knew that they were talking about a murder in the other room and that it was a serious matter, but I had to suppress a chuckle just the same. First of all, the details of Willard Highsmith's death had not saddened me at all. Second, the mental image of Gail Banner stuck naked in the desert by the dam should have struck a sympathetic nerve. After all, I hadn't liked it much when a couple of guys had thought that it was me streaking around. But I admit that I felt no such sympathy. Too bad I would never be able to tell Stitch and Bitch about this one.

"You walked home?"

"Very cautiously. I crossed the highway into the low desert that borders part of the golf course. Then I worked my way up the slope into my neighborhood and eventually got home without being seen. I got into my pajamas, slipped into bed, and lay there awake all night."

"Ms. Banner, I can understand why you fled the scene. But once you got to safety, did it occur to you that he might still be alive, in need of help?" Carson managed to sound curious rather than judgmental.

"Mr. Carson," she said, sounding so frosty that he could probably see her breath in the air, "have you ever seen a dead person? That was what I saw, there in the moonlight while I hid in the shadows. He was beyond any need for help. I, on the other hand, am in need of yours. Now."

There was another long silence before Carson answered. "You said that you weren't seen, but you were."

She sighed and said, "I was afraid of that. There have been a few strange looks around the building. Not much, just enough to make me wonder. How do you know?"

I heard Carson's desk chair creak and could imagine him leaning back in it. I doubted that he was enjoying this moment as much as I was, but he didn't sound terribly concerned, either. "The police are aware that a nude woman was seen walking through the Long Vista neighborhood at about midnight on Monday night. I don't know whether or not the witnesses know who it was they were seeing."

"Shit!"

With what sounded to me like some possible amusement sneaking into his voice, Carson replied, "Indeed. Deep shit." He paused—I could only imagine the deadly glare she must have given him across that desk—before continuing in a more professional tone. "My first piece of advice is that you go to the police and tell them everything. They will be as discreet as they can."

"But I don't want anyone to know about this."

"That ship, as they say, has sailed, Ms. Banner."

I heard Gail Banner get up out of her chair, and I could hear the tapping of her heels as she paced on Carson's threadbare carpet. I heard her rummaging in her purse again and then the click of her lighter and her first drag on a cigarette. It occurred to me that she hadn't asked Carson if she could smoke in the office, and if she had looked around at all, she would notice that there were no ashtrays. But I decided to cut her some slack on that. I figured that if I had run through the desert naked after swimming a couple of miles to get away from a murdered philanderer, I might take up smoking myself.

"No," she said finally. "Nobody knows about this, and maybe nobody ever will."

I could hear Carson's desk drawer open and again the sound of paper rustling. "You may as well take your money back," he said. "I haven't earned any of it yet. If it goes as you hope, you won't need an attorney. If it doesn't, you'll need a good deal more money than that."

I had to grip the edge of my desk to keep myself from running in and snatching the money out of his hand.

Now I had the final proof that my employer didn't know anything about being an attorney. He would never be able to pay my salary, so I might as well quit right now. The first principle of law, which he obviously didn't understand, was that you never give back any part of a retainer. I think I learned that the first night of my first law course. It was just my luck that I'd get a boss who didn't know it. I had sneaked a peek at the balance in the office checkbook the day before, and now I realized why it was so precariously low.

After Gail Banner left the office, Carson just looked at me and shook his head with a tight smile that warned off any questions. Then he said, "I'm going fishing. Tell people I'm out on a case."

Since I knew that his boat was out of commission, I wondered how he was going to do that. I suspected that he might have meant something else by the expression "going fishing."

"Will I be able to reach you?"

"Probably not," he said as he walked out.

He hadn't returned by the time I closed the office. There had been no calls. It occurred to me that this might turn out to be the easiest job in town —and that I might never get paid for it.

~ ~ ~

After dinner I found some time to sit with my knitting while my kids did their homework. I have to admit that I was feeling pretty chipper. A terrible man who treated good people badly was now out of their lives forever. A woman I didn't much like or respect, and who clearly thought she was better than everyone else, had been given a healthy dose of embarrassment. It was almost as if I were being rewarded for all those nights of sitting at home with my kids when I could have been out doing who-knows-what with who-knows-who.

My smugness was punctured right at bedtime. The phone rang and I glared at my daughter for receiving phone calls beyond the allowed hour. She was able to glare right back at me as she handed me the phone. The call was from Grant Carson.

"Bad news," he said.

Somehow he didn't have to tell me what the bad news was. I knew.

"They've arrested Ellen Highsmith," he said.

I nodded, though he couldn't see me. I choked a little before answering. "What happens now?"

"Can you come down and meet me at the police station? I'll understand ... the kids I know... but can you come?"

"I'll be right there." I hung up and looked at Kai, who was looking at me like I sometimes look at her. "You lock up and get to bed, sweetie. I have to go out."

"I knew it," she said. "You have to work late with Mr. Carson." She held her fingers up in quotation marks around the words *work late*. "Like I couldn't see this coming," she added.

I patted the couch next to me. "Sit down here for a minute, honey."

She rolled her eyes before parking herself on the other end of the couch and turning her face away from me. I let that go without comment and said, "It's Ellen Highsmith. She's been arrested for..."

"Murder! Oh my god!" She jumped up and threw her hands in the air. "She *couldn't* have done it, Mom! I've known her all my *life*!" It seemed that even my sensible down-to-earth daughter couldn't help acting like a drama queen, at least a little, given the opportunity.

I avoided mentioning that our having known Ellen for a long time probably wasn't legally relevant. Instead, I told her, "Mr. Carson is her attorney. I'm sure he'll get her out soon. Of course she didn't do it. But right now I have to go over and help."

I grabbed my keys, but as I headed for the door, I saw Kai sneaking a glance at the phone. "Don't even think about it," I said.

"What, mom?" Little Miss Innocent had no idea what I was talking about.

"It's past ten. Besides, if I were the one in jail, how would you feel if Ellen's kids got busy calling all their friends with the news?"

She sighed one of those you're-ruining-my-life-again sighs. "Fine!" Without another word, she stomped down the hall to her room.

~ ~ ~

Disclosure is a word that means that the prosecution has to show you what they've got on your client. The police aren't the ones who have to make disclosure, and the prosecution only has to do it later in the process, but Jack Miller stepped right over that boundary and began his own version of disclosure almost as soon as we arrived at the police station. He was waiting for us in the empty front lobby.

"The chief went for a warrant this afternoon and they searched High-smith's house. It's pretty routine to search the victim's house, and I was surprised that the chief got a warrant instead of just asking Ellen. Anyway, they found a gun—a .357 Magnum. Apparently it was hidden."

"Hidden how?" Carson asked.

"I'm told it was under a drawer in Highsmith's nightstand. I was assigned to other duties at the time so I've just read the report."

"The chief thinks it was deliberate hiding place?"

"That's his take on it."

"Who was the supervising officer?" Carson asked.

"Chief Rodriguez himself. He and Peggy Thomas conducted the search. She wrote the report."

Carson smiled briefly at the mention of Peggy and got back to the subject of the gun. "So the gun was concealed in a nightstand beside the bed. How do they know it was *his* nightstand?"

"Their beds are in separate rooms. The pistol was *underneath* a drawer resting on top of a thin piece of plywood that had been stapled under the drawer from the cabinet below—a prepared hiding place. It wasn't original to the furniture."

"Loaded?"

"Yeah, jacketed rounds."

This sounded awful, but I didn't quite know why. I interrupted Jack. "So what? What does that mean?"

Jack looked around nervously to make sure that no one was listening to him and lowered his voice. "The bullet that killed Highsmith went right through his chest, clean and fast. It wasn't a hollowpoint, and it wasn't a lower velocity pistol like a .38."

"Probably a high-powered rifle," Carson said. "If the shot was fired at much distance at all, even the .357 would have stopped in his chest, so the weapon you found couldn't have been what killed him."

"Not so fast. If the shooter was reasonably close, these bullets would have done the job. There is no slug for us to examine. It went into the lake." Then Jack added under his breath, "I wish this gun had gone with it."

It shocked me to hear him speak that candidly, and Carson even looked around nervously. "I'm sure I didn't hear you say that, Jack. Besides, did Ellen actually know the gun was in the house? She told me that she doesn't allow guns anywhere near her kids, and she sounded pretty…definite about it. Maybe she didn't even know it was there."

Jack thought about that. "It's possible that she didn't know."

Carson continued. "Actually, I'm glad you guys found the pistol where you did because if my client had used that pistol to shoot her husband, she *would* have thrown it in the lake. I think the fact that it was at her home indicates that she didn't shoot anybody with it. Has it been fired?"

Miller lowered his voice. "We can't tell, but it has sure as hell been cleaned. It was fully loaded, no spent cartridge."

"Doesn't prove a thing. I'm surprised you guys made the arrest." Carson looked at me and frowned slightly. Then he moved his head from side to side just once.

I knew I was supposed to be getting some kind of message from that, but I didn't understand in time. "Willard wasn't shot from up close," I said.

Carson looked up at the ceiling and rolled his eyes. "What she means is that we're *betting* that he was shot from a distance."

His attempt to cover for me didn't work. My cop friend faced me with a scowl on his face. "What do you know that you didn't tell us already?"

"Nothing."

"You told us you couldn't tell where the shots came from. You said that you didn't even think that it was gunshots at the time."

"I didn't. It just makes sense, is all I meant." I looked up at my frowning boss. "I've been thinking about it, and we've talked about it, and it would make sense that if I could see the boat that well from up on the cliffs…that someone could shoot him from up there. I mean, where else would they be? There's no way to get down from the top along there."

Carson asked, "What about that? What was the angle of entry? Wouldn't that help identify where the shot came from?"

"Inconclusive," Jack said. "The chief's pet theory is that Ellen was on the boat with him." He looked at Carson. "Naomi heard a swimmer. Rodriguez thinks it could have been her."

I bit my lip.

"So he thinks Mrs. Highsmith swam back to town with a .357 Magnum tucked in her swimsuit?" Carson said skeptically. "Then cleaned it and loaded it and hid it in her dead husband's room?"

"Remember that Willard was naked. There was that report of the naked woman."

"And how well do you think Mrs. Highsmith could swim with a couple of pounds of steel in her hand?"

Miller nodded. "The chief's other theory is that there was another boat —one Naomi didn't see."

I continued to keep my mouth shut. So far, I could see that Carson was letting the police develop theories that he thought he could explode easily if he had to. He had a few surprises ready if he had to bring Gail Banner into it.

"Wouldn't Naomi have heard another boat?" he said.

"Not if the killer was cool-headed enough to wait. How long were you up there before you left, Naomi?"

"Five minutes, maybe ten."

Carson said, "Highsmith was found in his boat, right? So even if someone shot him from another boat, it couldn't have been Ellen because *Highsmith* had their boat."

Jack checked again to make sure that no one was coming down the hall. "There's an officer back in the cell area," he said, "but Chief Rodriguez has gone home. Anyway, the Highsmiths actually own *two* boats. He was in their family boat, a nineteen-foot open-bow with a big outboard, but the furniture store also has a flashy inboard ski boat that Highsmith liked to race around in, one of those that's all nose and engine." He paused and looked at me and shrugged.

I said nothing.

"They keep the larger family boat at the marina and the ski boat on its trailer at the house." He halted for a second. "It's missing," he added.

"Jesus!" Carson said. "Are you sure? Maybe it's in the shop for repairs."

"We've been checking. So far, none of the shops have it."

"What does Ellen say?" Carson asked.

"Nothing. She hasn't said a word since we picked her up."

"And she waited until now to ask for me?"

"She hasn't even done that," Jack said. "According to Rodriguez, she hasn't said a word."

"Not even to you?" I asked, earning a stern glance from Carson.

"I've been ordered to stay away from her. The rest of the staff knows that, too, so my hands are tied. I don't know if she'd talk to me. I don't even know if she'll talk to you. I called you to fill you in, is all. If Rodriguez gets wind of it, he might be pissed off." He smiled, "Way I see it, it just makes sense to keep the defense attorney informed. We don't want to be accused of denying counsel, do we?"

"We're leaving," Carson said. "Get Rodriguez to call me in the morning even if she doesn't ask for me."

I opened my mouth to protest that Ellen had to see us, had to let us help her. But my boss gently steered me toward the door.

Chapter Eight

Fɪʀsᴛ thing Thursday morning Carson was standing by my desk trying to come up with a list of tasks for me that I hadn't already thought of. Three-Steps Larry walked in, nodded at me, and flashed a big smile.

"Hey, Grant, you got a minute? I need a little advice. Got something I'd like to run past you."

Carson's face showed mild annoyance as he answered, "You need some legal advice, Larry?" He turned to me. "Naomi, meet Larry Sabano."

I said, "We've met. Hi, Larry."

I guess I'd better explain about Three-Steps Larry. He'd earned the nickname because of a couple of events involving angry husbands. Supposedly, on two separate occasions, he'd sort of been forced to act out the lyrics of an old Lynyrd Skynyrd song—one where a guy begs for "three steps toward the door."

I should add that Three-Steps was not really my type. Sure, he was blond and muscular, with smile-crinkles around his eyes, and, yes, he usually wore a charming boyish grin. I could see how women might find him appealing, but he wasn't much for conversation beyond a handful of pickup lines, and he had probably never read a book in his life. It was hard to imagine him in any kind of relationship. Still, when we were on the same crew for a power plant overhaul in one of my temp jobs in the past, I found that working with him night after night had led to some interesting fantasies.

Three-Steps ignored me and walked right past us into Carson's inner office. I could hear him settling down into a chair in the other room, and he said, "Not a legal consultation—nothing that formal, you know? Just a little man to man between friends."

Carson winked at me and stepped into his office and closed the door. "I'm going to have to charge you for the time, Larry. This is my office during working hours, and things are piling up right now."

"Don't you have one of those free-initial-consultation policies?"

"Is this an injury case involving a rich person or a big corporation?"

"No, it's just a simple question."

"Then I don't have one of those free-consultation policies."

"I'm just kidding, Grant. Of course, I mean to pay you. This is business."

"Go ahead, Larry. But keep it short for now."

"Okay, you remember on Monday night when I ran that investment idea past you?"

"That wasn't on Monday night, Larry. I think that was on Saturday night."

"No, I think it was Monday night at the Lunker Room. It was about 9:30 or 10:00. Anyway, it doesn't matter. You were pretty soused by then—just like you were on Saturday night."

"Whatever," Carson said. "You asked me about a scam you were thinking of pulling."

"Scam?" Larry said indignantly.

"You were going to advertise an investment opportunity—a land development—and promise that the investors could not lose their money. If I remember correctly, the idea was going to require a lot of front capital."

"That's it. And it wasn't a scam, it was a business proposition."

"Larry, are you planning a fraud? Because if you're planning a swindle of some kind, you can't come in here and ask me questions about it in advance. That's not the way it works. I think I told you the other night that you have to go out and commit fraud and get arrested and *then* come see me and let me help you prove that it wasn't a fraud. I can't sit and help you plan it here any more than I could at the Lunker Room."

"You pierce my heart, Grant. I'm not looking for help with a scam. I'm …uh… thinking of providing an investment opportunity worth millions. There could be some fat legal fees in this." He paused and then added, "Huge."

"I don't know what you're up to, Larry, but I'm kind of busy these days."

Three-Steps Larry's voice took on just the amount of sad concern you would expect if he were a high-school actor in a school play. "Oh, sure, the Highsmith murder. I heard, terrible thing."

"Yeah, terrible." Carson paused for a moment. "Hey, you've had a couple of run-ins with the Big Chief. Where *were* you on Monday night? It would help my client if I could pin this on you."

Sabano was oddly quiet. "Don't even kid around about stuff like that, Grant."

"Gotchya!" Carson said. "Better figure your alibi for Monday." He chuckled. "Seriously, Larry, when you're ready to go into specifics about setting up a corporation or something for this investment, make an appointment with Naomi. I'm sure we'll have more time in a couple of weeks."

"In the meantime," Sabano said, "I'd like to give you a retainer—make it official, you know?"

"Make what official?"

"That you're my attorney on this matter. That you're my attorney of record for anything. That we have an attorney-client relationship."

"This was just a friendly chat."

I heard Larry Sabano squirming in his chair. Then he said, "No, really, I want to give you a retainer. How about a thousand bucks? I want you to know that I'm serious."

"The size of the retainer normally depends on the type of legal service you will need, but a grand will get things started for just about anything."

Now I heard Three-Steps walking across the room and rustling some paper.

A moment later Carson spoke again. "Usually, we take a check."

"So in this case it's cash. Surely you take cash?"

A chair squeaked as Carson stood up. I hoped he was taking the cash.

"I really do have a big thing coming up, Grant. There'll be lots of money in it."

"I hope I can be of help when the time comes," Carson said as he opened the door. Larry gave me a smile and a salute as he walked out.

After he left, Carson turned to me. "Don't hold your breath waiting for us to have a big corporate deal with Larry Sabano. That guy is all bullshit."

It seemed to me that a thousand dollars wasn't exactly bullshit, but I didn't say so.

~ ~ ~

The rest of Thursday went by without much news about Willard Highsmith's murder. Ellen spent the day in silence, according to Peggy Thomas when I met her for a late lunch in the park across from our office. She also told me that Captain Miller had been placed on leave. Officially, he'd accumulated too much unused vacation time, but actually Rodriguez had ordered him to take a few days off and to stay away from the Highsmith murder case. Jack's feelings about Ellen were no secret.

"I can understand why the chief sent him home," Peggy said, "but we're already short-staffed as it is."

"Busy, huh?"

"Everything's rushed, and then stuff falls through the cracks, even important stuff."

"Like what stuff?"

She shrugged. "Like getting all the forms done. Like putting things into the computer—I'm way behind on that. And getting evidence logged in while it's piling up. When Jack's there, he can check up behind me, like he did yesterday. I'd overlooked stuff when I was logging in a bunch of evidence. There was a Navajo medicine bundle—never saw one before, and I guess I just didn't pay attention. Anyway, he pointed it out to me, and I logged it. With him gone, mistakes like that might not get caught."

"A *jish*? Whose was it?" I asked.

"It was from the search at Ellen's. I hadn't logged it into the list of stuff that was in the evidence box, and Jack brought it to my attention—first time I'd noticed it."

Now, Jack was a white guy who had moved to Sage Landing when he was in grade school. And medicine bundles are never just floating around in plain sight, so how would he know a *jish* when he saw it? I tried to think back to the sings I'd gone to when I was in high school. Had he been there with Ellen, watching the singer with his buckskin bag of sacred objects? "What did it look like?"

"It was a very small pouch tied with a thong," Peggy said, holding her thumb and forefinger just a couple of inches apart, "which was probably why I hadn't noticed it at first. Looked like leather or some kind of hide, with beading on it. It was pretty but kind of grubby, like it had been handled a lot."

"Yeah, that's not actually a *jish*—uh, medicine bundle. Which is good, because those shouldn't be lying around anybody's house." Or sitting in an evidence box, for that matter. "It sounds to me more like a little pollen sack. Lots of families might have them, from their grandparents or something like that."

Peggy brushed invisible crumbs from her lap and stood up to head back to the station. "Well, for now it's listed as a medicine bundle, and I'll check with the chief to see if he wants me to change it in the log."

So Jack Miller hadn't actually known what he was looking at. Still, I was surprised that they had it at all. Thinking about it, though, it seemed more likely to be something Willard Highsmith would pick up up in some kind of shady transaction than something Ellen would have. On the other hand, I recalled what she'd said about not being able to cross the coyote's path without pollen to pray over it. Maybe she really was more religious than I'd realized.

~ ~ ~

On Friday morning I got a call from the police station before Grant arrived at the office. Chief Rodriguez had gone personally to Gail Banner's office at the high school as soon as she got there, and they had left for the station right after that. The high school kids sure had plenty to talk about now.

She called for Grant in what sounded like a state of controlled hysteria. I told her that Mr. Carson would come to the station as soon as he got in.

I was glad he told me to go with him to meet with her. After a few formalities, we were ushered into a room where Mrs. Banner was waiting for us. She wasn't in handcuffs or anything, but she looked plenty prisoner-like as she stood to shake Carson's outstretched hand.

"I guess your predictions proved correct," she said. "Here I am."

"Under arrest?" Carson asked.

"Not yet." She looked toward me. "Can't we talk privately?"

Carson gestured for me to sit down. He even pulled a chair out for me. "This is a private as it gets. I need my assistant to take notes and be able to remind me of everything that goes on here at the station."

She sat down across the table from me and tried to smile as she nodded assent. "As you said yesterday, I was seen on Monday night. By Tuesday night a couple of my least-favorite students had told friends that it *might* have been me that they saw."

"Sounds like idle speculation, malicious innuendo. Wouldn't make it to court."

Mrs. Banner shook her head. "Small town, Mr. Carson. Some other kids heard it and told their parents. One of the parents called a School Board member who, in turn, called Chief Rodriguez."

"That was last night?"

"Yes. I don't know what happened after that, but the Chief came to my office first thing this morning and asked if I was willing to come to the station to help in his investigation. He was kind enough to let me drive myself over here after he'd left the school."

"Has he interviewed you yet?"

"No, because I asked to see my attorney."

"A wise move."

She laughed "Says the attorney, but it didn't seem to help me any with the chief."

"Nope, never seems to be the move they want, but you need to be very cautious with every move you make now."

Mrs. Banner put her elbows on the table and clasped her hands in front of her face. "Will Rodriguez give out any information about this?"

"Absolutely not," Carson answered, "but, as you said, it's a small town. Everyone knows by now that Highsmith was murdered. A lot of people know that Rodriguez came to see you this morning and that you left the school shortly after that."

I chimed in with, "By tonight everyone will know that, so even though the police won't say anything…."

"I know," she said. "What now?"

"Go ahead and tell the chief everything you know. He won't hold you after that. I'll stay with you until that's over." Carson turned to me. "Naomi, please go back to the office and hold down the fort."

I walked back to the office and waited. An hour later, Carson came in carrying two large cardboard cups of coffee and a check for three thousand dollars. He gestured for me to follow him into his inner office, handing me the check and one of the coffees after I sat down. I set the check on his desk where I could admire it while he explained.

"This turn of events weakens the case against Ellen Highsmith in three ways."

I reluctantly looked up from the check. "Great! How?"

"First, it eliminates the possibility that Ellen was with her husband on their boat. She wasn't the mysterious swimmer you heard."

"If Gail Banner owns up to that," I said.

"Don't worry. She already told the chief. She'll just try to explain it in such a way that it doesn't implicate her in the murder."

I took a sip of coffee and thought about that. "Okay, what else?"

"Second, it makes it very unlikely that Ellen shot Willard from their other boat, the missing speedboat."

"Because…?"

"The timing—Ellen would've had to get home, hook up the speedboat, drive out and launch it by herself...park the van. You get the picture."

I tried to think like a juror. Those were both good arguments for Ellen's case, though they didn't bode so well for our new client, Mrs. Banner. "You said three ways it was good for Ellen?"

"Most important, this makes it nearly impossible that the pistol found in Ellen's house could have been the murder weapon. Even if she is a hell of a pistol marksman, Ellen couldn't have hit Willard from anywhere within sight of the boat. And, actually, a hell of a marksman would know better than to try a pistol shot at that distance."

Again channeling my inner jury member, I asked, "Lucky shot, maybe?"

"Not out of the question, but at any distance, a pistol bullet would have lost too much velocity to go cleanly through Highsmith's chest."

"So why is Rodriguez still holding Ellen?"

"Motive, for sure, and until something proves otherwise, she had opportunity."

"She was in Tuba City at the time of the shooting."

He gave me a look. "Says the coyote, but no one else so far."

I didn't much like his skepticism. Hoping to change his attitude, I told him about the little pollen pouch that had been taken into evidence from Ellen's house. He didn't seem very impressed, so I moved on. "What about Gail Banner?"

"They won't hold her for long is my guess. At least not for now."

And with that, he was done with the subject. He stood up and threw his cardboard cup into the trash. "Let's close up shop and go out to lunch. We'll eat out at the marina if it's okay with you. I want to take a look at my boat."

While he was driving me out to the marina, I thought of another question. "What about the pistol? You explained that it couldn't be the murder weapon, but where did it come from?"

"Rodriguez filled me in on that yesterday after I left the office. Registration records showed that it was originally bought in Salt Lake City by a Utah a resident who lives in Bluff. He told the sheriff out there that he sold it at a yard sale a year ago. He was out of work at the time and held a big yard sale—sold a lot of valuable stuff, including several guns. He said it had been very busy, and he'd made no notes or records about the sales."

I conjured up a mental map of the vast territory that is generally called the Four Corners region.

"Bluff, Utah, is not all that far from Kayenta," he continued, clearly reading from the same mental map that I was using.

The distance was about seventy miles or so. That's not very far by high-desert standards, and big yard sales out there would routinely draw people from a hundred miles away.

"And Ellen's mother lives in Kayenta," Carson went on, belaboring the obvious. "Did Highsmith go over there very often?"

"I don't know. Sometimes, maybe."

"And how about Ellen?" He was gazing straight ahead, eyes focused on the road.

I didn't like where this was going. "Look, she told you that there were no guns at her mother's home when she took the kids over there Monday afternoon."

He still didn't look over at me. "Rodriguez verified that Ellen stayed for dinner that day, but she left Kayenta before seven."

This was getting tiresome. "But she turned around between Kaibeto and Sage Landing. She drove all the way around to Highway 89 and came up here that way." That was the rest of the story, and the point needed to be made again, because he had never shown what I considered proper confidence in what Ellen had said.

He looked over at me before saying, without any expression at all, "After being stopped by a coyote, you mean."

Now I was the one avoiding eye contact by turning to look straight ahead through the windshield. "Am I to conclude that Chief Rodriguez isn't buying that?"

"It's pretty hard for him to believe. I admit that it's pretty hard for me to believe. What about you?"

I just shook my head. Yes, it was unusual, but it was certainly plausible, and it was all we had to go on. Before I could decide how to answer, Carson spoke up again.

"Will the pollen pouch help us show that Ellen was serious enough about traditional Navajo beliefs to have done what she says she did?"

For all I knew, it might. But that really wasn't the point. "The main thing for me is just that—what you just said. The fact that she *said* she turned around. I've known Ellen since elementary school, and I don't think she's ever lied to me."

"But you don't sound like you think she's really all that religious."

I thought about my answer for a moment. It's not that I was trying to be cagey, but I had been turning that question over in my mind for days. "Religion is a funny thing. It seems to me that for most people it comes and goes," I said. "There are periods of your life when you feel religious. Other times, you don't. I think that can happen moment to moment or at least day to day sometimes."

"I'd have to take your word for that," Carson said.

We drove into the parking lot at the marina and parked. On our way into the restaurant I said, "But it's not going to be very convincing to the prosecution, is it?"

"Other things are working for us. The pistol is pretty much out of the question now, for one thing. Let's hope that some other helpful stuff comes up."

"How much of Gail Banner's money are we going to keep?" I asked, and I couldn't help smiling.

"That depends on how much my boat repairs cost me." Carson laughed.

"And what about taking money from two clients in the same case? Couldn't they have conflicting interests?"

Carson looked at me with an expression not unlike my son used when I caught him sneaking candy into his room. "That's probably not a problem. It might be a bit iffy at some point, but they haven't charged Gail Banner with anything. If they *do* charge her, they'll be dropping charges against Ellen. You see? We won't ever end up defending both of them."

I gave him a stern-mother look. "You probably shouldn't have taken retainers from both of them."

"Nope," he said.

~ ~ ~

After a nice Friday fried-fish lunch, during which I had more coffee and Carson had three beers, we went down to the docks. It occurred to me while we walked that my daughter would have raised serious objections. I was now on my way to Grant Carson's notorious cruiser, the *Deep Inn*. I had to admit that I was curious about how he had decorated the interior.

As it turned out, I didn't get a chance to see that because all he was interested in was opening the cover of an engine compartment and poking around. It appeared to me that he knew just about as much about what he was looking at as I did, which was next to nothing.

He glanced up at me. "Does it look to you like any work's been done in here?"

"How would I know?"

"Well, look at this. It's dusty and sandy in here. I think it looks about the same as the last time I looked in here. Margolin said I needed some engine stuff, but the engine is all closed up and dusty."

"Engines," I said, "plural. You have two engines. You're just looking at one of them. The cover on the other one is over here."

He looked up at me with a frown. "I knew that." He turned around and opened the other engine cover.

I had to admit that I couldn't see any signs of work on either engine. "Do you remember what he said was wrong?"

"Drive clutches? Something about the drive and a clutch. Actually, more than one clutch, I think."

Now I was getting a chance to show off a little. Even though I knew practically nothing about boats, I knew that this one had inboard engines with outdrives. A person couldn't live on this lake all of her life and go boating countless times and not know a few basics. "The drives aren't in there. Those are the engine compartments. The outdrives are those things with the propellers on them that are tilted up at the back of the boat."

Carson stepped back and looked over the edge. "These?"

"Yes, sir."

"And the clutches are in here somewhere?"

"Got me," I said. "That was the extent of my knowledge. These are the engines, those are the outdrives."

"Well, it doesn't look to me like anything's been done back here either. Supposedly Margolin's discovered all kinds of bad parts, rare parts, exquisitely valuable parts, that have to be replaced. But how would he know that if he hasn't dismantled these drives?"

I just shook my head and shrugged.

"I mean there should be parts lying all over the place and grease and stuff like that, shouldn't there?"

"Or he put it all back together. Did you agree to have the work done?"

The question seemed to stump him. "Not exactly, sort of, I think."

"If I were a repair man, and I didn't have a firm commitment to go ahead with the repair, I'd probably put everything back together so that it wouldn't get all rusty and dirty."

Carson leaned way over and stared at one of the drives and then the other. "I don't think these have been taken apart at all. He's talking about at least several hundred dollars in repairs. Drive clutches, all kinds of names of parts, stuff that's hard to get and expensive."

I didn't want to argue with my boss and I certainly didn't want to give any endorsement to Chuck Margolin, but it seemed to me that Carson was overlooking a point. "Isn't this a pretty old boat?" If memory served me, this big cruiser had been for sale for a couple of years before Grant Carson had come to town and bought it and renamed it. In fact, it might have been for sale for four or five years, maybe more, and it had been referred to more than once by friends of mine as "that old cruiser."

"Well, yeah, but that's part of its charm. There's woodwork on this boat that you can't even get today—extinct wood. You should see the stateroom."

He stepped toward the doorway that led down, down, down into the very depths of infamy.

I wanted to see the interior, but I suddenly got cold feet and caution prevailed for once. All I needed was for someone to see us walking down into the boat's innards. My kids would hear about it by dinner time, and I'd never hear the end of it. "No thanks. I'll take your word for it, but if it's an older boat, maybe it's true that the parts are hard to get."

"It's not that old. Well, it's not really old. I mean these are Volvo engines. They still make Volvo marine engines, don't they?"

He didn't even seem to notice that I had declined his invitation to go inside the *Deep Inn.* That was a little disturbing in its own way, but I managed to stay on topic. "I think so, but the models change. I'm not the one to ask about this stuff. What about Abe Bingham? Doesn't he have a nice boat? Maybe he could give you some advice."

"He did. He advised me to be careful about Chuck Margolin. That's why we're here today."

I looked along the floating dock toward the shoreline and saw a man starting out toward us. "Speak of the devil," I said.

By the time Margolin reached the boat, Carson had straightened up and put on a smile. "Afternoon, Chuck," he said.

Margolin nodded with his own broad smile. "Ready to do some horse trading, Grant?" he said. "I've still got that legal work for you."

"Oh, well, I've decided to keep things on a cash basis, Chuck. I wanted to go over the costs on this job again, but I'll be paying you for the work."

Chuck Margolin's smile disappeared. "I thought we were going to keep things more informal."

Carson shook his head. "I got to thinking about that, and I decided that neither one of us wants to get into any tax difficulties. Have you got a written estimate ready?"

Margolin was quiet for a moment. "Let me see if I can remember some of what my man said." He looked skyward. "These drives have sliding clutches." He paused again. "And you got your clutch dog springs... and tilt clutch cover gaskets." He paused again, and it looked like he was running out of steam. "Then everything is times two—you got two drives. And this is all old-model parts."

"So you *will* write that all up and give me an estimate, a firm estimate?"

"Sure." Margolin looked down at the dock. "It might even come out a little lower than I thought before," he said as he turned to walk away.

"Good," Carson said. "Always glad to hear that."

We closed the engine covers while Chuck Margolin got out of earshot.

"Why do you suppose he would be lowering the price?" I asked.

"Because when he had to itemize the parts, he couldn't come up with a very long list. It has occurred to Mr. Margolin that he is about to give something in writing to an attorney." Carson patted the top of an engine cover, friendly but cautious, like it was pet that wasn't very well trained.

While we drove back to town, Carson was unusually quiet, and I figured he was brooding about his boat. But he surprised me as we drove up to the office.

"Let's hope we don't find out that guy in Utah also sold Highsmith a deer rifle," he said.

We walked over to the office, and I unlocked the door.

"Do you think she could shoot one?" he asked as he followed me into the room.

I knew she could plink with an old .22 that we fooled around with as teenagers, but that was different. I was pretty sure it was different. "Carson, she was the homecoming queen, for god's sake. Where would a girl like that learn to shoot a rifle?"

Chapter Nine

I took the weekend off, and, as far as I could tell, so did most everybody else in Sage Landing. I wouldn't have heard anything at all had it not been for a couple of hard-working friends. Peggy, who'd pulled a weekend shift at the police station, let me know that Ellen was still not saying anything to anyone. Wanda, who'd been patrolling the Park Service land along the river, called me on Sunday with the juicy news that my boss had spent Saturday night camping down at Lee's Ferry. His camping companion had been an attractive assistant manager from the supermarket. Everyone knew that her boyfriend was out of town on a tour of duty with his National Guard unit, and Carson wasn't her first rumored dalliance. As far as I knew, though, he was the first one who was about twice her age.

For all the weekend's peace and quiet, Monday morning began with an interesting development in the person of Dr. Banner, husband of the naked night-time walker. He arrived at our office shortly after I opened and announced that he had an appointment with Mr. Carson. I was unaware of this, but I didn't let on.

Sure enough, Grant Carson showed up at the office bright and early only a few minutes after Dr. Banner. He even had shoes on. They went into Carson's office and closed the door for complete privacy.

"I think I may need to retain your services, Mr. Carson."

I held my breath and leaned toward the wall.

"I gathered as much from what you said on the telephone last night, Dr. Banner. What can I do for you?"

"This is a very delicate matter. Are you sure that we have enough...uh... privacy?"

"Our office is small, as you can see, and some of what is discussed in here may be overheard by my professional assistant from time to time. But I assure you, Dr. Banner, that Ms. Manymules is the very soul of discretion. In all my long association with her, I've never known her to betray a professional trust."

That made me wonder how much Dr. Banner knew about the relatively short time Grant Carson had been in practice in Sage Landing. It also made me wonder how much Dr. Banner knew about how long I had been a paralegal—or sort of a paralegal. Nevertheless, it seemed to satisfy Banner because he continued in a lowered voice.

"It has occurred to me that I may be implicated in this Highsmith thing."

"The death of Willard Highsmith?"

"Yes."

Carson was quiet for a moment, and I figured that he must be weighing what he'd just heard against what he already knew. Finally, he said, "I'm already involved in that case in a peripheral way, of course. I can give you general legal advice, but if it happened that you were actually indicted, that is to say a defendant, I might not be able to take your case. Well, I could not take your case under my current circumstances. However, if circumstances were to change by the time of that unfortunate eventuality, I might be able to defend you."

If Banner's reaction was anything like mine, he was trying to sort through what Carson had said. Was Carson agreeing to be his attorney or not? Eventually, Dr. Banner said, "I'm sure that I'll never be a defendant in the case. I had nothing to do with his death," but his voice lacked confidence. "I was hoping you could tell me how to avoid being...involved."

I was pretty sure that Grant Carson shouldn't be giving any legal advice to Dr. Banner—not for a fee, anyway. After all, he already officially represented Ellen, the main suspect, and he'd also sort of agreed to defend Gail

Banner. As I understood legal ethics, that had been at least a minor mistake. And here sat Dr. Banner, saying that he might himself be a suspect in this murder. For Carson to even suggest that he *might* represent Dr. Banner seemed to present multiple conflicts of interest.

"As I said, Dr. Banner, I can give you legal advice. I would require a retainer of a thousand dollars. In the event that you are never seriously implicated, that would be sufficient. Again, though, if a conflict of interest were to arise, I might have to refer you to other counsel."

"I understand."

"Why do you think you might be implicated in this case?"

Banner didn't answer immediately. "I am not the fool that people might think," he began. "I know about Gail's occasional indiscretions. But even though I don't care about that, some people may think of them as a motive for revenge. I think that Gail may have… seen Highsmith a couple of times. That's kind of surprising, even amusing, in some respects, but it doesn't bother me."

"I understand."

"In a conversation with Gail this weekend, it came to my attention that she arrived home late on Monday night and found that I was not there."

"What else did she tell you about that night?" Carson asked.

"Nothing, really. She said to me in a rather accusatory way that although circumstances had kept her out late that night, she had arrived home to find me absent. It was her suggestion, actually, that people might believe that I had something against this man Highsmith."

I heard Carson's pencil scratching out some notes. "Which is not the case?"

"Other than that the man was a local joke, I never gave him a thought."

"Has your wife discussed any…consultations she might have sought recently?"

Dr. Banner answered, "Yes, she told me that she'd spoken with you about the possibility that her friendship with Highsmith could in some way prove a legal embarrassment. She assured me that they were just friends. That's crap, of course, which is why I'm here. If, in fact, Gail was involved with

Highsmith in more than a friendship, there are those who might think that I was jealous."

"Jealous enough to kill Highsmith?"

"Exactly."

"You ask for my legal advice, Dr. Banner. I've got to ask you if you have any information—anything at all—that might have a bearing on Willard Highsmith's murder."

"None whatever. Actually, I know nothing about his death except what I've read in the newspaper. He was shot?"

"Apparently," Carson said.

"His wife has been arrested."

"That is correct. To be clear, she is my client."

Dr. Banner was quiet for a moment and then responded, "More power to her, and to you, Mr. Carson. I can tell you that if I am ever a suspect myself, it will not be for long. If absolutely necessary, I can prove beyond any doubt that I was elsewhere at the time of Highsmith's murder. I understand that it took place on the lake?"

"That is the current scenario," Carson said.

"I was in town. I think that's all I need say about that for now."

"If you have no evidence to offer, my advice to you at the moment is to remain silent and go about your business."

It sounded like Dr. Banner coughed once. Then he was quiet for a moment. "For this advice you are charging me a thousand dollars?"

"No, I'm throwing in something extra. If you get called in for questioning on this matter, go ahead and ask that I be present as your counsel. If you were actually charged, Ellen Highsmith's defense would no longer be necessary and I could then represent you. I am very familiar with the case. Of course your retainer would be applied toward your defense costs. You'd have the advantage of immediate access to defense counsel that was already fully up-to-date on the case."

There was a long moment of silence.

"Will you accept a check?" Dr. Banner said.

"Certainly."

~ ~ ~

When Dr. Banner had gone, Carson came into my office, all smiles. He handed me the check with a flourish.

"What do you think of that? What a delightful turn of events."

I looked at the check and thought of the combination of things that it could do. It would help with the boat repairs. It might buy some curtains for the office window. Most important of all, it could pay my salary next week. It occurred to me that Carson might want some money of his own, too. "What would be the position of the Arizona Bar on this matter?" I asked.

"Let me tell you something, Naomi. At the risk of sounding crude, I look at this as a refund of what I paid for the very…thorough…exam that I got from Dr. Banner a couple of months ago."

I couldn't help laughing at that. "I'm not sure that the Bar Association would accept that in evidence, but I see what you mean."

Then the absurdity of Gail Banner and her husband hit me, and I just kept on laughing helplessly, which made Carson laugh, too. It wasn't very professional, I guess, but that's what was going on when the door opened and Abraham Bingham strode in. He was dressed in khaki pants with a matching shirt, which, together, looked vaguely like a uniform. Although his feet were clad in sturdy high-top work boots, he wore a nice black knit tie. He was wearing a black hardhat, and for a moment he reminded me of a soldier.

"Is this a joke I can hear?" he asked.

"No, it would violate client confidentiality," Carson said, causing us both to start laughing again.

Bingham smirked. "And I can see that you are very serious about that. Carson, have you got a few minutes?"

"Sure," Carson said, "would you like to step into my office?"

Bingham walked over to the partition wall, slapped it with his open hand, and said, "What's the point?"

That sent Carson and me into more giggling, and I said, "Have a seat out here, then, Mr. Bingham. It's all the same to us."

"I can see that," he said.

Carson tried to scowl at me, but he couldn't pull it off. Abraham Bingham went ahead and sat down in the nearest chair and removed his hardhat.

"Okay, this is serious, Carson. I want a legal document."

"I already told you, Abe, that I can't get you a divorce from either of the two women that you aren't married to who don't live in this state."

Bingham nodded. He turned to face me. "I guess you know all about this?"

I managed to say nothing.

"I'm not going to divorce either one of my wives, Carson. Both of them, bless their hearts, have made it abundantly clear over the weekend that they could not possibly live without me. But I have managed to figure out a way to take better control of my household situation. What I need is a prenuptial agreement."

Carson looked astonished, and I guess I did too. Up until now, we had assumed that Bingham wanted a divorce or two from his wives, to whom he was not actually married as far as any federal, state, or local government was concerned. Moreover, we assumed that he would be seeking this action in Arizona, although he was a resident of Utah, as were his wives. Now it seemed that he wanted a *prenuptial* agreement, or perhaps two, for marriages that had never occurred in Arizona or any other state, and it was hard to see how a man could ask for a prenuptial agreement for any sort of marriages that had already happened, such as they were.

Clearly enjoying himself, Bingham looked at our expressions for a good thirty seconds before explaining. "I don't want it for my wives. I want it for my fiancé."

It pained me to think that I wasn't going to be able to share this at that evening's textile arts meeting. It would have almost certainly given me celebrity status as winner of any regional competition that ranked the juiciness of insider news. The reality that it would just have to stay inside was just plain frustrating.

"Abraham, I had no idea you were getting married," Carson said. "Will that be here in Arizona?"

"No, it will be a small ceremony out at my house in High Creek on Sunday. Nothing formal. I hope you guys can come."

Carson smiled and nodded. I didn't know if the nod meant that he would attend the wedding. As for my own attendance, I wouldn't pass it up for the world. How often was I going to get a chance to see a plig wedding? "I'd be happy to," I said.

"And what about your two lovely current wives?" Carson asked.

"They will be matrons of honor," Bingham said. "Look, there's no use in your trying to understand our way of doing things. The point is that I'm about to be married again and I want a clear understanding with this new wife before she comes on board."

"How much understanding does she already have?"

"Oh, she knows both of my wives. She's known them for years, longer than I have. I'm a relative newcomer to the community out there, but Henrietta is practically a native of High Creek."

"Henrietta? Isn't that the name of the woman you introduced me to the other day?" Carson asked. He looked over at me. "You must have noticed her, Naomi."

I thought back to the woman who had been sitting with her arm on Abraham Bingham. I'd heard his wives described as young, but the woman I had seen didn't seem to fit that picture. I nodded and said nothing.

"She's got experience at running a household with young sister wives. She's been married in the community before. Her husband passed away and his other wives left the area. I always admired the way she ran her place."

"Her place?" Carson said.

"She was the head wife."

"Head wife?" Carson said. "I didn't know that it worked that way. I'm afraid that I don't know much about your community's practices—household rules, that sort of thing."

"Out at High Creek we don't have a lot of formal rules. It's not like over in Colorado City where it's much more traditional and religious. High Creek is more secular in its practices these days. Hell, we've even got guys out there who only have one wife. We don't care—that's their business."

While Grant Carson remained speechless for a moment, I reflected on how open-minded Abe made High Creek sound. They even tolerated monogamists.

"So Henrietta is going to be the head wife?"

"Right, she's going to keep them other two in line, so to speak."

There was a brief silence. I was pretty sure that Carson was wondering what the other two thought about the prospect of being kept "in line," because I sure was, but he evidently decided not to go there.

"And why do you need a prenuptial agreement?"

"It's her idea. I've got a lot of property. If something should happen to me, Henrietta wants to be taken care of. Nothing unreasonable, you understand, but some security. The way we do things a widow has no pro-tection under the law. She's been through all that and was left standing in the desert with nothing. Kids got everything, such as it was, and Henrietta didn't have any kids. Can you do something for her?"

Carson took a legal pad off of my desk and grabbed my pen. "How much security do you think you want to provide for Henrietta?"

Bingham looked up at the ceiling for a moment. "Half a million should do it."

It was hard for me to keep a straight face after that. I wondered immedi-ately if Abe might want a fourth wife while he was at it. He was beginning to look downright eligible.

Carson assured him that we could come up with just the right document, and he accepted a five hundred dollar retainer. We set up an appointment for the next week. I was pretty sure that accepting money for legal services in a state where you were not licensed was called the unauthorized practice of law. But I figured that Grant Carson knew what he was doing.

~ ~ ~

Our telephone rang a few minutes after Bingham left. Without thinking, Carson picked up the phone and took the call himself. I thought this was a breach of protocol for an attorney who had an office manager, and I made a mental note to train him better.

"That was Peggy," Carson said after he hung up. "I'm being summoned to the police station again. It seems that Dr. Banner has been taken in for questioning and has requested that I be present."

"Shall I go out and get you some rubber gloves?" I asked.

"Yes, those dishwashing ones with the little knobs on them," Carson said.

Before we could indulge in another round of unprofessional mirth, Carson put Dr. Banner's predicament into context by mentioning that every person they took in for questioning meant that they were looking that much further away from Ellen. With that, he left the office, and I sat there hoping that he was right. Part of me was worried that the questioning just made them rule other suspects out. He hadn't returned by the time I closed up and went home to get ready for my Monday night meeting, so I couldn't ask him about that.

Naturally, I was expecting that the conversation that evening would begin immediately with the subject of Highsmith's murder and was surprised when it didn't.

When I got there, Wanda was talking about the movie company that would be snarling traffic all over the area in a few months. Our giant lake and beautiful sandstone attracted film crews every couple of years or so.

"What's this one?" I asked.

Wanda rolled her eyes and said, "Does it matter?"

She was right. Whatever it was, it would be getting in everyone's way for weeks. Still, I wondered if the production company might need the services of a local attorney. I made a mental note to ask Carson if he'd ever done any work like that.

Sue Gallo, who did Frank Armstrong's sister's hair, started us in a different direction when she said that Frank was going to get a liver transplant.

Not being surgeons or hepatologists, we couldn't think of much to say about that, aside from wishing Frank Armstrong well and hoping for the best. Along the way, though, we found out that Frank was dating a young woman who was only slightly older than his daughter. Ranger Wanda told us that she knew a young park service intern who'd met Frank over the summer. This woman was only twenty-two, and we all deduced from various bits of information that Frank had to be in his mid-forties. In itself, that might not have been worthy of comment. But with Frank having a daughter who was eighteen... well, that put it in a different light.

I had to sit there biting my tongue because I didn't dare say a word about Frank Armstrong and his daughter, and I didn't know anything about his girlfriend. Finally, someone brought up the subject of Highsmith's murder, and all the faces turned to me. Cursing the pledge of confidentiality, I said nothing, and my jaw began to ache from holding back. It wasn't that I knew all that much, but I sure had theories, and I couldn't share those, either.

I wasn't in the spotlight for long, though. When Maggie said she'd heard that Dr. Banner had been arrested that afternoon at his office, everyone's gaze turned to Lucille Farneth, his medical file clerk. Of course, I could've clarified the question myself since I knew that Dr. Banner had been brought in for questioning but not arrested, but I bit that back, too.

Anyway, everyone looked to Lucille for confirmation of the arrest rumor. She dropped her knitting into her lap, turned red, and burst into tears.

"No, he wasn't arrested, and you all are terrible," she said, looking wildly around the circle. "We... I mean we all are terrible. Talking about this as if it were just... just nothing. People's reputations are involved, reputations they've spent years building."

"I... we... I didn't mean anything, Lucille," somebody said. I didn't know who, because I was too busy watching poor Lucille.

"And he wasn't there," Lucille sobbed. "He wasn't anywhere near the lake when Highsmith got shot. He absolutely wasn't anywhere near the lake."

Well, that lowered the level, as they say. There wasn't a woman in the room who couldn't figure out the source of Lucille's emotional outburst, and none of us pretended that we couldn't figure out where she must have been during the meeting the week before. For a minute we all sat without speaking, not quite knowing what to say under the circumstances. Revelations like this weren't unusual in a small town. But they also weren't generally connected to a murder investigation that was getting more complicated every day.

After Lucille calmed down, Alice asked her quietly if anyone knew about her and Dr. Banner, and I almost laughed. One sure thing was that now a whole room full of people knew it.

I wondered if the police did.

After the meeting, Wanda and I paused beside her Park Service jeep.

"How's your Bull Banks murder going?" I asked. "Got any suspects?"

"Nope, strange scene, though—hard to figure out. How about you guys? Got any suspects?"

"Tons of 'em," I said.

Chapter Ten

O N Tuesday morning I could hardly wait for Carson to get into the office so he could tell me about what had happened to Dr. Banner on Monday afternoon. After the previous night's revelations, I knew that Banner couldn't have killed Highsmith, and I wondered if Carson knew it, too. As my foul luck would have it, though, Carson arrived late and we didn't have time to catch up, because we had a pretty full schedule. He surprised me by wearing a nice suit, and socks as well as shoes.

The first meeting on his schedule was with the Armstrongs, to go over the final revisions of their family trust. I knew that, but what I didn't know was that Carson had arranged a bail hearing for Ellen that was to take place just after lunch. Now he just mentioned it in passing, as if it were no big deal, and he also let me know that Dr. Banner would be coming into the office at around three o'clock. We barely had time to run through the final check of the trust before they arrived.

Carson was standing next to his office door. After they walked past him to sit down in front of his desk, he handed me an envelope and said, "Please take care of this as soon as possible, Naomi," before following them in and closing the door.

I opened the envelope and found a note from Ellen specifying where I could find the clothes she wanted to wear at this afternoon's hearing. In addition to a key to her house, there was also a brief scrawled note from

Carson. It asked me to go to the Highsmith house and get Ellen's clothes and take them to her at the jail. He wanted me to get it done while he was talking with Frank and Linda Armstrong. Frankly, that was one tension-filled event that I was just as happy to miss.

To tell the truth, unlocking the front door of the Highsmith house and walking into it sort of creeped me out. Ellen was in jail, the kids were in Kayenta, and Willard Highsmith was dead.

The house had been closed since Wednesday morning, so it seemed to me that the air was stale—probably my imagination, but I left the door open anyway. Everything about the empty and silent house got on my nerves. I could tell that the house had been searched—drawers left open, books lying down on the shelves instead of lined up like Ellen had had them—but it wasn't too bad, and I was relieved that the police had shown some respect. I opened the refrigerator to see if there was anything I should throw out. Then I decided to believe that Ellen would be home later today, anyway, so I abandoned any kitchen tasks for the time being.

Following Ellen's directions, I went to the dresser in her bedroom and opened the bottom drawer. The contents surprised me, but not as much as the fact that she intended to wear these clothes this afternoon at her hearing. Folded neatly in the drawer was a long brown wool skirt. There was also a box containing traditional silver and turquoise jewelry, and I selected the pieces that she had requested: the silver concho belt, a modest squash blossom necklace, a heavy turquoise ring. In the top dresser drawer was the simple tortoise shell hair comb that she wanted.

I opened the closet door and found the muslin bag that her note said would be hanging at the back. Inside was a maroon velvet blouse with long, full sleeves and buttoned cuffs. The plain black Oxford shoes that were on the list were packed neatly in a box on the closet shelf.

I'd never actually seen Ellen in a traditional outfit of this type. But I remembered a photograph of her mother and her where she was wearing clothing like this, perhaps these same pieces. And when I thought about it, I remembered her telling me that Highsmith had insisted that she wear traditional clothing at their wedding, which had been in Flagstaff. She hadn't shown me any wedding pictures, though, and I'd never asked to see them.

I stacked everything up and got out of the house as quickly as I could. Then I drove to the police station and turned it all over to Peggy.

～ ～ ～

I arrived back at the office just in time to see Frank Armstrong and his daughter leave. Carson followed them out for a word of farewell at their car as I went into the office. A moment later he returned.

"Schedule a meeting with Frank Armstrong for ten o'clock tomorrow morning," Carson said. "He says he wants to talk to me about some other legal matter. How did things go at the house?"

"I found everything okay. I was a little surprised at what Ellen wanted to wear. She doesn't normally dress that way even for special occasions."

"That was my doing, I'm afraid," Carson said. "I asked her if she had a traditional outfit like that, and luckily she did."

I hesitated for a moment, unsure whether or not to question my boss's decisions. But I felt I had to say something. "I'm not sure that's such a good idea."

He looked at me and raised his eyebrows.

"I mean I don't like it, I guess."

"How so?"

"What you're doing is using her, posing her like a museum piece. The same way that Highsmith did."

"Not exactly. Those clothes actually belong to her. She has worn them before. It's not like she's putting on a costume."

"I don't see the difference," I said. "This kind of... of... Buffalo-Bill showmanship is... it's degrading."

Carson nodded his understanding. After a moment's silence, he spoke again. "So far, the only alibi that Ellen has given us is one that is pretty weak, and it depends heavily on her credibility as someone who values traditional Navajo practices."

I didn't say anything. He waited to let that sink in for a little while before going on. "All we're going for here is bail. If I can raise enough doubt in the judge's mind, Ellen will get out of jail and be with her kids at least until her trial."

That was true, and I couldn't be too angry at what Carson was trying to do, even if I wasn't very happy about how he was doing it. I was surprised that he had gotten Ellen to go along with it, and I'm not sure that I could have brought myself to do the same thing. Still, I had to admit that he was right about the case. We didn't have a strong alibi, and the slender one that we did have might work better if Ellen wore clothing that was recognizably traditional.

His voice sharpened. "Naomi, you realize that it was Ellen's own actions that gave me this idea, right?"

I said, "I don't understand," but that really wasn't true. I knew exactly what he was talking about.

"All that bullshit about having you translate for her while she spoke Navajo and told me about the coyote." He smiled. "Ellen speaks English as well as you do—as well as I do. But when she told that story in Navajo, she was putting a velvet blouse on it and a silver squash blossom around its neck."

I crossed my arms and looked down at the floor.

"And you went along with it," Carson continued. "Don't tell me that you didn't know what she was doing."

"She and I speak Navajo sometimes. We used to, anyway, when we wanted to say something that we didn't want some of the other kids to understand."

"As I remember it, you looked surprised when she switched to Navajo."

"Yeah, a little. But you're making it sound like she was just putting on an act. Like it was calculated. And manipulative."

Carson was shaking his head vigorously. "No. No, that's what I thought at first. But here's what I think now. She wanted me to *hear* that the place where she'd encountered the coyote was a different world. She wasn't putting on an act. She was helping me realize that I *couldn't* understand,

and she was asking me to believe anyway." He looked away toward the window and added, mostly to himself, "So now I have to see if we can get the legal establishment to do that, too."

I could see what he was trying to do. It still bothered me, but there wasn't any point in arguing.

Still gazing out at the sand that had started to migrate from beyond the parking lot, he said, "Look, Naomi. Some of the practice of law is straightforward interpretation of statutes. But some of it is about making impressions, so that people can be open to a story that's different from the one they already have in their heads."

I began to rearrange things on my desk, stalling. "I want her to get bail," I said. Then I changed the subject. "How did things go with the Armstrongs?"

He turned back to face me again. "Pretty well. He signed the trust, over Linda's objections. She hated the twenty-year payout terms, but Frank was adamant. He came right out and told her she should use that time to grow up so that she can take care of herself when the money's gone."

"That had to be hard for her to hear," I said, qualifying for an understatement-of-the-year award, "but I hope it puts Frank's mind at ease. Word is he's going in for surgery."

"Thursday in Phoenix," Carson said. "He wants to talk to me tomorrow morning about something else. God knows what he has on his mind at a time like this."

With an unstable daughter, a life-threatening illness, and upcoming major surgery, I could see that Frank had a lot to think about. But I knew of one thing more, and it sounded like Carson didn't know it yet. "Did you know that he has a girlfriend?"

Carson looked surprised. "No. I didn't. But if it's someone he's serious about, he really shouldn't be doing this family trust right now."

"I thought you said he already signed it."

"He did." Carson shook his head. "What do you know about this girlfriend?"

"I've just heard that he has a girlfriend, is all. Rumor has it that he's been dating a woman he met this summer."

"He hasn't said a word to me, but there isn't any reason why he should, I guess, especially in front of Linda if she doesn't know about it."

"I understand why this trust is a good thing if Armstrong dies," I said, "but how good is it for him if he lives?"

Carson thought about that for a moment. "Maybe not so good, if he is starting up a new romance. As things stand, Frank is terminally ill. Chances are he'll die before long. That's the expectation that he and I have been operating under. I didn't know that he was giving any thought to long-term survival. Or to maybe expanding his family."

"Maybe he isn't," I said. "All I heard was that he was dating someone. Besides, his trust is revocable, isn't it? He can change it if he wants to, can't he?"

"Yes, but holy shit. I'd rather eat broken glass than sit in a room with those two again to talk about money." Carson headed for the door. "I've got to grab a sandwich and get over to court. Close up for lunch and then hold down the fort until I get back. Remember that Dr. Banner will be in later."

I took Carson's advice and hurried across two parking lots to the supermarket deli. Once I had selected a reasonably fresh looking sandwich and a small salad, I sat down to enjoy a leisurely twenty-minute lunch and watch the bustle of noontime grocery shopping.

About a minute after I sat down, an arm reached over my shoulder and set a soda beside my paper plate. I turned to see Jack Miller standing behind me, looking very outdoorsy in uncharacteristically casual clothes. He wasn't relaxed, though. He seemed tightly wound and tense, practically bouncing like a prize fighter heading for the ring.

"You forgot to get something to drink," he said as he slid into a seat across from me. "How are things going with your new job?"

"Fine," I said. "How are things going with your long-overdue vacation?"

"Cool. I didn't think that I wanted any time off in the middle of all this, but the chief was right. I really needed a rest. I've managed to get out on a couple of hikes that I have been putting off for years, and I've been able to get my boat off of its trailer and onto the lake at the perfect time of year."

"I'm glad to hear it." I waited a moment, unsure that I wanted to ask the next question. "Did you know that Ellen has a bail hearing today? I hope she can bring the kids home."

Miller nodded. "I know. The chief told me to stay out of her case so I'm not going to the hearing. I hope this is the end of it for her. I'm sure they'll find out who really killed Highsmith before they get around to trying Ellen." He looked at me over the top of his paper cup as he started drinking his soda.

"You got a favorite suspect?" I asked.

"Have you?"

I honestly couldn't think of a good answer to that. I didn't suspect Dr. Banner because of what I knew, but maybe his son could have done it. I suspected Gail Banner, but only a little bit. "I honestly don't," I said.

"What about Dr. Banner? I heard they questioned him yesterday."

Before answering, I mentally trotted out the confidentiality yardstick that I'd developed as we had acquired more clients: when it came to information, speculation, or conversation about a client, I couldn't say it if I wouldn't mind everyone, including my boss, seeing it in the weekly *Sage Landing Gazette*. Period. And this one was a no-brainer, so I just shrugged.

Jack Miller raised his eyebrows and tilted his head. "Really?" He frowned. "Well, there's got to be someone whose alibi doesn't hold up."

I stared at him meaningfully. It took him a while, but he got it.

"Um...so, Ellen's," he said, his voice low. And sad. "I hear they interviewed the people down at Tuba City, but no one could clearly identify her. You know, clerks don't pay a lot of attention to what their customers look like, even when things are slow. And customers don't pay much attention to other customers unless they know them personally. So all they've been able to get is a statement that some customers came and went between nine and ten o'clock. Some of the customers were women; most of them were Native Americans."

"Nothing else?"

"The cash register tape says they sold four chocolate shakes between 9:00 and 10:00. Two of those orders were for just the shakes, like Ellen's. The other two were with food."

I couldn't think of much to say that wasn't at least borderline confidential, and Jack didn't want to talk about anything but Ellen's situation. Consequently we just made half-hearted small talk—the weather, the high-school football game, stuff like that—for a few more minutes, and then I excused myself, saying that I had to get back to work.

~ ~ ~

Banner arrived before Carson got back that afternoon, and I ushered the good doctor into the inner office, assuring him that Mr. Carson would be back very soon. Then I paid attention to being as quiet as possible while I did some filing. Grant Carson arrived a few minutes later and smiled broadly at me before joining the doctor. I could only assume that the smile meant that Ellen had gotten bail. Carson closed the door, and I sat down to listen.

"Let's go over what we have here, Dr. Banner," I heard Carson say. "What about the rifles that the police found in your home?"

"Found is hardly the right word, Carson. The rifles weren't hidden or anything. They were in a gun case where they belonged."

"Several rifles, I understand. Three high-powered ones."

"Deer rifles, hunting rifles, yes. My son and I hunt deer every year, and we've gone up to Wyoming a couple of times to hunt antelope."

"Any of the guns missing?"

Banner paused. "No, nothing was missing, and none of the guns have been fired recently."

"But the report says that two of the deer rifles have been cleaned recently. Why is that?"

"The late deer season in North Kaibab is coming up in November, and we both have permits for this year. When the hunting season is approaching, Mark gets kind of excited about it. He usually starts to fool with the rifles about this time—takes them out and cleans them. Sometimes he'll drive out in the desert someplace and test the scopes by firing a few rounds, but he hasn't done that this year, so they haven't been fired."

Carson paused, and I could hear his pencil scratching across a notepad for quite a while—was he taking down a word-for-word transcript?—before he continued. "Were you aware that he'd cleaned the guns recently?"

Sounding defensive, Banner answered a little too quickly. "No, but that's not unusual. He's very responsible about guns."

I couldn't help rolling my eyes at that. If Mark was responsible about guns, they were just about the only things he was responsible about.

Carson didn't make any comment about Mark's reputation. He just asked, "As I understand it, the police didn't keep any of the guns, is that correct?"

"That's right. They told us that they'd just inspected them and recorded their serial numbers. They returned them later. Is that significant?" Now he sounded hopeful.

"It means that they're not taking them in as evidence yet. That's a good sign. It means that at this point they don't consider you or your son a suspect in this murder."

"My son? Why would they ever consider him a suspect?"

Carson was quiet again for twenty seconds, which is a very long time when you're trying to listen to a conversation through a wall. I knew it was twenty seconds because I had a stopwatch going on my computer screen. Billable hours don't just track themselves.

Finally Carson said, "Your son is certainly old enough to commit murder. Depending on what he may have heard around town and how he felt about it, some could assume that he had a motive. The hunting rifles provide him the opportunity. Where was he the night that Highsmith was shot?"

"I assume that Mark was at home."

"You assume?"

"I wasn't there. I believe I told you that."

"You said that you could prove beyond a doubt that you weren't out at the lake shooting Highsmith."

"Right," Dr. Banner answered, "but I wasn't home at all that night. We went over all this at the station."

"Did the police ask you about Mark's whereabouts?"

"No. When you talked to my wife, Mr. Carson, didn't she say that Mark was at home?"

"I think she *assumed* that Mark was asleep in his room when she got home. I'm sure that the police will follow up on that question with each of you as time goes along."

Dr. Banner raised his voice an octave. "Follow up on Mark? What's the point? Everybody knows that Highsmith's wife killed him."

"I certainly don't know that," Carson said. "This is very much an open case and the police will be questioning you again. They will also want to inquire about Mark's whereabouts."

There was another period of silence before Dr. Banner answered. "And my wife's as well? I assume that she will have some explaining to do. As I understand it, she has already spoken with the police."

"Haven't the two of you discussed this with one another, at least some of it?"

"I'm afraid that at this point we are not very forthcoming with each other, Mr. Carson. I am confident that I can't be charged with his murder. I gather that Gail is equally confident."

"But the two of you haven't spoken about this?"

"We have certain... understandings, and they do not necessitate speaking to each other much."

Carson let that statement just sit there for a while before he said, "Mark is seventeen years old, right?"

"Yes."

I heard Carson drop his notepad on his desk, and then he finally asked the obvious question. "Do you and your wife think that he is *unaware* of your...understandings? Do you imagine that the entire town is unaware of them?"

Dr. Banner didn't exactly yell, but he definitely took it up a notch. "It's a small town. I assume people make guesses and gossip, but our marriage details have no relevance in this case."

Carson answered calmly, with exaggerated patience. His voice dropped to a near-whisper. "These kinds of…uh…marital arrangements result in multiple murders every year… no, multiple murders a month… in this country. If the police begin to examine these arrangements, all three of the people in your house will become suspects. You say you're sure of your alibi, and I have reason to believe that your wife is confident that she won't be charged. So far, we can be less sure about your son. Let's find out about that before very long."

After another period of silence, Dr. Banner said, "Deer rifles?"

"It may be that the murder weapon was a high-powered rifle. The police have not told me that, you understand?"

"But that's your guess?"

"I've merely pieced it together from what I do know about the case. There are probably a thousand deer rifles in this town, maybe more. And you're not the only people in town with some kind of reason to kill Highsmith. Unfortunately for Highsmith, there are a lot of them."

"But, as you imply, I am one of them, and my wife is one of them, and even my son is one of them. It makes those two recently cleaned deer rifles look important." I could hear Banner smack the arm of his chair. "What a mess."

The men were through talking, it seemed, because I heard Carson get up and step around his desk toward the door. I managed to get a fistful of files in my hands and open a file drawer before the two of them came out into my office. A minute later Dr. Banner was gone.

"Do you think he can really prove that he was somewhere else?" Carson asked me.

"I…I know he can."

"You know? Well, the police know where *you* were so you can't be Dr. Banner's alibi."

"But I know who can," I said. "I really hope she doesn't have to come forward."

Carson shook his head. "You know, I had no idea how busy things were on Monday nights around here. I'm starting to believe that I'm one of the tamer sorts in Sage Landing."

"Don't worry," I said, "your reputation as a wild man is secure, but you aren't the only busy man around."

"Or busy woman," Carson said. "For every busy man, there's a busy woman."

"Well, almost." I shrugged my shoulders. "I know a few men and a few women here in town who could throw that calculation off."

CHAPTER ELEVEN

WEDNESDAY morning brought in a fresh surprise when Frank Armstrong came in to see Carson. The first thing he did was ask what sort of additional fee would be required to get Carson's opinion on a criminal matter. Carson replied that he would need more information before he could answer that question.

"Murder," Armstrong said.

Jeepers. My eyes widened and I held my breath, but the man in the other room couldn't see that. I wondered if it was possible that Highsmith's killer had just walked in and was about to confess to my boss. For Ellen's sake, I really hoped so.

"Are you saying that you killed Highsmith?" Carson said with an air of calm that I would never have been able to pull off.

"Don't be ridiculous. If I had killed the bastard I wouldn't be telling you about it. I'd be long gone." Armstrong paused for a moment and then added, "I guess I might be gone anyway before long."

"Well, we hope not."

"Those are the odds, though. Anyway, I didn't kill Highsmith, but there's a chance I'll come up as a possible suspect."

My mind started to do two things at once. I continued to listen closely to the conversation in the other room, but I also started doing some financial calculations. We had already taken money from Ellen, Gail Banner, and Dr.

Banner on this case. Now it looked like we were going to get more from Frank Armstrong. It seemed pretty clear to me that we were getting further out on an ethical limb here, but I'm no lawyer. One thing was certain, and that was that Carson could afford to pay me for another month or so.

While I was running the stuff about ethics and money through my mind, Carson was asking Frank Armstrong for a further explanation.

"I threatened to kill him, for one thing."

"In public?"

"Yes, there were a half-dozen witnesses."

"How long ago was this?" Carson asked

"Over a year...August of last year."

"Maybe they've forgotten about it. Has anybody said anything to you?"

"Not yet, but they won't have forgotten about it. It was pretty dramatic. I was waving a gun around at the time."

Well, yeah. I'd probably remember a scene like that if I'd been there. Carson just continued, "Where was this?"

"Down at the marina at that flashy racing boat of his. He was just coming into his slip. There was another man crowded into that one bench seat along with my daughter and another teenage girl. Four or five people were loading up a houseboat a few feet away."

"Did you recognize anybody?"

"The people at the other boat were locals, but I couldn't tell you their names. I don't know if they knew who I was exactly, but I've seen them around since then. I can tell they haven't forgotten it."

I could hear Carson taking notes, and I hoped that he was planning to have me hunt down those witnesses. I couldn't believe that I hadn't heard anything about this confrontation when it happened.

"I take it that this was about your daughter?"

"She was underage—still just under seventeen then. I don't care what people say about how wild she was, or is. The fact is that Highsmith was over three times her age. There are laws about that. I could've had him arrested."

I could hear Carson's chair squeak as he leaned back. "Not for taking her out water skiing, Frank."

"Oh, don't worry, she'd already told me all about it—thrown it in my face." Armstrong lowered his voice to a near whisper. "He was doing her up one side and down the other, Grant. She was a kid, and he was old enough to be her grandfather. Well, almost."

Thinking back to what Wanda had said about Frank's new girlfriend, it seemed to me that he was in no position to be casting aspersions on relationships across generations. Meanwhile, Carson scratched out a few more notes before he said anything. "What kind of gun?"

"An old Browning .32 automatic. It was loaded, and I was prepared to shoot the bastard, but I got cold feet and just did a lot of threatening and swearing instead."

"I'd call it good sense, rather than cold feet, Frank. After this swearing and threatening, what did you do?"

"I nodded at the other people and walked away. I still had the gun in my hand where anybody could see it, all the way back to my car."

I heard paper rustle as Carson turned to a new page on his notepad. "You're right about one thing, Frank. I'm surprised that you haven't been questioned by now. Where were you Monday night a week ago?"

"Then you'll take my case?"

"This isn't a case. You haven't been arrested, and maybe you never will be. Until you're charged, it isn't a case. I'm just going to give you some general legal advice. Ellen Highsmith is my client, and she *has* been charged. It is in her best interest, probably, that I tell the police about you. Unless you can tell me where you were when Highsmith was shot, I'm going to have to do just that."

"Don't you and I have some sort of attorney-client privilege? How can you say that you could go to the police?"

I thought to myself that old Frank Armstrong had hit the nail right on the head. That's why we shouldn't be handing out legal advice like it was Halloween candy, when Ellen was our client. This had conflict-of-interest written all over it. Surely Carson could see that. But Grant Carson seemed to practice law in a way peculiar to him.

Sidestepping the question, my boss just said, "Get me off the spot here, Frank. Tell me where you were when Highsmith was shot."

"Last week's *Gazette* said that it happened Monday night. In one of his boats on the lake, right? Well, I wasn't there. I wasn't near the lake."

"Were you alone? Were you with your daughter?" Carson paused briefly. "Or perhaps someone else?"

"Let's say I was alone, fishing down on the Colorado."

"Did anybody see you at Lee's Ferry?"

"Let's say I went down the ropes up here at this end—camped out at the bottom."

I really wanted to believe Frank Armstrong's story, but I had my doubts. People have two ways to fish the Colorado River from here at Sage Landing. The conventional way is to drive about forty-five twisty highway miles down to Lee's Ferry, launch a boat, and drive it back up from there about fifteen river miles to the dam, fishing anywhere between the dam and Lee's Ferry. But there's another way to go, where you don't need a boat. Just a little ways out of town there's a trail down the north side of the canyon wall about a half-mile downstream from the dam. It's steep, and there's a sheer drop, so there are a couple of stretches of rope spiked into the sandstone face. The Park Service doesn't like it—don't ever mention it to Wanda, because she'll bite your head off before you can say "rainbow trout," but you can hike the trail down to a limited stretch of shoreline at the bottom to fish, and then climb back out. If you do it at the right place, it's pretty safe. I used to do it all the time when I was a kid.

My doubts about Frank's story had to do with his medical condition. A person has to be in decent shape to go down the ropes, and climbing back out takes real strength. I didn't doubt that Armstrong had done it a few times, but I was sure that he hadn't done it recently.

Carson stopped writing on his tablet, and when he spoke, his voice was patient. "If you absolutely had to do so, Frank, could you provide a reliable witness who could prove that you were not on the lake, or on the lakeshore, when Highsmith was killed?"

After a pause Frank said, "Yes, if I had to, but it would involve someone that I'd rather leave out of this."

"Someone other than your daughter?"

"Yes."

"Okay," Carson said, "then I'm going to give you some legal advice and send you a bill, Frank."

I just sat at my desk with my head in my hands. Carson continued talking. "Here's the advice. Go to see this person, whoever she is, and make sure that she is willing to come forward if necessary. Get whatever other proof you can as to where you were. People may have seen you. If you bought anything late that night, find the receipt. Anything. Then go on down to Phoenix and try not to think about it and have your surgery."

After a silence Frank said, "Can you represent me if they arrest me?"

Since this was not anywhere close to the first time that Carson had fielded that question, he was ready with a quick response. "If they arrest you, they will have dropped charges against Ellen Highsmith. Then I could take your case."

I didn't like the answer that I was hearing through the wall at all. So far, Carson and I knew of three and maybe four other suspects besides Ellen. Okay, so some of them had pretty good alibis, but some of them didn't, at least not yet. It seemed to me that instead of taking money from every potential killer who walked in the door, we should be casting suspicion on all of these people and maybe getting Ellen out of the spotlight.

After he'd ushered Frank Armstrong out the front door, Carson stood with his hand on the doorknob before turning around to look at me with a kind of sheepish grin. I looked back at him with what I thought was stern disapproval.

"What?" he said.

"Aren't there some rules?" I asked. "Doesn't the Bar Association have some sort of guidelines?"

"Don't worry about it, Naomi. Let me worry about it." He was still smiling so I figured it was okay to be a little more direct with him.

"Have you always practiced law like this?"

"Not always. Once I took it seriously." His smile was beginning to fade.

"What happened?"

He sank onto a chair across from my desk. "Sooner or later you've seen too much to take things so seriously. Then you get tough and you do it the way it's done, or you get out. In my case, though, I didn't quite do either one."

"You moved to Sage Landing instead?" I said.

Nodding, he said, "I came here for the boat, but it turned out that the boat needed a little more income than I have if I don't practice law. As you can see, I practice as little of it as I can."

"What do you mean you came here for the boat?"

I'd lived long enough in this boating playground to learn that the notions people had about boats were seldom rational, so it wasn't a surprise when he looked at me as if it should be obvious.

I just stared back at him until he decided to explain. "I was a prosecutor down in Phoenix. I pretty much hated the job, and the District Attorney had grown to pretty much hate me. Things were kind of getting out of hand. I hadn't quite figured out what to do about all that, but I was talking about it with some of my friends, and one of them told me about this great deal on a boat."

"The boat you have now?" It didn't seem to me that the boat I'd seen could be priced low enough to have been anything like a "great deal." I managed to avoid saying that out loud, but my face just couldn't keep a secret.

"Yeah. The *Deep Inn*. Don't be so skeptical. Anyway, I drove up to take a look at her and got this romantic idea to sell everything in Phoenix and come up here and live on the boat with my savings and my Army pension. That was the plan."

"You were in the Army?" I said, trying not to sound shocked. I couldn't picture that at all.

"For several years. Then a service injury got me a discharge."

"Oh." Something in his voice warned me not to ask for details about the service or the injury or the discharge, and I left it at that. So did he, continuing instead with what had happened when he got to Sage Landing.

"Well, as it turned out, that didn't quite cover the bases. For one thing, you're not supposed to live aboard a boat at the marina, so I rented a little place in town. For another, my money didn't go quite as far as I thought it would, so I opened this office for some extra income. That was the revised plan."

I smiled. "Only now it's kind of piling up and getting complicated. Now you need an assistant. Before long you'll need a calendar and a watch and maybe a briefcase. And some more socks."

"God forbid," Carson said. "But just look at how the money rolls in now. If I'd known, I'd have paid more attention a long time ago. The past few days alone have brought in... let me see..."

"Depending on what you charge Mr. Armstrong, something over seven thousand dollars," I said. "Some of it is even ethical."

We heard the slamming of two car doors out in the parking lot, and both of us turned to look toward the door. I expected to see policemen enter, but when our front door opened, two regular civilians walked in. Well, not exactly regular, because they sure weren't from around here. The first one, with the broad shoulders and beefy arms of a professional football player, was dressed in nice casual clothes that were tailored to fit him well. His slacks were pressed, his blue camp shirt draped nicely over his flat mid-section, and he looked like he could pick up my desk and toss it over his shoulder without breaking a sweat.

The second man was somewhat smaller, a couple of inches shorter than Carson, and thirty pounds lighter. He was dressed like someone on Miami Vice, wearing a pale linen sport jacket with the sleeves rolled up, and a black polo shirt tucked into pastel pants. His hair was a little long and carefully windswept, too. I noticed that he wore his ivory suede loafers without socks. "Grant Carson?" he said, extending his hand. "I'm John Rice. Have you got a moment?"

Carson stood up to shake the outstretched hand. Then he nodded at the other man, which gave him a brief moment to take in the whole picture—slick guy in trendy suit, and big guy in remarkable shape—before answering. "I've got a moment. What can I do for you, Mr. Rice?"

Rice looked at me and smiled politely. He looked back at Carson and nodded toward the door his office. At least he knew better than to point his finger at it. "Could we talk in your office?"

"Sure," Carson answered, smiling briefly at me as he did so. "Come on in."

Rice looked at the football player. "Could you wait for us out here, Fred? This won't take long."

Carson's smile disappeared, as did my own. Our little office secret was about to be discovered, and there was nothing we could do about it. I made one try at fixing the situation. "Fred, why don't you and I go get a cup of coffee. I'm due for a break, and I could use some company."

"Thanks just the same," Fred answered as the door to Carson's office closed. "I'll wait here for Mr. Rice."

A couple of seconds later, Rice began speaking in the other room. Fred looked at the wall quizzically for a moment and then looked at me and smiled as he sat down.

"I understand that you represent Larry Sabano," John Rice said as clearly as if he were sitting next to us. Fred grinned at me and nodded at the same time that Carson answered his boss.

"Mr. Sabano is a client of mine."

"Like yourself, Mr. Carson, I am an attorney. I represent a small New Mexico corporation. We've had some dealings with Mr. Sabano in the past and have been trying to contact him recently, but he seems to have dropped out of sight. Would you know how we could contact him?"

"Dropped out of sight? I hardly think so. He's probably just out of town on business. He travels quite a bit."

"When did you last see him, if you don't mind my asking."

"I think you know that I can't answer that—client confidentiality."

"You saw him on Thursday. We know that because my client has spoken with Larry since then. That's how we learned that you were his attorney. The last time we were able to talk to him was last Friday. You're sure you haven't heard from him since then?"

Instead of answering the question, Carson asked one. "Mr. Rice, is your client involved in a land purchase with Mr. Sabano?"

"Land purchase? No, our trades with Larry have never involved land." He sounded amused. "Are you under the impression that Mr. Sabano is in the real estate business?"

Carson cleared his throat.

Rice chuckled, and even though it was a rather quiet chuckle, Fred and I could hear it very well through the wall. "So Larry is now representing himself as a land speculator?"

Sounding just the tiniest bit flustered, Carson said, "I don't know that he is representing himself, as you say, as anything in particular."

"Well, well. He certainly is an interesting fellow. Anyway, Mr. Carson, we really need to get in touch with Mr. Sabano. There are large economic interests at stake, and it's in your client's best interest to talk to us as soon as possible." John Rice paused briefly, and his voice sounded much less friendly when he continued. "That is my card. On the back I have written two telephone numbers. One or the other will reach me or my staff at any time. When you have an opportunity to do so, please, advise Mr. Sabano to contact me immediately."

"Immediately?"

"Frankly, his absence is causing my client to mistrust Mr. Sabano. This kind of mistrust can have serious consequences."

Fred and I heard Carson open his desk drawer. We could almost hear him dropping Rice's card into the drawer—or maybe that was my imagination. "I don't think we have a specific appointment with Larry, but I'm sure he'll turn up here before long. I'll give him your card and the message."

Fred and I heard the sound of chairs creaking as the two men in the other room stood up. As the door opened, Rice continued. "The consequences really would be quite serious, Mr. Carson. I guess that's all we can say at this time."

"Thanks for dropping by," Carson said as Fred hefted himself from the chair and the two men left our office.

As soon as they were out of earshot, Carson said, "If I didn't know any better, I'd say that Sabano has tried to pull one of his little scams on the wrong people." He didn't seem particularly worried.

I patted the wall beside me. "You realize that his assistant heard everything that was said in your office?"

"Yeah, we've really got to do something about that. Good thing we've got some money, huh?"

"It was a little embarrassing," I said. "That guy Fred thought it was pretty funny."

But my boss wasn't in the mood to be practical. "Well, I thought *he* was pretty funny," Carson said. "The other guy too, John Rice. How long before those pearly white suede loafers turn red from sand exposure?"

"Fifteen, twenty minutes tops," I said. "I made the mistake of wearing new white sneakers to a softball game one spring. They were pink by the time I got to the bleachers."

"Damned shame, ruining a spiffy pair of shoes like that," he said. As if he knew anything about spiffy shoes, or cared.

Chapter Twelve

I went out for lunch intending to get some downtime while enjoying a deli sandwich at the supermarket, but Jack Miller had other plans for me. Before I could even get inside the market, he called my name and beckoned me to come over and talk to him. Sporting a very uncharacteristic Hawaiian-print shirt and baggy shorts, he was standing in front of the frozen yogurt place next door and was just finishing off a cup of chocolate swirl. I was hungry, and it annoyed me that he was eating at the same time that he was delaying my lunch.

"Two days in a row, Jack?" I smiled in spite of myself. "We've got to stop meeting like this."

"I've got to talk to you," he said. "It's important." He said this without looking at me. But he kept looking around the parking lot and sort of facing away from me as he spoke. It was kind of comical—reminded me of one of those movies where the two undercover agents are trying to pretend they don't know one another while talking to no one out of the sides of their mouths. I figured that the tourist outfit was supposed to be a disguise.

"Jack, come on. I was just going in to get a sandwich. Why don't you come in and talk to me while I eat."

"It's too crowded in there, Naomi. Actually, I shouldn't be seen talking to you anyway. Why don't you get your sandwich to go and meet me somewhere else?"

"I'll get a sandwich and go on back over to the office. We can talk there in private."

He leaned past me to toss the frozen yogurt cup into the trash can. "No, I can't be seen in Carson's office. We should get out of town. Meet me at the old picnic area out by the campground. Nobody from town will be out there."

"I haven't got that much time for lunch, Jack."

He started walking away as he said, "It's important, Naomi. Call in sick or something. Just don't tell Carson that you're meeting me." He stopped at a car I didn't recognize and got in without another word.

I wasn't sure what I ought to do. I could take the afternoon off easily enough without lying about being sick, and Jack's cloak-and-dagger routine had convinced me that he thought he had something important to say. I wanted to find out if he could tell me anything that might help Ellen. On the other hand, his behavior was making me nervous. I pondered the situation for a moment as he drove away.

After grabbing a pre-made sandwich and going back to the office to leave a brief note for Carson, I drove out to the lake. When I got to the old picnic area, I parked close to one of the concrete tables and settled in to wait for Jack. A minute later his bright floral-printed shirt appeared in the brush. Obviously he'd parked the car somewhere else and walked here.

"Where did you park?"

"Further out by the gravel pit. I didn't want the cars to be seen together."

"So do you plan to look at me now while you talk to me?" I asked.

He ignored my question and kept staring out at the lake. "What's your boss's current thinking about this case? Who's his prime suspect?"

I'd been thinking about that same question quite a bit, and I didn't like the answer that I'd come up with. I was pretty sure that Jack wouldn't like the answer either. But I was damned if he'd get me to say it after I'd been all huffy with Carson about knowing the rules of confidentiality and all that. Not to mention wanting to stick to my personal confidentiality yardstick. With my eyes on his face, I took a big bite out of my sandwich and then shook my head, pointing at my mouth in the universal sign for *can't talk because my mouth is full.*

Miller looked around the area before sighing. "Okay," he said. "Just listen, then. I figure it's Ellen he suspects. How can he defend her if he doesn't believe in her?"

I took another bite, smaller this time. The sandwich was still ice cold and a little soggy from its plastic-wrapped hours in the deli case. It had almost no flavor at all.

Jack went on. "Actually, they don't have near enough to bring her to trial at this point. It's just that as long as the chief thinks she did it, he's not going to look much of anywhere else. He'll keep trying to find something that puts her at the scene while he ignores all the other possibilities."

I knew, of course, that Ellen wasn't capable of committing murder, but I had to agree with Carson that her alibi might not be very convincing, and that no other viable suspect had turned up yet. Also, the chief had brought in other people for questioning, so it wasn't really true that he was ignoring other possibilities. I was pretty sure that Jack knew all that. I asked, "Like what other possibilities?"

"Like the Banners, for instance."

"What about them?"

"Gail Banner does have a story," Jack said. "What she has is just a story. What if she simply shot Highsmith and jumped in the water and swam home? Maybe he got a little too kinky for her."

I shrugged.

"Maybe Highsmith had a gun on the boat and she used it and threw it overboard. The lake is at least four hundred feet deep along there. That makes a lot more sense than the idea that Ellen came out in Highsmith's ski boat and shot her husband."

This called to mind the image of Gail Banner streaking through her neighborhood in the dark, without a stitch on, and I couldn't help smirking a little.

As if he could see what I was thinking, Jack grinned and nodded his head. "If she was trying to establish an alibi, it would make perfect sense to walk the streets naked. She probably hoped that she would get caught before she could get home. Then she could tell her story about the mysterious gunshots that came out of the dark."

Jack's version of the events made little sense to me. If Gail Banner had planned to kill Highsmith in advance, she would have thought of a much better plan, one with a decent alibi. If, on the other hand, she shot him in some sort of struggle, all she had to do was take the boat back to the marina and call the police. I chewed my bland sandwich in silence for a moment while I thought about it.

Jack spoke up again. "It doesn't hang together too well, does it?"

Again I shrugged.

He wasn't done yet. "What about the boy? Mark. He had a motive."

Beginning to feel a little bit like a mime in my efforts to keep the exchange of information one-sided, I tilted my head to one side, hoping that he'd take that as meaning "well, maybe—tell me more."

He did, raising his voice to a near shout and getting very red in the face. "He's got guns, damn it, *and* he knows how to use them, *and* he wasn't in school that Monday, *and* he hasn't been there since."

Now, that was interesting. No one had mentioned that before. "Really?"

"See, that's just the kind of thing that I mean. The chief hasn't even looked into that. He doesn't even know that Mark wasn't in school. He's not investigating anybody else."

"How do you know about it?"

Jack took a deep breath. He gazed at the lake, probably deciding how much to tell me. Then he turned those heart-melting, bright blue eyes back to me and said, "You know I'm not supposed to be investigating this case, right? I'm under orders to take time off and stay away from this because the chief doesn't think that I can be objective. But he isn't doing anything so I've been checking out a few things behind his back."

"Man! You're going to get in trouble."

"I'm being careful."

"You could get fired, Jack."

"I can't just do *nothing*, Naomi. I can't!"

"So you found out that Mark Banner hasn't been in school. What else?"

"There's more to it than that. I'm not supposed to say anything about juvenile records, but you can get Carson to do some checking."

"He wouldn't do that," I said. "Who could he ask?"

Jack's face became unreadable. "Don't worry. Anyone who's been on the force for the last few years will know about Mark Banner's police record, but nothing has ever come out in public."

"Don't play games with me, Jack. If you know something that could help Ellen, tell me what it is."

"No. Carson is a lot more likely to believe something that he discovers on his own. Just check the Banner kid out. When you do, I think you'll have something to work with."

He stood and walked away without another word. A moment later he crossed over a low sandy hill and disappeared from view. I stared for a moment in the direction he'd gone and tried to evaluate what he'd said. He was thrashing like a striped bass on a hook, trying on first one theory and then another.

The idea that Mark Banner might be a suspect is one that I had never taken seriously, but now Jack had all but said that Mark had a secret criminal record. His mother had said that he was home when she got there, but that was hours after the murder, and she might not have known for sure where he was. Jack clearly thought that Mark hadn't been there at all. That was something that we really should check out. Still, it was hard for me to imagine that a seventeen-year-old boy would have committed this murder. Besides, wasn't he sort of a client of ours? It had become so hard to tell.

I rolled my sandwich wrapping into a tight little ball and tossed it into a nearby trash can. Then I retrieved it and put it in my pocket, realizing that the Park Service probably wouldn't empty out the containers in this area again until spring.

As I got into my car, it occurred to me that I'd be going right past the marina on my way into town, giving me a good chance to see the inside of Carson's boat without his being there.

It wasn't that I was actually afraid of Grant Carson or of his intentions. So far he had been a perfect gentleman with me. I just didn't feel like going inside the *Deep Inn* with him. I was curious about his infamous pleasure boat, though. I couldn't deny that. So when I got to the entrance of the marina parking lot, I turned in. I even thought of a good excuse for going out to the boat. Carson was anxious for its repairs to be completed. He was worried that Chuck Margolin would find a way to screw him over instead of getting the work done right. I could say I was in the neighborhood at lunchtime and decided to check on it for him.

I found a parking spot near the top of the access ramp and walked down to the docks. There wasn't a soul in sight as I strolled out to the boat. I climbed aboard and made a pretense of looking at the outdrives. I was surprised to see clear indications that work had actually been done on them. There were shiny new bolts here and there, and both drives sported clean new props.

I walked forward a few feet, looked around, and then reached down to try the latch that would let me go below. At first, I thought the door was unlocked, but it turned out that the latch was actually broken. The door opened easily, and I peered into the dark depths below. I fumbled around for a light switch and found one. When I flipped it on, the cabin below me was flooded with fluorescent light. Obviously the batteries on the cruiser were well charged.

I stepped carefully down the steep stairs and found myself standing in a small salon. Its furnishings included a small couch and comfortable chair as well as a sizable dining booth. In the forward left corner was a spacious galley. On the counter next to the sink was a partially finished convenience meal, one of those camping dinners that don't need freezing. Then I realized that I could smell the warm food and that it must not have been long since it had been removed from the microwave. I'd interrupted someone's lunch, and now it was time for me to leave.

I was halfway up the steps when a man's voice spoke behind me.

"Stop, Naomi! Wait a minute."

I didn't stop, though. I scrambled up the ladder steps to get out of the cabin, but someone grabbed a fistful of the back of my blouse. I lunged forward, popping all the buttons off of the front, and that gave me enough reach to get a firm hold on the sides of the doorway. My assailant released his grip, and I lurched up out of the cabin with my shirt hanging from my arms and my lace bra shining in the sunshine. The term "bodice ripper" came to mind, though this situation sure wasn't anything you'd see on the cover of a paperback romance novel. I whirled to face my attacker as I pulled my blouse back together. Holding it closed with both hands kind of put me at a disadvantage, defense-wise, but I guess I thought I'd kick him or something.

Standing down in the hallway across the salon stood Three-Steps Larry, grinning awkwardly up at me.

What do you do at a moment like that? What I did was yell, "Did you break this goddamn door?" and immediately felt like an idiot. Not only was it obvious that he must have broken into the boat, but it was just as obvious that I should be getting out of there without any further conversation. There was nobody around to help me if I needed it, and Three-Steps didn't have what I considered a good reputation.

"Naomi, hang on a minute. Yes, I broke the latch and let myself in. I'm sorry. I'll pay for the repairs. But I had to get out of sight, you know? And Carson's boat seemed like a good place to do that. I'm sorry about your shirt, too. I'll buy you a new one as nice as that one. Okay?" When I didn't say anything, he went on, "Is anybody around on the docks?"

I did a mental calculation before answering. Even if he had further mayhem on his mind, I was sure that I could get onto the dock and run halfway back to the parking lot before he could get up out of the cabin and come after me. So hanging around a little longer to find out why he was here seemed reasonable, even if there wasn't anybody on the docks. "There are some guys inside the work sheds, and remember that all of these boats are visible from the restaurant and the bar and half the rooms in the hotel."

"I know, I know. I'm not coming up out of here, don't worry."

I glared at him with all the venom I could mobilize as my pulse started to come back down out of the stratosphere. "*Don't worry*! Hey, when someone rips a person's shirt off her back, that person gets pretty worried, pretty fast. Yeah, you'd *better* not be coming up out of there. Asshole."

He looked down at the floor and said, "I'm so… Naomi, I didn't think … I didn't want you to… I couldn't…"

Since he didn't seem capable of finishing a sentence or uttering a proper apology, it was up to me to move the conversation forward. I stuck with the obvious and demanded, "What the hell are you doing down there?"

"I was eating lunch."

"Besides eating lunch. What's going on, Three…I mean Larry."

"Three-Steps Larry," he said, "I know. I bet I've heard that name more often than you have."

"Is it true?" I blurted without thinking. I sat down at the edge of the hatchway.

Three-Steps Larry just smiled at me. "Like most legends, it's partly true." Personally, I would've called it a rumor rather than a legend, but I kept that to myself. He moved over to the dinette and sat down. "There used to be a guy in town named Phil Malcolm. Did you know him?"

"No."

"Anyway, he was married to a woman named Beth, and I knew her from …well…from the business I was in at the time. She didn't much like Phil anymore, and she'd started to like me. So I was hanging out with her at the Lunker Room one night, and in walked her husband."

"And he was carrying a gun?"

"That part of the story is true, and so is the part about him pointing the gun at me and telling me to stay away from his wife."

"And the 'gimme-three-steps' part?"

"That just comes from the Lynyrd Skynyrd song, I'm afraid. I actually just told him that I was leaving. All of this was pretty loud. He was shouting at me from fifteen or twenty feet away and I was shouting back at him to be heard over the noise in the bar."

"And he let you leave."

"It was way more humiliating than that. He told me that I'd better run before he changed his mind." Three-Steps smiled uncomfortably.

"And so you ran?"

"Yeah. Kind of a loser moment in my life, but there have been quite a few of those."

"At least he didn't shoot you."

"Well, actually, he *did* shoot me, just not then and there. He shot me a couple weeks later when I was having lunch with his wife at the steakhouse. He went to jail for that. Still there, I guess. Beth found the whole thing too embarrassing and left town. Never saw her again."

"Are you sorry about that?" It was one of those times when I just kept asking personal questions instead of minding my own business.

Larry's smile vanished. "It doesn't matter anymore. What does matter now is that some guys may be looking for me. Have they come to see Carson?"

I called up a mental image of John Rice and his lackey, Fred. "This morning. What have you gotten yourself into? They seem like men I wouldn't want to fool around with. One of them said he was a lawyer from New Mexico. The other one—I think he must've been a football player or a professional wrestler. The lawyer's name was John Rice."

Three-Steps Larry lowered his gaze to the tabletop again. "What did you guys tell them?"

I slid back down into the salon, folding my arms to keep the front of my shirt closed, and sat across from him at the dinette. "Nothing. What was there to tell them? Carson said you were out of town—that you were in and out of town a lot and he didn't know where you were."

"Good. What else?"

"Nothing else. Oh, that guy, Rice, he said they'd talked to you last Friday, but that you'd dropped out of sight since then."

"He said I dropped out of sight?"

"And he said that you told them that Grant Carson was your attorney. He said they'd had dealings with you before. I got the impression that they actually knew you."

"I don't know this guy John Rice, but I've met his boss a couple of times. I used to sort of work for him."

"What did you do to them?"

Larry looked all around the salon, but not at me. "What makes you think I did anything to them? Why would you assume that?"

"Come on, Larry. There are two guys looking for you. You're hiding out here on Carson's boat. The men who are looking for you seem pretty serious, and you seem to be pretty seriously hiding from them. I notice that you haven't gone to the police. What am I going to make of all that?"

Three-Steps stood and stepped over to the galley counter and touched the dish that held the rest of his lunch. He picked it up, put it back in the microwave, and punched a few numbers before turning back to face me. "Don't make anything of it. Just forget it. Those guys are mistaken, but you won't convince them of that, and neither will I. I've just got to stay out of sight until they decide to leave town."

I leaned over and rested my forearms on the table, still crossed over my button-free blouse. "So you're just going to stay here on Carson's boat? How long can you hold out here?"

"This boat is built for living aboard. She has a large water supply and lots of room in her holding tanks. She's plugged into the dock for electricity. If all I needed was beer and wine, I could live here for a long time without being seen. Unfortunately, Carson doesn't see the need to keep too much food on board. I've got a few more of these ready-made dinners in the cupboard, and there is some cereal, but no milk."

"Does Carson know you're here?"

"Hell, no. Carson sure wouldn't take that kind of risk for me—not if he knew about it. Are you going to tell him?"

"I won't have to, Larry. He'll be coming out to check on his boat repairs any time now. I'm surprised he hasn't already been here."

Three-Steps stopped the microwave before it had finished and retrieved his lunch. He sat back down at the dinette across from me again and savored his first bite before saying anything. "Then you'd better tell him. I don't want him to be surprised when he finds me."

"Why don't you just leave his boat?"

"Because it's the best place I can think of. I've got my car tucked away where no one is going to find it. As far as anyone knows, I'm out of town—just like Carson said. Those guys have got no real reason to think that I'm anywhere around Sage Landing." He went back to munching his hot food. Linguini in some kind of cream stuff, it looked like.

"Chuck Margolin's mechanics are going to be working on the boat any time now, too," I said. "They might call the cops if they find you aboard."

Larry shoved some food around with his fork. "They're all finished with the boat. I watched them pack up their stuff before I came out on the dock."

"Well, then."

"I'm keeping a careful watch," he said. He stared down at his lunch again for a long moment, and I got the impression he was trying to decide whether to say more. "I have a favor to ask."

"Besides not telling Fred on you?"

"Besides that." He looked up at me, and his face softened. "I've got a dog. I was in a panic and in a hurry so I took her to the vet and put her in for boarding. They were booked up and said they could only squeeze her in for a couple of days. I'm overdue now."

"Let me get this straight," I said. "You're here hiding out, afraid to go outside, and you're worried about your dog?" I had a soft spot for dogs and for men who treated them kindly, but I didn't have either one in my home just then, and a dog wasn't going to be my first choice.

"I can take care of myself. My dog can't."

It seemed to me that he was probably right. He would be pretty safe here, if nobody ratted him out. I had to ask myself if I had a reason to be that rat, and I couldn't think of any. I didn't know what he might have done to John Rice, but I didn't know Rice either. At the moment, I sort of liked Three-Steps Larry, and I didn't much like John Rice.

"I'll tell Mr. Carson," I said. Then I got up and climbed back up to the deck. I added, "and I'll pick up your dog, and maybe I'll bring you some food."

My warm feelings about Larry faded quite a bit after what happened next, which was all his fault. If he hadn't destroyed my shirt, I wouldn't have had to go right home to change out of it before anyone besides Larry got an eyeful, and before my kids got home. I could only imagine what they'd say, and avoiding that conversation was weighing on my mind as I sprinted in, changed, and then dashed out of my house. What I'm saying is that I just wasn't paying attention to my surroundings.

Anyway, as it turned out, getting the dog was easy. The kennel was overcrowded, so it was strictly no-questions-asked when I explained that I was there to get Sabano's dog. It turned out that she was a sweet mutt and I didn't figure I'd have any trouble with her once I got her home. I thought that my biggest problem would be convincing my kids that they couldn't keep her.

I was dead wrong about that.

Chapter Thirteen

My biggest problem turned out to be that John Rice's man Fred had been posted to watch my house, and I'd been too preoccupied to notice him following me when I left to get the dog. But I noticed him now, as I left the vet clinic. I was no sooner back on the road with the dog sitting beside me than Fred pulled out behind me and made no attempt to disguise the fact that he was following me.

By the time I got back to my house, John Rice was sitting in front of it in another car. I tried to look casual, parking in my driveway as if everything were perfectly normal. Fred pulled in behind me, blocking my car. Rice got out of his car and walked up beside me. He gestured for me to roll down the window, but I didn't.

"Ms. Manymules," he said.

"I can hear you, Mr. Rice. I don't want to let my dog out."

"That's not your dog. I think it's Larry Sabano's dog, and you know how I know that? I know it because you don't have a dog. You have a daughter named Kai and a son named Len."

While I fought to keep down my lunch, Fred got out of his car and walked up to the passenger side door so that I had no escape route, not that I thought I had one anyway.

"This is going to get you guys in trouble," I said as I rolled my window down about two inches. "I'm sitting here in my driveway being threatened by two strangers from out of town. How long do you think that can go on in this neighborhood?"

"It doesn't look to me like you're being threatened, Naomi. You seem a little nervous, though. What's your problem? A couple of businessmen whom you met earlier today are simply talking to you in your driveway. Frankly, you act as if you have something to hide."

The dog put her paws up on the passenger-door armrest and started licking the window and wagging her tail while Fred placed his palm against the glass.

"When did you hear from Larry?" Rice asked, leaning a little closer to the window's narrow opening.

"He called me just before lunch and told me about his dog. I said I'd pick her up and take care of her until he got back to town." I noticed that every time I said the word "dog," the pooch looked at me briefly.

"Back to town?" Rice brought me back to the subject at hand.

"Yes, he said he was out of town and was going to be delayed for several days. He said the dog had to be picked up because he was overdue getting back. I said I'd take care of her for him." The dog looked at me for a second and then went back to trying to lick Fred through the glass.

Rice leaned down to look over at the dog like he expected her to contribute useful information as he continued, "All right. Where was he calling from?"

"He didn't say, and I didn't ask. It didn't occur to me." I wondered if any of my neighbors were watching and if any of them would think it strange that I was sitting in my closed car while two men talked to me. I hoped that they were being nosy as hell and had already dialed the police.

Flashing a look of mock dismay, he shifted his eyes from the dog to me, like he was surprised that I'd been the one who answered. And like maybe her answer would have been better. "Apparently we didn't make it clear enough this morning that we are very serious about talking to Larry right away." He leaned even closer to my window.

"You made it plenty clear," I said quietly.

"Please understand that I am hoping to keep this matter between Mr. Sabano and myself, Naomi. Our business has nothing to do with you." He straightened up and gestured toward Fred. His subordinate backed away from the other side of the car and walked back toward the car that was parked behind mine.

Rice continued. "I'm going to call you on the telephone this evening, Ms. Manymules. At that time, I will expect you to tell me where I can find Three-Steps Larry."

"I don't know where…."

"Please find out," Rice said. He sounded polite enough, but I was pretty sure he wasn't a gentleman.

About the time that Rice climbed back into his car, my stomach won the argument that I'd been having with it. The dog found that disgusting.

~ ~ ~

After cleaning up the car, changing clothes again, setting some dishes out for the dog, and writing a note for my kids, an hour had gone by before I got back to the office.

Carson was sitting at my desk looking at something on my computer. "You failed to mention that you would be away quite so long. We've had a lot going on here."

I could've hit him. "Oh, really? Really? Well, we've had a lot going on out on the goddamn *streets*, too. Want to hear about my last couple of hours?" I could feel tears starting to roll down both of my cheeks and I quickly wiped them off with my fingertips.

He looked up, surprised, but didn't answer my question. "I've done some checking on Dr. Banner," he said. "It seems that he has something going on with one of his employees, a woman named Lucille Farneth."

"I knew that. I told *you* that."

"No you didn't. You said…"

"That's what I meant. You didn't expect me to name names. I told you that Dr. Banner could prove that he was somewhere else and that I knew it."

He nodded thoughtfully and looked at me, finally seeing that I was radiating anxiety and wearing a whole different outfit than I'd started the day in. "So you did," he said. "Naomi, what happened at lunch?"

I could feel my face crumple and my throat close up. I took a deep breath. "John Rice," I said, and I couldn't control my voice. "John Rice and that guy Fred." Just like Three-Steps when I'd surprised him at the boat, I didn't seem to be able to complete a sentence. "John Rice and that guy Fred. They threatened... they threatened...not in so many words. Politely."

"They threatened you politely?"

Carson came around the desk and put his arms around me. I put my head on his chest and sobbed. "...and my kids. And I threw up. And I had to change clothes twice and find something to feed the dog."

Then I realized that I was getting tears all over Carson's semi-clean T-shirt and that one of my feet was planted firmly on top of one of his sandals. I looked up at his face and saw that he was taking the pain quite well considering that he wasn't all that young and I wasn't all that light. I got off his foot and backed away from him.

"We need to know more about Banner's son," I said. "Apparently he has some kind of juvenile record that ties in here."

Carson sat down and lifted his foot, looking at it as if to examine the sandal for damage. "Did Rice tell you that?"

"No. I have a source who wishes to remain anonymous."

He stood again and walked without any discernable limp toward the door to his inner office. "Come in here and sit down, Naomi. We need to make some sense of this." As soon as we sat down, Carson started rummaging through his desk and finally came up with a pretty sizable pistol that had been buried under papers in his lower left drawer.

"What's that?" I asked. Then I clarified my question. "What kind of gun is that?"

"It's a .45 automatic."

Keeping my eyes on the gun, I smiled faintly. "It's a good thing you couldn't find it and grabbed the four-iron instead last week. If you'd charged out there with that thing you might have been arrested."

He laughed. "Or you might have taken it away from me and shot High-smith with it before someone else beat you to it." Then the smile left his face. "Can you handle one of these?"

The gun looked enormous lying there on the cluttered desktop. Just picking it up would be a challenge. "I've only fired a handgun a few times in my life," I said. "Never one that big—just a .22 revolver."

Carson pulled up his T-shirt and tucked the small cannon into the top of his pants. "Then this one wouldn't do you any good. Do you still have the .22 revolver?"

"It wasn't mine. It was...uh... it belonged to a friend of mine in high school."

He nodded and I could tell that he was too sharp for me and my see-through face. "It was Ellen's, wasn't it?"

"Uh… no. It was her grandfather's. We took it out plinking a couple of times."

"Plinking?"

"Plinking. It means..."

"I know what it means. More than that, it means that Ellen Highsmith knows how to handle a pistol."

"That doesn't mean anything, Carson. Everybody around here knows how to handle a pistol—and a rifle and a shotgun."

"Everyone?"

"At least a little, yes." I looked at the gun-shaped outline that the .45 was making in the front of his T-shirt. "I wish right now that I knew how to use one a lot better." My tears started up again. "And I wish that I'd had one an hour ago."

I went on to tell him about picking up a friend's dog and about being followed and about Rice's implied threats. I didn't mention Three-Steps Larry yet. Carson listened with a kind of steely grimace, and I saw a different man across the desk than I had seen before. This man wasn't the laid-back, semi-retired lawyer that I thought I knew. He was some earlier man from before law school. This was the leaner muscle that showed still.

When I finished my story, he said, "I don't want you to go to a store for this, but I want you to have a handgun, and I don't have another one. Who do you know?"

"Who do I know who has a gun?" I looked at him and smiled as if at a question from an innocent child. "Everybody." I paused because he looked as if he hadn't understood me. "I think I may know a few people who *don't* have any guns. If my ex-husband hadn't taken his with him, I'd have four or five myself. I could probably borrow a handgun from any of a dozen people within an hour." I stood up and walked toward the outer office. "And I'm going to get on the phone and do that right now."

Without offering any explanations, I was offered a plethora of firearms, no questions asked. Within twenty minutes, a .38 and a box of ammunition were sitting on my desk. A friend's brother had brought them in and laid them on my desk without saying a word. The pistol was one of those shiny chrome ones with a very short barrel. Carson, who'd overheard the telephone conversations, of course, stayed in his office when it arrived.

"Are we through getting packages now?" Carson asked through the wall.

"For now," I said, "but we may be getting a rocket launcher later."

"Then come on back in here and let's figure this out."

I started to put the pistol in my purse but thought better of it. I shoved it in the waistband of my pants before going into Carson's office.

He looked at the pistol butt sticking out of my waistband and said, "You can't just go out on the street and shoot those guys, you know?"

"Well, where can I shoot them, then?" I was only half joking.

"Are you sure that you could do it?"

"Shoot one of those bastards?" I said, picturing myself firing the shiny little pistol at Fred. "Sure. In a heartbeat." That mental picture triggered a long-ago memory. "Actually, I *have* shot a guy before—my cousin Billy, when we were kids."

"Wow! So you would know all about having a juvenile record."

I laughed. "It wasn't like that. We were just fooling around, plinking, with his old .22 rifle. He hung a saddle blanket over a fence wire and took a shot at it from about fifty feet. When we got up to look at the blanket to see if he'd hit it, we found the bullet lying on the ground right under the blanket. Billy discovered that the bullet had gone through the first layer of the blanket, but not the second. It had fallen out between the folds."

"So you shot him?"

"I'm getting to that. Okay, so Billy got this theory that a horse blanket was as good as a bullet-proof vest. He stood back a few feet from the blanket and shot it again and the same thing happened."

"The bullet only went through one fold?"

"Yeah, so then he wanted me to shoot him."

"I missed something there," Carson said.

"He said we had proof that the blanket would be like a bullet-proof vest, as long as we folded it. He put the folded blanket up against his chest and told me to shoot him. I wasn't convinced, so I said no. He wouldn't give up, though. He said he'd hold the blanket across his butt instead. Eventually he talked me into it. He turned around and stretched the folded blanket tight against his backside, and I plugged him."

"But this time the bullet went right through the blanket," Carson said, "didn't it?"

I nodded. "Like a hot knife through cold butter."

"Because he held the blanket tightly across his rear end instead of letting it hang loose and absorb the energy."

"Right, so I shot him in the butt. The bullet went into him more than an inch—bled like a son of a... I thought our grandmother was going to kill us."

"Kids." Then his smile faded. "So what's this business about the Banner boy?"

I answered his question with a better question. "How can we find out about his juvenile record?"

"Theoretically, we can't, but I know someone who might be able to help us."

"Do you think Peggy would do that?"

It was his turn to look at me as if answering an innocent child. He said nothing. Then his expression changed. "Oh, I almost forgot. Chuck Margolin called and said that my boat was ready."

"I know. I went by there at lunch."

"Went by there? The marina isn't on the way to anywhere. Where were you?"

Boy, this withholding-information stuff is difficult. You have to choose your words carefully—especially with a guy who used to make a living by nailing witnesses in a courtroom. "I met a friend out at the lake. On the way back in, I decided to drop by the boat to see if it was finished."

Carson stood up. "Well, let's go look at her. Hell, let's take her for a little ride."

I stayed put. "Maybe not," I said. "It might not be a good idea for us to go out there right now, not if Rice is watching us."

"Why not?"

"Three-Steps Larry is out there."

"Out there, as in on my boat?"

"He's hiding."

"On my boat?" Carson slammed the palm of his hand down on his desktop. "That son of a bitch! He'd better not be messing up my boat."

"He acts like he thinks that Rice and Fred are going to kill him. I told him to stay put and that I would pick up his dog and bring him some food."

Carson sat back down in his chair. "I don't need this. I'm not involved in whatever it is that Three-Steps did to these guys. I've got all that I can handle with the Highsmith case."

"You mean with all three or four of our Highsmith murder-suspect clients?"

In his current state of mind, my subtle criticism was lost on him. "Exactly! Whatever this other thing is, this thing with Sabano and Rice, I haven't got time for it."

"I don't think that explanation will go very far with Rice," I said. "I think he intends for us to make time for his problem, and his problem is Larry Sabano."

"That's not my…"

I raised my voice to interrupt his rant. "Carson, he threatened my kids."

That got through to him. It reminded him that Rice had handed me a big chunk of that problem just an hour ago. To Carson's credit, that had made it his problem, too. "Right, yes. I'm sorry, Naomi. What, exactly, did he say?"

"Rice said he was going to call tonight and he expected me to tell him where to find Larry." After a moment I added, "Maybe I will."

Carson leaned back in his chair and stared at the ceiling for a moment as if considering that possibility. "You'd get stuck with the dog," he said.

"That's the only down side, though."

"That, and being responsible for whatever happens to Three-Steps Larry."

"I could live with that a hell of a lot better than with what might happen to my kids."

We were interrupted by the arrival of Mike Rodriguez. I was sitting where he could see me in Carson's office, and he came on in.

"Hello, Naomi," he said with a smile before turning to face my boss. "Where's your client, Grant? She's supposed to stay home."

I briefly wondered which of the two female clients he was talking about. My boss was quicker on the uptake.

"Isn't she there?" Carson asked.

"She is not, and I'd better not find out that you knew otherwise. It's a condition of her bail, as *you* know." So he was definitely talking about Ellen, and I wondered where she had gone.

Using my most soothing voice, I said, "Ellen is probably out shopping." I gestured vaguely toward the chair next to me and went on, "Why don't you sit down here and tell us what's happened?"

The police chief crossed his arms and leaned against the door jamb. He was a pretty tall guy, solid and well-muscled. With his trim uniform buttoned tightly over the regulation bullet-proof vest—no saddle blanket here —he more or less filled the doorway. "We have more questions for her— about money. A lot of money."

"Highsmith had a lot of money that we didn't know about?" Carson asked.

"Insurance that we didn't know about," the chief said, "and that Ellen didn't tell us about. New insurance. She told us that there was a policy that would pay the mortgage on the house. She failed to mention that there were new policies on her and her husband—corporate policies through the business."

Carson glanced over at me. Either he didn't know about these policies, or he was doing a good job of looking confused. He turned back to Mike. "How much?"

"Half a million, each."

"Over and above what we know about?"

"Over and above, and only two months old," Rodriguez answered. "It sure goes to motive, doesn't it, counselor?" Suddenly he looked down at me, directly at the pistol butt sticking out of the top of my pants. Then he turned his head and looked at Carson's waistline. "What the fuck is going on here?" He raised both of his hands about chest high like he was surrendering or something—talk about being dramatic.

"We were about to go rob a bank when you came in," Carson said.

I gave him a mom look. "Shush," I said before looking up at Mike.

"Some men threatened…" I stopped and cleared my throat. "Some men threatened me and my children," I said. "We're just getting ready to defend ourselves."

Chief Rodriguez sat down and kept his hands conspicuously out in front of him. "A direct threat?"

"More like a very skillfully worded implied threat," Carson said, "made by people who have cultivated their ability to do that."

"Related to the Highsmith thing?"

"No. This is something else. We're just not sure what." His expression darkened, giving me another glimpse of that pre-law-school steel and muscle. His voice was gruff when he went on, "But the next time I see either one of them, I'll tear his…"

The chief interrupted him. "Okay, okay. Calm down, counselor. Can't have you taking matters into your own hands. Stay away from them. I've known Naomi for a long time. I'll have my people keeping an extra watch. What are we looking for?"

Carson, answered, still visibly agitated. "A slick New Mexico attorney named John Rice, staying somewhere in town. He has a mountain of a guy named Fred with him. They think Naomi has information that they want. It's privileged information, and she's not going to give it to them."

Rodriguez nodded solemnly. He turned to look at me. "Do you know how to use that thing?"

"Sure. Sort of. Maybe." Now that I thought about it, it'd been more than fifteen years since I'd tried to shoot soda cans out in the desert, and I hadn't been very good at it even then. I might be kind of rusty, but I sure wasn't going to say that.

Mike Rodriguez leaned back in his chair and sighed. "Well, don't let them get too close, and please make sure that they're facing you. It's hard to make a defense plea if the bullets are in the back."

"You can't be serious," Carson said. "Is that all you've got to offer her?"

"Of course not," Rodriguez said, standing up abruptly. "I'll find out where this guy Rice is staying, and I'll confront him directly. He'll come out with a denial—say it was an unfortunate misunderstanding—all that shit. You know that, but I'll make sure he gets the message. I'm the chief of goddamn police, and this is *my* town." He paused for a second and then added, "That'll probably do it, but don't pass up a chance to shoot him in the chest if he gets near you, Naomi."

"I'd hate to cross you if I were an out-of-town attorney," Carson said.

Rodriguez glowered. "You don't want to cross me if you're an in-town attorney, either. Find your client and get her ass back in her house," he said as he stomped out of the office

We looked across the desk at each other and both spoke simultaneously.

"I can't handle this," is what I said while Carson muttered, "This is too much for me." That made us laugh, but just for a second. Then reality returned.

"A couple of weeks ago I was only worried about my mortgage," I said. "Right now I don't even think I can count up all the things I'm worried about. What does a nervous breakdown feel like?"

Carson pulled the .45 out of his waistband and laid it on the desk. I think it was probably poking him in the gut. He'd put on a few pounds since he bought those pants. "Give me a few more hours, and I'll tell you all about it. I think I'm starting my mental collapse as we speak."

"Seriously, this will take both hands." I leaned forward and held up my index finger. "First, there's a shady character threatening my kids." I raised another finger. "Highsmith was murdered *and* my friend is the prime suspect." That was just one finger because the murder part didn't worry me, just the Ellen part. I unfolded a third finger, saying, "A nice friend of mine is having an affair with someone whose whole family is implicated in the murder." The final finger and the thumb. "Ellen might lose her kids."

Carson looked at my hand, which now had all five digits stretched out. "You're losing count."

I waggled the thumb—problem number five. "I've got to get some dog food," I said. "Not important, considering, but still…."

"And Three-Steps is probably fucking up my boat," Carson said.

I nodded, extending the thumb and first two fingers of the other hand. "And you'll probably be disbarred, and I'll lose my job." Problems six, seven, and eight.

Carson was quiet for a moment before adding the most immediate worry for us both.

"And where the hell is Ellen?"

Chapter Fourteen

I gave my kids a generic warning about watching for strangers—murderer on the loose in town and all of that. I also kept them home all evening. They could tell something was up.

I kept my borrowed pistol out of sight but close at hand all evening long, waiting for Fred to show up at my door, but he never did. Rice didn't even call. That's the way it is with men. They say they'll call, but they usually don't. The only call that came in was from Carson. He said that he wanted me to go fishing with him the next morning and that we wouldn't be getting an early start. He said to wait for him at home and he would pick me up at ten in the morning.

I slept fitfully with the pistol under the covers next to me all night long. I repeated all my warnings to the kids at breakfast and told them they'd have to stay home after school. They promised that they would. Usually they could be trusted when there was a murderer loose in town. Still, I drove them the few blocks to their schools—yes, they rolled their eyes—and told them to stay there until I picked them up in the afternoon.

Carson was almost on time. He showed up about fifteen minutes late and any observer would have known that he was going fishing. Four fishing rods were sticking up out of the back of his pickup truck, and a large ice chest was clearly visible. He was wearing a canvas vest from which dangled all manner of fishing paraphernalia. He also sported a crumpled khaki hat that was decorated with at least a dozen colorful flies.

I didn't have a fishing costume so all I could add to the illusion was myself in old denim pants and a plaid flannel shirt. I would have worn a hat, but I was having a particularly good hair day and didn't want to spoil my luck. I was carrying an old day pack of Len's into which I'd stuffed the pistol and a fistful of extra bullets, along with the usual purse necessities.

I opened the truck's passenger door and stood for a minute, looking up and down the street. Nothing.

I climbed in and said, "Nobody seems to be following us yet. What's up?"

Carson started the truck and shifted into gear. "Oh, that. Well, the chief requested the pleasure of Fred's company this morning, and Mr. Rice's, too. They're all spending a little time together at the station." Still, he waited at the stop sign a few beats longer than necessary, looking in the rear-view mirror, before turning north toward the lake.

I turned to look through the back window, too, just in case. Seeing no menacing vehicles—no vehicles at all, in fact—I turned around and changed the subject. "Ellen is out on the reservation," I said. "I called her mother last night. Ellen had told her that she was going out to stay at her grandfather's place for a few days."

"Not allowed," Carson said simply.

"That's nuts. It's practically in town. Her granddad lived only a couple of miles past the power plant. It's not like she took off for parts unknown."

"It's exactly like she took off for parts unknown. Her bail specified that she had to stay in town. It was very clear. I'll give her a call before we go out to the boat."

"You can't. There's no phone out there."

Carson drove along in silence until we pulled up in front of a grocery store. "I'll worry about that later. Now we're going to go in and buy beer for our fishing trip."

"We don't need it," I said. "Three-Steps said that there was plenty of booze on the boat."

"*Was.* That is the operative word. I have no doubt that Sabano has been drinking my supply. Now it will be depleted—it was already getting low."

"We should get more food. He said there wasn't much to eat in the galley."

Carson was already half-way out of the truck, but he stopped and frowned at me. "Ha! That's funny! Like I'm going to encourage him to stay in my boat? Not gonna happen. He's like a stray cat—feed him and he'll move in. No, instead he's going to get hungry and move on."

"So why bring more beer?" I asked. Sometimes Carson's logic escaped me.

"Conversation starter." He closed the truck door and walked into the store.

As we drove to the lake, Carson went back to talking about Ellen. "The reservation is a different legal jurisdiction. She's done more than leave her home and leave town; she's also left the state of Arizona, sort of. She's now in the Navajo Nation and under both tribal and federal jurisdiction."

"I'm sure that never even occurred to her. We just think of that part of the Rez as a suburb of Sage Landing. We'll just drive out there when we get a chance and talk to her. It's no big deal."

"It's a big deal to Mike Rodriguez. You can bet on that. Do you think he knows about her grandfather's place?"

I had to think about that for a moment. Ellen had spent a lot of time with her grandfather when she was a child and a teenager, but Mike wasn't from around here and might not know that. "I don't know. Maybe."

"What about Miller?"

"Jack would probably think to look out there, but he's out of the loop right now. He's on forced vacation so Rodriguez isn't going to ask for his opinion."

Then something else came to mind. Maybe she was trying to enhance her connection to traditional Navajo ways by going out to the Rez in a time of trouble. However, if she were strict in her traditional beliefs, she would probably not go to her grandfather's house, because he had died there. Way back in the past, avoiding a house where someone had died meant that you just stayed away from his *hogan,* which would eventually melt back into the earth. These days, of course, property ownership and mortgages and all that made it harder to leave a house and its spirit undisturbed.

Carson interrupted my train of thought. "No phone, you said? Is this place a modern house?"

"It's a nice double-wide mobile home, like half the houses in town. It's got a well and electricity and everything—used to have a nice vegetable garden and a stand of corn."

We pulled in at the marina as I finished my description. Carson simply nodded and started unloading the truck. We carried all the fishing junk and the beer out to the boat and set it aboard. If we were being watched, I couldn't tell it, and I said so when we climbed aboard.

Carson said, "The question is whether or not Larry has already given himself away. When I talked with Rodriguez last night, he told me that Rice was staying out here at the Sage Marina Hotel. That's probably just a coincidence since it's the nicest hotel in the area, but it could mean that he's been watching the marina."

"What's his room number?"

"Rodriguez didn't say. Why, what difference does it make?"

"I know the numbering system that they use at the resort. If I knew his room number, I could tell you whether or not his room looks out at the marina. Half of the rooms look out at the beach on the other side."

"Did you work the front desk?"

I laughed. "I used to deliver pizza out here. Lots of it. I wasn't always a legal professional."

"I think you have to work for a better lawyer than me to be considered a legal professional," Carson said as he uncoupled the electric line that connected to the dock. "Cast off those lines, will you?" He walked over to the ignition panel and started the engines. They both started instantly.

I untied the two lines that held us in the slip and Carson started lowering the drives so that he could back us out into the marina. It occurred to me that under different circumstances this could be a lot of fun. However, given the current situation, I made sure that my little pack with its pistol was lying close to me as I sat down. I also looked Carson over to see where he was carrying his .45. It was tucked into the middle of the back of his pants, mostly covered by the fishing vest.

We cruised slowly out of the marina at below-wake speed and headed for the buoy line that would let us open up the engines. When we reached it, the cruiser leaned back and started to gain speed rapidly. Carson steered to the right and kept the boat tightened along the base of the cliffs as we headed south toward the main channel. We were out of sight of the marina within minutes.

"Larry, you son of a bitch, you broke my lock," Carson shouted over the engines.

The cabin door opened and Three-Steps Larry reached up and set an open beer can next to Carson's hand. He looked at me with a question on his face and I signaled that I didn't want a beer. He shrugged and climbed up on deck with one for himself. "Sorry about that," he said. "You didn't leave the key where I could find it." He had a cocky smile on his face.

Carson must have finished about half his beer in the two long swallows that he took before he spoke again. "I'm sure glad you gave us a retainer, Larry, because you're turning into a real pain in the ass."

"Well, you've got to do something for that kind of money, Grant. What kind of supplies did you bring me?"

Grant narrowed his eyes. "If you think I'm going to let you keep hiding out on my boat, you are even more deluded than usual."

I stood and headed down to the galley to put the beer we'd brought into the tiny fridge. While I was checking out the cupboards to see if Grant had been right about the depletion of supplies, the two men said nothing to each other. I was glad to be out of all that awkwardness and took my time. A few minutes later, I had to brace myself against the counter to keep my balance as Carson made a wide left turn to ease the cruiser into the main channel and head east. I thought about the Colorado River, which once would have been running fast and deep right under where we were, and I pictured what it must've looked like here before it swelled into a lake.

Before long, the engines cut back to idle and the boat settled down. I cautiously climbed the stairs again. We were now bobbing midway between the cliffs at the edge of town and the sandy island that I'd gazed at as the moon rose before all this intrigue started. The guys, still not talking, were looking in different directions.

"It should've been right along here," Carson said. "Right, Naomi?"

"Further," I said. "Down at the mouth of that next canyon. Highsmith's boat was floating out about two hundred feet from the cliff."

Carson moved the boat further to the east until we were floating just about where Highsmith's boat had been when I first saw it. "Right about here," I said. I began to look along the top of the cliffs and a moment later found what I was looking for. I pointed upward and said, "I was in that chute there at the top. I was hiding."

The guys both gazed at where I was pointing. Shielding his eyes from the sun with his hand, Carson said, "It looks to me like it would have been pretty easy to fall right out of that crack and drop a couple of hundred feet."

"For a few seconds I thought I was going to do just that," I said. "Anyway, I could see the boat from there in the moonlight."

Carson turned to look toward the canyon that came from the south and broke into the main channel at this point—the one where I'd thought some-one had tossed a couple of cherry bombs. "Look over there, Naomi."

Three-Steps Larry and I both started to scan the cliff tops between the side canyon and the cleft where I'd been hiding. At first it was hard to see anyplace where the gunshots might have come from.

A moment later, Larry spoke up. "Maybe not on the town side," he said. "Look across to the other side of the canyon, at the cliff wall facing us—the part we can see, anyway." He pointed his finger. "It looks to me like there's a fault running down from the top over there, maybe even a trail. See it? Looks like it dead-ends maybe fifty feet below the top. Right over there."

"Yeah," Carson said. "I see it. What do you think, Naomi?"

"Could be," I said, looking at the spot that Larry had found. "It looks like a ledge slopes down along there and comes out on top a few hundred feet back—hard to be sure from down here."

"You think you could've heard someone shooting from there?" Carson asked.

Three-Steps answered for me. "Hard to tell. In the canyons, some places amplify every whisper. In others, you can't even hear a thunderstorm." Then he had a question of his own. "If someone wanted to come out to that place on the east wall, where would they have to start?"

Carson looked at me. I didn't have an answer, but I tried to construct a mental map. "There are no roads that I know of coming down that side of this canyon. I think the closest one goes down to a point two canyons to the northeast. It would take forever to walk from there."

"How far back does this canyon go?" Carson asked.

I thought about that for a minute. "Two, maybe three miles, I think. Maybe a little more."

"There must be trails out there," Three-Steps said. "There are trails everywhere on this desert."

"Sure," I agreed. "There will be trails running along the top up there. They would run southward from here. Sheep probably graze up there, for one thing."

Grant Carson reached down to the control panel of his boat, turned off the engines, and squinted up at the cliff. "Did Ellen's grandfather run sheep?"

Then it hit me as if something physical had actually shoved my chest. Of course her grandfather had run sheep, and if I had my mental geography right, he might even have grazed them as far as the lake. Not trusting my voice, I nodded. On my mental map, Ellen might now be standing about two and a half miles south of us beyond the end of this canyon.

"Could you get from his place all the way to here?"

There would be lots of rough ground between here and there, but I figured it might be possible for an experienced desert rat like Ellen. If the trail was good, the Ellen I had known as a teen could have made it out here in less than an hour in the daylight. But she wasn't a teen anymore, and there wouldn't have been any light. I knew that because I'd watched the moon rise over the lake while I stood there, just before hearing the shots.

I shook my head. "I doubt it…maybe."

Larry walked to the back of the deck and sat down on the upholstered bench there. He seemed to be studying the rocks around us for a moment, and then he turned his attention to the island across the channel. He looked along its shore to where the island ended, perhaps a quarter of a mile northeast of us. "So you're sure the shots came from up there somewhere?"

Carson shrugged. "Chief Rodriguez thinks they probably came from another boat. The other Highsmith boat is missing, and Rodriguez thinks that Ellen came out here on it and shot Willard. I think the shots came from up on top somewhere, but I'm guessing."

Three-Steps was staring at the island again.

"I couldn't tell where they came from, but I heard two shots," I said. I couldn't remember whether or not I was supposed to tell people that, but since it was my own story instead of anyone else's secret, it seemed okay to say it. Besides, I wouldn't have minded seeing it as a headline on the *Gazette*. "Only one bullet hit Highsmith—went all the way through him —but I'm pretty sure I heard two."

Carson frowned at me and shook his head slightly—an older man's way of telling a younger woman to stop talking. "So, Larry, what have you got *yourself* into?" he asked.

Three-Steps sat silently and continued to study our surroundings. He chose his words carefully. "I don't know, exactly. Nothing." He crossed his arms and didn't seem inclined to say more.

Carson, impatient now, said, "So John Rice..."

Larry interrupted, "Look, I know who John Rice is, and I know who he works for. Those guys got it in their heads that I did something they didn't like, so they came all the way over here to find me."

He sounded like he was lying. "You must have done something," I said.

"No, they just have to *think* I did something. There's not a lot of legal process in their world." He looked back northward toward the island. "Obviously they *think* I did something to them. It doesn't much matter whether I did or not."

"What's your connection with them?" Carson asked.

Instead of answering, Three-Steps stood up and paced around the deck for a moment. "I'm ready for another beer. How about you?"

Carson shook his head, and Larry went below and brought up another can for himself. He waited until he had opened his beer and taken a gulp before he continued. "Let's just say that I used to buy things from them sometimes and get hired occasionally to do things. Best if I don't go into that. Anyway, that was a long time ago. And I don't owe them any money —quite the contrary."

"The contrary?" Carson asked, raising an eyebrow. "So they owe *you* money?"

"A while back, quite a while, they owed me a whole lot of money. They stiffed me on the money and threw me under the bus with the DEA."

"Ouch!" Carson said. "Did you end up doing time?"

"Not that time. But I was in holding for weeks waiting for a trial. I ended up getting a tough lawyer—on my own dime. Then, when I tried to get the fuckers to square things up with me, a couple of their guys nearly killed me. I was in the hospital about a week. Seemed like a good time to get out of New Mexico."

On the one hand, I tried to be pretty open minded. I knew a fair number of adults in Sage Landing who smoked a little pot. Okay, some of them smoked a lot of pot. I had nothing against them. Toleration is a good thing. I reminded myself of that often. Sage Landing was not a place to be intolerant.

On the other hand, I had kids, and we lived in a very small town. It doesn't take much drug traffic to have a big impact on the teenagers in a town this size. One dealer could do a lot of harm.

If I was following the story that Three Steps was telling, it would be hard to make myself believe that he was talking about something other than drugs. So toleration wasn't called for here because I was becoming less sure that he wasn't hurting anyone.

"Let's assume for a moment that you're not lying to me," Carson said. "Let's assume you haven't done anything to these guys, but that they think you have. What's the way out of this?"

"I don't know. You understand that I have no idea what they think I did." He sounded very unconvincing. "Even if I could figure that out, I don't know what I could do about it. If, for instance, they think I have some of their money or something, I don't." He paused. "More likely they think I'm doing business in their territory without their permission."

"Are you trespassing on them?"

"No. I told you I don't deal in their products any more. I was never very good at it. They used to tell me that all the time."

"Where'd you get the money you gave me?"

Larry coughed and seemed to be choking for a second. "Swallowed wrong," he said. "Savings... my savings account. I took it out of savings that morning."

"And I could check on that?"

Three-Steps didn't answer.

My toleration was slipping, and I felt a frown creeping into place on my face. If I understood this conversation correctly, I'd just heard Larry pretty much admit he'd been a dope dealer. He wasn't talking about selling cars or timeshares. No, what I had just heard was that he'd been dealing dope around *here* because he'd been living here for several years.

Then I started to recall scenes with Three-Steps in them—the kinds of scenes that take place right in front of you without your noticing them. Three-Steps playing pick-up basketball in the park across from the high school. Three-Steps hanging around at the shopping center and joking with the young guys there on weekend nights. Girls a few years older than my daughter flirting with Three-Steps Larry outside the new movie theater.

Larry noticed my frown because it had turned into a glare that was directed at him. "What?"

"Tell me we're just talking about marijuana here," I said. "Just tell me that, at least."

He shook his head. "Usually, yeah. Mostly just grass."

"Mostly!"

"Jesus! I said that was all in the past—over. Cut me a little slack here, Naomi."

"Drop dead, asshole."

Everybody and everything went silent. There was no wind. The lake was calm. The engines were off. I closed my eyes and felt the slight motion of the water under the boat. The only sound I could hear was the gentle lapping of the water against the boat's hull. I thought *this was what Willard Highsmith was hearing just before the shots that killed him*, and I shivered.

CHAPTER FIFTEEN

AFTER Carson gave Larry some forceful instructions, including—I'm quoting here—"quit fucking up my goddamn boat"—we drove back into town. Still fuming, I had half a mind to sic the thugs on Larry instead of helping him hide. But Carson vetoed that, saying, "You're a legal professional, remember?" I started to protest. If he could use my own words against me, I could use his, and he didn't seem to have any trouble justifying his own bending of the rules. But I thought better of it and took a deep breath.

Carson took the opportunity to change the subject, launching into a review of the various suspects we knew about in our murder case, ending with Ellen. His mind was really on that ledge and trail we'd seen in the canyon, but he didn't include them in his rundown.

I waited to see if he was going to share what he was thinking about that and what it might mean for her case. When it was clear that he wasn't going to, at least not without being asked, I said, "About the canyon…" but couldn't seem to find anything to say about it.

He could, though. "About the canyon, it's not our place to go find evidence that might be damaging to Ellen. It's not our place to speculate about how she might have done it, if she did it. That's the prosecution's job, so just forget about the cliffs and all that."

"Right. Good." I could tell that he was still troubled, though, and a moment later he made it clear what he was thinking.

"On the other hand, what do you think Ellen would say to a possible plea bargain if the subject came up?"

I avoided the question. "What about Mark Banner?"

Carson nodded. "I talked to a friend last night about the boy's history. He *has* been in some serious trouble, but it was covered up, and, of course, it's officially part of his juvenile record. Therefore, it's theoretically inaccessible."

"Sure, I understand. So what did he do?"

"A couple of years ago he and a couple of other young rowdies, including Linda Armstrong, were killing cats in town—hunting them for sport."

I shuddered. I'm not exactly a cat person, but still. "That's pretty rough. I don't remember anything about that. You'd think that with gunshots going off around town there would've been quite a bit of talk."

"They weren't using guns; they were using slingshots, shooting those steel balls that you buy in sporting goods stores. They had a couple of heavy-duty slingshots that they bought through some hunters' magazine. According to my friend, they got really good at it."

I rolled my eyes. "Carson, her name is Peggy," I said. "Peggy Thomas or Deputy Thomas, but most people call her Peggy."

He grinned. "I don't reveal my sources, especially those who could get in trouble by sharing information. Anyway, the kids were apprehended but the Banners kept them from being charged. Actually, at that time the stray cat population of Sage Landing was a problem. Chief Rodriguez decided to take a boys-will-be-boys attitude."

"And girls-will-be-girls. I guess."

"It's pretty clear that Linda Armstrong is an unusual girl. In lots of ways."

I couldn't argue with that, but I wasn't exactly sure what *he* meant. "How so?"

"She has a certain…reputation. Her relationships …"

"She's open about what she does. But then, so is Gail Banner, and it doesn't seem to get her into much trouble."

"I'd say that they're both a little excessive, wouldn't you?"

Ah, the old double standard. I didn't like it, not at all. "What do you think they do that you don't, Carson?"

"We're not talking about ridding the neighborhood of cats anymore, right? We're talking about, um, dating behavior?"

"We're talking about sex. You do what *you* do, and you're some kind of Romeo-hero. But just let a woman do the same thing? She gets a whole different 'reputation.'"

We had to stop for the traffic light at the edge of town so Carson looked over at me. "Okay, point taken. Getting back to Mark Banner, let's put it in the worst possible light and say that he has a history of killing things in cold blood. Put that together with the fact that he might have resented Highsmith's affair with his mother."

"And add in the fact that he can get his hands on a few deer rifles."

Our conversation was cut short when we arrived at the office because our front door was open. When we walked inside, Jack Miller was sitting at my desk, this time wearing camouflage pants and an olive green T-shirt. All he lacked was some black grease under both eyes, and he could've been an extra in the new Rambo sequel.

The place was a mess. Some papers were strewn on the floor, all the desk drawers in both rooms were open, and the file cabinet in the outer office had been emptied and knocked over. There hadn't been much in it to begin with, so it didn't take long to scoop up the scattered files. Shuffling through them quickly showed us that there probably wasn't anything missing. And, thank goodness, my computer was intact.

I looked at Jack. "What happened?"

"This is the way I found it when I came to see you guys this morning. I've been here about an hour waiting for you."

"I guess I should've come by this morning before we went out to the lake," Carson said.

"What good would it have done?" I said. "This must have happened last night. We couldn't have done anything this morning."

Jack nodded toward the filing cabinet lying on the floor. "Kids aren't likely to have done this."

"No," Carson said. "The guys who did this aren't kids. They were looking for specific information."

"Why make a mess?" I asked.

"It's also a warning," Carson said.

Miller stood up. "Who is warning you and about what? Has this got anything to do with Ellen?"

I was about to say no, it's a whole different thing, but something made me stop. Where had Three-Steps been when Highsmith was shot? And Rice and Fred, where had *they* been? Who knew what anything had to do with anything else at this point? I'd have to think about that for a little while, somewhere quiet, so I could sort through everybody and map their whereabouts and draw dotted lines and make big red circles. And it was looking like I'd need to do that soon, before everybody in town had to be accounted for.

"Maybe," I said. "Some guys from out of town. We're not ruling anything out." Carson looked sharply at me but said nothing.

Jack said, "A guy named Rice?" and shrugged when I looked surprised. "I keep in touch with some people in the department even though I'm on vacation."

I looked at my boss to see whether or not he wanted me to answer, but he answered for me. "The office was probably tossed by John Rice or by someone working for him. It's not the first message he's sent us, but you'll never prove it. Let's get back to Ellen." Carson fixed his eyes on Jack. "What do you think would be the prosecutor's take on this Highsmith thing if it turned out to be a domestic-violence situation, say some sort of a fight, for instance."

Miller's face flushed beet red. "A fight between Ellen and Highsmith? That's bullshit, Carson. The man was at least fifty pounds heavier than Ellen."

"She wouldn't stand a chance. That's what I'm saying."

"Are you talking about a plea bargain? Are you thinking of asking Ellen to plead to manslaughter? In the first place, she didn't do it. In the second place, you'd never be able to talk her into a plea *because* she didn't do it. What the hell are you thinking?"

Carson took the mess of files and papers from my awkward grip and set them on my desk. "I'm just exploring the possibilities, Jack. Who knows what's going to turn up as this investigation goes along? It wouldn't be the first time I advised a client to plead down because I thought they might be convicted even though they were probably innocent. There's a history of domestic violence here. Under the circumstances, we might even be talking about immediate probation for her."

I thought that Jack was going to raise his fists. He had balled them both up at his sides. I touched his arm, and he looked up at the ceiling for a second before continuing in a low growl, "I'm warning you. Don't you dare offer a fucking plea for her. Don't you dare try that. I'm not kidding, Carson. You'd better start looking in another direction."

"Calm down, Jack," I said. "We're not doing anything like that. It's just that things don't look so good right now. Ellen has violated her bail by leaving home. She's probably just out at her grandfather's place, but that's a violation. And her alibi is thin. You know that."

Still glowering, he said, "Did you look into the Banner kid?"

Carson glanced quickly at me. So much for my source-who-wanted-to-remain-anonymous. "We're doing that," Carson said. "Thanks for the anonymous tip. It's true that there's a bad history there, and we may be able to go somewhere with it. At least it ought to cast some doubt in that direction. We'll certainly work on it."

Jack finally unclenched his hands and sat down. He didn't seem any happier, but he had sort of run out of steam. "Anything else?"

Carson leaned against my desk and gestured for me to sit down. "There's another slim possibility. This guy Rice is hanging around. Maybe he had a beef with Highsmith. It's not likely, but we might be able to raise some doubts there, too. Don't get the idea that I've given up on Ellen's defense."

"Rice works for a New Mexico company owned by Carlos Deguerra. Ever heard of him?"

Carson shook his head. "No, should I have?"

"Well, if you were a cop or a prosecutor up here in the Four Corners region, you would've heard of him."

"What would I have heard?" Carson paused and looked around the room. "No, let me guess. I would have heard that he was a narcotics dealer, probably a big one, right?"

"Not exactly. It would be more accurate to say that you would've heard he was *suspected* of being a narcotics dealer. He is also suspected of laundering money through a variety of restaurants and bars and other high-cash businesses. Also suspected of murder. And of jobbing out other murders. He's been arrested a few times, but never brought to trial. Why would his boys be interested in you?"

Carson sidestepped the question by asking, "Why do you think they would be interested in *anything* in Sage Landing?"

Jack shrugged. "I heard that Rodriguez was talking to those guys at the station this morning, but he's sure not going to tell me about it. I'm thinking maybe Rice is interested in something that happened on the lake the other night, but it was nowhere near here."

"What happened?" Carson asked.

"It was up at Bull Banks, or near there. A houseboat was drifting out on Bull Banks Bay closer to the north shore. It was a top of the line boat, worth at least a hundred grand. Registration says it belongs to a small New Mexico insurance agency. The insurance agency is owned by an investment corporation. I haven't heard anything about the corporation yet."

"So maybe Rice is missing a boat," I said.

Miller nodded. "Or boats—there was a high-end inflatable floating nearby. More likely Deguerra is missing a boat or two. I doubt if the boats are really the issue, because there were two dead guys aboard the houseboat —shot to death."

"When did they find all this?" Carson asked.

"Park Service picked them up on Tuesday a week ago at about noon. They towed them into Bull Banks and dry-docked the houseboat. A representative of the insurance agency tried to claim it on Thursday, but it's being held pending investigation. FBI is in on it."

"Because the lake is federal," said Grant, explaining in my general direction.

Ignoring him, I turned to Jack and asked, "What else do they know about it?"

"Give me a break, Naomi. I'm lucky to have heard that much. I'm on vacation, remember? It doesn't sound like they've discovered anything significant yet. My bet is there's a narcotics team going over it, but I'm just guessing. I did overhear that FBI forensics is having trouble figuring out who shot who."

All of a sudden I wasn't feeling so good. It seemed to me that I had somehow gotten into the middle of a very scary situation. John Rice and his thug were bad enough. Now we were harboring the man they were looking for—a drug dealer—and his fugitive dog. Three-Steps wasn't a fugitive from the law, at least not yet, but from people who were far more dangerous. And now there were more dead people involved, even if they'd died seventy-five or eighty miles up the lake.

I'd ridden this train of thought more than halfway to full blown-terror when Jack stood up abruptly. He said, "I've got to be going," and headed for the door.

I turned to Carson and said, "Me too. First I'm going to pull my kids out of school. Then I'm going to go home and lock the doors and try not to think about all this. I hope my new dog knows how to bark. So far the only thing she's done about John Rice is try to lick Fred's hand."

~ ~ ~

I had a lot of friends in the school district office so it wasn't difficult for me to get my kids out in the early afternoon. I said that we had family business to attend to. It wasn't hard to convince the kids to go home, either. They liked school, but they were kids after all, and now there was a dog to play with. Since it was a Thursday afternoon, their instincts told them that they might well parlay this into a Friday off as well.

After I had a quick lunch, it occurred to me that my daughter's behavior was a little off. She hadn't sat in the kitchen with me to talk. She hadn't spent much time with the dog, either, even though she'd been begging me for one since she was six years old. Instead, she'd gone directly to her room and turned on her music—softly, which was not normal for her. The more I thought about it, the more I realized that she'd looked a little somber when I picked her up.

Sure enough, her door was locked. I knocked. She opened it promptly, which was a relief, but then she gave the lame and completely implausible excuse that she'd been napping. That wasn't like her either so I brought on the showdown.

"Okay, Kai, what's going on?" There's a stance I take that is an unmistakable signal that I'm not to be fooled with. My daughter knew the stance very well.

"Nothing with me," she said. "Don't worry."

I stepped into her room and closed the door behind me again, relieved in spite of myself at not smelling smoke of any kind. "Honey, you're worried so it must be something important. Out with it."

"It's over now, anyway. Some bad stuff was happening to a friend of mine, but it's over now. I just found out about it, is all."

When Kai said 'a friend of mine,' she meant one of three or four people she liked well enough to worry about. It occurred to me that at the present moment the most likely would be Ellen's daughter, also named Ellen, who'd always been called Elle. But Elle was not in school this week because she was with her grandmother in Kayenta. Before I could start asking her about the short list of other possibilities, Kai spoke up.

"Elle," she said. "I've been talking to her."

"Talking to her? I thought she was at her grandmother's."

"They came into town and she walked over to school to get stuff from her locker while her grandma was getting groceries."

"How could you talk to her when you were in class?"

Kai looked away. "She caught me in the hall between classes and said she needed me to come talk to her."

"How did you manage that?"

"I was going to P.E. so I begged off from class."

"From P.E. class?"

"Yes."

"I don't remember that we were excused to visit friends during P.E. class when I was in school. How did you pull this off?"

"Cramps."

I remembered that all right. I used to get out of P.E. class the same way from time to time. Now I had a dilemma that faced most mothers from time to time. Should I pretend that I had never done such a thing and be stern, or should I just let it go and try to find out what was going on? Luckily, that wasn't a tough choice this time.

"What about Elle?"

Kai blushed. "It's over now. It's nothing."

I sat on the edge of the bed and patted a place beside me. "Why can't you talk about it? What happened?"

Kai sat down at her desk and turned her office-type chair around to face me. "It's not her. She hasn't done anything. It was her dad—her stepfather. It doesn't matter now."

My stomach was in knots all over again. "God, no. What all did he do to her?"

"No, not what you're thinking, Mom." Kai shook her head slowly and deliberately from side to side and put her right hand over her heart as if making a pledge to me. She paused for a moment, considering carefully what she would say.

"He'd only *talked* to her about…stuff… sort of. Hinting and…well… touching sometimes. It was getting worse."

"I'll kill him!" I said.

That made Kai laugh. "I thought you already did that."

"What?"

"I've heard you say you were going kill him at least a hundred times," she teased.

"Well, fifty maybe." Which was true enough, but not really a subject for joking around just now. "So what actually happened with Elle?"

"He never, you know, never really did anything. She said it was like he was trying to…convince her…that it would be okay. She feels really guilty, though."

I ran that through my mind for a moment, trying to understand. It was a situation I'd never known personally. I couldn't imagine what Elle was going through. I reached out and put my hand on my daughter's back. "Why?" I asked the world in general, wondering why some things went like that.

"Because. She decided to keep it secret from her mother but…" Kai answered softly to the question I hadn't meant to ask.

"Oh my god! She told Ellen?"

"No!" Kai paused again, trying to find words she could use to explain this to an old person like me. "She couldn't. She feels guilty because she didn't…she felt dishonest. It's like she was hiding something, but it wasn't her fault."

"Of course not!"

"Mom, you know how things were with her mom and him… how he got… if she told her mom…"

She didn't have to finish. I knew exactly what was left unsaid—her mom would confront the bastard and get herself beaten to a pulp.

~ ~ ~

I tried to soothe Kai with some bullshit about everything being okay, and she tried to pretend that she'd been soothed. To keep the kids occupied while keeping my own mind off everything that would probably be keeping me awake all night long, I announced that we'd sit together in the middle of the living room floor and have a picnic-and-board-game extravaganza. We used to do that a lot, so I shouldn't have been surprised by how enthusiastic they both were about the idea. Kai got busy making grilled cheese sandwiches for an early dinner while I heated tomato soup and poured it into mugs. Meanwhile, Len spread out an old blanket on the floor and carefully arranged our old Monopoly set in the middle, taking the opportunity to snag the race car token for himself. He said it brought him luck. Kai chose the battleship, saying that a battleship was bigger than a race car and therefore luckier. I took the top hat, saying that I had faith in my excellent Monopoly skills and therefore didn't need any luck.

We ended up having a really good time. The low, late-afternoon sun was shining through the window as we slurped warm soup. We tried to keep the greasy sandwiches away from the monopoly money and took turns keeping the dog away from the sandwiches. It felt cozy, and the effort to accumulate piles of wealth while driving our nearest and dearest into bankruptcy proved to be very absorbing. So absorbing, in fact, that by the time Kai and I had to admit that Len had thoroughly beaten us both, it was completely dark outside.

The kids got busy cleaning up the living-room picnic area while I went around double-checking the door locks and closing all the curtains. I turned on the light in my bedroom and walked past the dark window, reaching for the drapery cord on the other side of the open curtains so that I could draw them closed. Just then I heard Kai teasing Len about what a hard-hearted landlord he'd been any time either of us landed on his properties, and I stopped and turned toward the door, intending to holler "She's right, you're one mean slum lord!" at him.

But I didn't.

The bullet smashed through the glass and caught me on the back of my head just as I heard something outside and froze in place. Then it was pitch dark everywhere.

CHAPTER SIXTEEN

WHEN I woke up, I didn't know where I was, but I knew that I was blind. With some difficulty I raised my hands to my head and found that it was covered in bandages from the bridge of my nose back to the nape of my neck. I also felt a wave of nausea.

Before I could panic too much, I heard a voice. "Hold still, Naomi. Don't move your bandages." The voice was Carson's. "You're in the hospital, you're okay. It's Friday afternoon. Your kids are at home right now with Peggy. They were here most of the night."

It took me a moment to realize that he had answered almost every question I would have asked him, except the first one. "What's wrong with me?" I began to shake, and my voice cracked, "I'm blind."

Carson gently took hold of my hands. "You were hit in the head."

"I was shot?"

"Not exactly, not by a gun. At first they thought you'd been shot, but they took a steel ball out of the back of your head. Someone put it through your bedroom window. Luckily, it didn't have enough force to go all the way through your skull. It cracked a dent in the bone and lodged under the skin. The doctors here think it might have messed up your vision." The tone of his voice changed a little as he added, "Temporarily."

"Temporarily?"

He squeezed my hands, taking just a bit too long to answer. "They're pretty sure it's temporary. There's a specialist on her way up here from

Phoenix. She'll tell us for sure after she runs some tests and looks at your X-rays. In the meantime, they don't want you using your eyes."

I pulled my hands away from his and put them back up to feel my head, just to be sure that it was all still there. "You said *someone*. Do you think it was Rice?"

"That was my first thought, too, but he and Fred were both busy being highly visible in the marina restaurant all evening."

I lowered my hands slowly until I felt the sheets again. Considering the weapon used, there were a couple of obvious choices next on the suspect list. "The Banner kid?"

"He's missing. It turns out that he's been ditching school off and on for the past couple of weeks. Mike Rodriguez got a warrant to search the Banner house this morning. I haven't heard yet what they found. Oh, and Jack Miller is back on the case. I think the chief is starting to take a serious look at other suspects now."

I blurted, "It's funny, because I was just starting to think that maybe Ellen had…."

"I was too. I guess you could tell when we talked yesterday." Carson's voice had moved a little further away, and I heard the springs of a chair squeak.

"Well, yeah. Your question about the plea bargain kind of tipped me off." I shifted around in the bed a little because I became aware that my back was getting numb. When I reached back, I discovered that there was nothing between my backside and the bed sheets because my open-at-the-back hospital gown was open at the back. I ran my hand around to be sure that I had covers over me as I continued, "Do you suppose they'll give me a few minutes alone with Mark Banner when they catch him? I could save them a lot of court costs." I tried to turn my face toward where I thought Carson was sitting.

"It's funny that you should say that because I was thinking a moment ago that if Miller is the one to catch him, he might not get back to town alive." His voice didn't sound like he was kidding. "I'm going to go out and call your house. I'll be back."

I'm not sure that I heard Carson's footsteps go all the way out of my room before I fell asleep. It would be nice to say that my sleep was easy and dreamless, but it wasn't. My dreams were amazingly coherent and linear. I dreamt of Ellen's conviction and imprisonment. I dreamt of myself wandering through town with a white cane. I dreamt of John Rice kidnapping my children. Maybe I wasn't dreaming at all, but just fretting in a drug-induced stupor.

At any rate I was awakened sometime later when Peggy Thomas walked in, talking with someone. After a nurse introduced herself and did some fussing with a blood pressure cuff and thermometer, she helped me rearrange my pillows and promised to be back soon. Peggy helped me get a drink of water and told me that Laura Dumfrees was at the house looking after Kai and Len. I could hear her smiling as she told me about when Laura showed up at the door to take over so that Peggy could come see me. "God help anyone who tries to mess with them. Laura brought her aluminum softball bat. She said it's been a rough week at work, so she's taking a mental health day. She'll be looking out your windows, hoping for a chance to pummel someone."

Then Peggy settled in for a chat, like she was having coffee in my kitchen instead of trying to keep me thinking about anything but being blind. I guess that as a legal professional I should say she began to catch me up to date with the latest information on the case. I heard her scoot the chair closer to my bed. "Did Carson tell you that we went over to the Banner house with a search warrant this morning?"

"Carson went with you with a warrant?" I was still a little foggy.

Peggy patted my arm and chuckled, "No, Honey, Jack Miller and me. I was asking you if Carson told you about the search that *Jack* and I did this morning, but it sounds like he didn't."

I tried shaking my head and was rewarded with more nausea.

Peggy went on, "Well, you knew that the Chief and I went over the other day, Right? Don't nod!"

Too late. "Ouch, yes. So why'd you go back?"

"Because that time we just asked for cooperation and looked around. This time, Jack and I went with a warrant and did a thorough search."

"Did you find a slingshot?"

"No, but we found some steel balls, the kind they use for hunting." I felt Peggy touch the covers on my bed. "How do you feel, Naomi?"

"I feel like hell. My head is aching, and all of these bandages feel like I've got an electric blanket wrapped around my skull." I could complain for a couple of hours without even slowing down, but that wouldn't make me feel any better. "Tell me more about what you found. Do the steel balls match the one they took out of my head?"

"Exactly." Then she added. "Well, they're not like bullets, you know? They're just hard polished steel balls about three-eights of an inch in diameter. I mean they don't get rifling marks from a gun barrel like a bullet would, so the one that hit you couldn't tell us where it came from. But it was the same size as the ones we found and just as shiny."

"Where did you find them?"

"They were hidden outside in the garden shed. Gail Banner said that they must have been left over from years ago. Talking about that made her nervous. You know why, right?"

"Animal control, vigilante style."

"Right. So, later, Dr. Banner said they weren't his son's and accused us of planting them."

"Both of the Banners were there? At the same time? Together?"

"Both of them insisted on being home while we searched, but I wouldn't say they were actually together."

"Wouldn't they have seen something if the evidence had been planted?"

When she didn't answer, I prompted, "Peggy? Are you still here?"

"Cool your jets, Naomi. I have to think back. I don't know. Maybe. Gail Banner was following me around while I searched Mark's room. Jack went outside and looked in the backyard and the garden shed. Dr. Banner left to go back to his office at some point in there, but I'm not sure when. Anyway, the steel balls were in a small plastic bottle. Jack said it was on a shelf inside an empty flowerpot. The bottle had Mark Banner's fingerprints on it."

"Just *his* fingerprints?"

"Just his, no one else's. The ammunition—the steel balls—had no fingerprints on them, but that didn't mean anything, since they could've been poured into the bottle right from whatever box they came in."

I sat quietly against the pillows and thought about this for a moment. "It makes no sense that Mark Banner would attack me."

"If he's the killer…."

I shook my head, which was still a mistake. I winced and changed position. "But I'm no threat to him. I'm not a cop or investigator."

"Well, you're trying to prove that Ellen didn't do it."

"Yeah, but…. Did you find anything else in his room?"

Peggy laughed. "Some really sexy magazines."

"Yeah? Anything I'd like?"

"Very definitely not," she answered.

The whole thing still wasn't making any sense to me, and I said, "I just don't see it." Peggy didn't laugh. I gave up on feeble attempts at gallows humor and went on. "Mark may have killed Willard Highsmith, I guess, but he had no reason to go after me."

"That's what Rodriguez says. Besides, if he wanted to kill you, why wouldn't he use one of his guns?" I heard Peggy stand up and move around a little.

I tried to follow the sound and keep facing her. "Grant was here earlier." I used Carson's first name, because I wondered how Peggy would react. Nothing. Of course, I couldn't see her face. So much for sleuthing blind. "He said that Mark is missing. What's the story on that?"

From across the room she said, "Nice view of the parking lot, Naomi. You're not missing anything." Her footsteps came back to the chair, and I heard her sit down. "Grant is right. Mark Banner hasn't been seen for a couple of days. Actually, his parents can't account for his time with any accuracy. It seems like they don't keep very close tabs on his whereabouts. He has his own truck, and when he's home he spends a lot of his time in his room. The parents come and go independently themselves, and they aren't always aware of whether he's home or not."

I considered that information for a little bit and satisfied myself that I was doing a better job of tracking my kids than the Banners were theirs. In view of what I'd just heard, though, I resolved to pay even more attention to where my kids were and what they were doing. Then a new question came to mind. "What about John Rice, that lawyer?"

"He and his assistant are still in town. Rodriguez went out to the marina and talked to them again after you were… hit. They were full of denials, of course, but they got the message. I don't think they'll get near you or the kids."

I put both of my hands up to my head. "Maybe not, or maybe *they* did this."

Before we could continue speculating, we were interrupted by a bevy of medical personnel. There was soothing talk, the dimming of lights, and finally the removal of bandages. High drama, but as soon as the cotton balls were off of my eyes, I could see perfectly. Thoughts of long-term sympathy and possible disability income faded away. I would've done a happy dance if I'd been wearing pants.

I thanked the doctors and nurses and listened to explanations of why they'd been worried, etc. They said something about where vision lives in the brain. Apparently it's at the back and down low. All and all, it was about fifteen minutes before Peggy and I could get back to our conversation. She was standing by the window again and signaled for me to join her. "Come here," she said. "Look at this."

"What?"

"That attorney, Rice, and his goon are sitting out there in the parking lot. Grant just drove in."

I got out of bed, clutching the back of my gown to close the gap while looking around for a robe. There wasn't one, so I just held on and hoped for the best. I got to the window in time to see Grant Carson get out of his car and slam the door before he started marching toward Rice's car. "He was here at the hospital when I dozed off. Where did he go?"

Peggy just shushed me and kept looking out the window. The whole scene was taking place two rows out into the parking lot below, and we couldn't see everything because of some of the cars in between us and the action.

"What's he going to do?" Peggy said.

"My bet is he's going to get his ass kicked. Have you seen Fred?"

Before Peggy could answer, Fred got up out of the car and scurried around to put himself between it and Grant Carson. I figured that John Rice was sitting inside, with just the car door and window between him and whatever Carson and Fred were going to do next.

"He's big," Peggy said.

"Grant is big," I said. "This guy is enormous."

"And buff."

With the sharpened sense of hearing that I'd developed during my recent brush with blindness, I could hear a slight note of admiration in her voice.

There was no time for me to comment on that, though, one way or the other, because Grant Carson didn't pause for conversation. He shot a swift right jab to Fred's chin. Fred's head snapped back a couple of inches, and he might've lost his balance for a second. Then he looked fine. Carson, on the other hand, had begun to flex his right hand and shake his head.

It was Fred's turn to throw a punch, and he did so with surprising speed and accuracy. It caught Carson in the belly and doubled him over. Grant backed up against a nearby car and slumped to a sitting position on the pavement. Fred lowered his fists and apparently said something to him. Then Fred leaned back against his car and folded his arms across his chest.

After a moment, Carson managed to stand up without much difficulty. He looked pretty good, actually. Then he leaned over and picked something up, and Peggy let out a gasp.

"Is that a... that's a gun!"

"Jesus!"

But Carson laid the .45 on the hood of the car where he was standing. Then he hitched up his pants and puffed out his chest. Next, of course, was the ritual raising of his fists.

Fred got into the spirit of things by taking off his jacket and removing his own firearm, shoulder holster and all. By this time John Rice had rolled down the car window, and Fred handed him the gun rig.

Next came the dance of the Bantam roosters. Now, bear in mind that neither of these guys was a Bantamweight, but there is no image to be drawn by my describing this as "the dance of the heavyweight chickens." You see what I mean.

Fred stood cautiously while Carson sort of circled—his chin occasionally making little jerking thrusts. Carson had his fists up in front of him. Fred didn't. Then John Rice apparently said something to Fred that distracted him because he turned his head. Carson took the opportunity to move in and land two solid blows. To tell you the truth, it didn't look fair to me. I mean, Carson kind of blind-sided the big lug.

Fair or not, though, Fred did go down, and you could see that Carson had some real gristle and not a little experience. He stood back in a sportsmanlike stance while Fred got to his feet. This time, the larger man did raise his fists to join in the dance of the roosters.

"This is kind of exciting," Peggy said.

"Aren't you a cop?" I asked.

"So?"

"Isn't this illegal?"

"I'm off duty."

"Don't you want to keep Carson from getting hurt?"

"He's not going to get hurt. He's going to teach that guy a lesson."

I felt a little disloyal betting against a man who had kept vigil at my hospital bedside, but I answered, "Ten bucks."

"You're on."

Fred tried a few jabs, but Carson dodged them. Carson tried a few jabs, but Fred dodged them. Then Carson landed a pretty good right to Fred's belly and stepped back to watch Fred fall.

But Fred didn't fall. Instead, he caught Carson with an uppercut. The only reason the blow didn't kill Carson was that he was a little out of reach, having stepped back to gloat a second earlier. He went down like a stone.

No, that's not it. A stone would have bounced on the pavement. Grant Carson went down like a sack of potatoes. Actually, I don't think they package potatoes in a sack that big. I'm talking maybe two hundred pounds of potatoes here.

I have to admit that Fred turned around after he dropped Carson. He spread his hands on the hood of the car and leaned his weight on them, so maybe he was hurting a little too.

Peggy started to turn toward the door, but I grabbed her. "Too late," I said. "You can't decide to be a cop now."

"How about a girlfriend?"

"You think he wants a girlfriend to see this?"

She stopped tugging toward the door and relaxed. "You're right."

"Peggy, we never saw this."

Her eyes glued to the window again, she nodded and said, "Saw what?"

Then the sack of potatoes got up off the pavement in one swift movement and slammed into Fred. Again, it didn't seem quite fair. I mean Fred wasn't properly prepared. There had been no warning, no continuation of the rooster dance, no preliminary raising of the fists, *and* Fred's back was turned. Actually, I was surprised that Carson could move, much less move fast and hit hard.

Fred was pretty surprised too. The body slam had caught him in the back and lifted him about a foot off the ground. That had to hurt.

When Carson stepped back, Fred went down to the pavement on both knees before toppling over on his back. That had to hurt too. Then Carson delivered a very unsportsmanlike kick to the kidney. Hurt, hurt, hurt.

Did you ever see one of those martial arts movies in which a man lying on his back sort of *flings* himself upward? I've never known how they could do that. Anyway, Fred did it as if he had a big spring attached to his back. In a split second, he was standing again and had landed two or three punches. One, I'm sure, landed square in Carson's face. It was really something to see, and I had money on Fred so I was kind of proud of him.

Peggy let out a gasp. "Did you see that?"

"Amazing!"

Even at this distance, we could see that Carson's face was bloody. "Forget about the bet," I said magnanimously.

"Bullshit," Peggy said. "Double it."

"I hate to take advantage…"

I was interrupted because Carson lunged forward and grabbed Fred by the face. Now, that can't be an easy thing to do, but he stretched both hands out as if they were talons and simply grabbed Fred by the face. Then he brought that face downward to meet his rapidly rising knee. It was pretty painful to watch. First, I was witnessing a hurtful event in the life of a fellow human being—that, in itself, is painful. Second, I had twenty bucks riding on Fred, or maybe just ten bucks since we hadn't exactly settled that. At the moment, it looked like money down the drain either way.

But my man Fred got up again remarkably quickly and seemed to be ready to go back into the fray. He looked pretty damned fit except for all the blood on his face.

Suddenly, though, Carson stood immobile, his hands up in the air. He was staring toward the car window behind which John Rice was still sitting. Peggy and I couldn't see inside the car. Fred turned and looked toward the window himself. Then he stood straighter and backed a couple of steps away from Carson. He picked up his jacket and walked around the car and got in. A moment later Fred and Rice had driven away.

"I'd call that a draw," Peggy said.

"Game called on account of a gun, I'd say."

Peggy was all smiles. "I guess we're even."

"My boss is a hell of a lot tougher than he looks," I said as a sort of apology for my disloyalty. Besides that, I admit that I really was impressed.

"Fuckin' A!" Peggy said.

I've never been able to figure out why people say that, but around here we say it a lot. Probably some language scholar has written a paper on its origins. Probably his graduate advisor read it and was impressed and raised his thumbs and said, "Fuckin' A!"

CHAPTER SEVENTEEN

B Y eight o'clock on Friday evening I was back at home. The kids were just fine. My friend Laura had stayed with them all day, bright purple softball bat close at hand, in spite of their protests that they could look after themselves. According to my kids, Carson and some other guy from town had repaired my bedroom window. Alice Yazzie had brought the St. Gerome Altar Society ladies to clean up the shattered glass and make sure the carpet was bare-feet-friendly. Three-Steps Larry's dog was still just a dog, but she was growing on me. She even managed to look concerned when she stared at my bandaged head. Actually, she was just thirty pounds of brown dog with her regular brown dog face pointed in my direction, but I felt her sympathy. There wasn't much left for me to do but thank Laura and wave good-bye—I turned down her offer to leave me the neon-purple metal bat —before I took some painkillers and went to bed.

I woke up Saturday morning without much of a headache and feeling pretty good. It took me a while to realize that my borrowed pistol was no longer in my bed. When I questioned my daughter about it, she reached into the back pocket of her jeans and handed me the little .38.

"I found it after they took you to the hospital. After what happened I figured that we needed it. I didn't say anything to Len or Laura, but I've been carrying it around ever since."

"You didn't say… what, they didn't see? How did you carry that around without their knowing?"

"I wore your long sweater." She sat down on my bed and gave me a worried look. "What's going on, Mom?"

Now my heart ached far worse than my head did. My smart, fierce girl. Taking up arms to protect her brother and her home. I didn't know what to say because I couldn't even guess at an answer. Still holding the gun in my hand, I decided to admit ignorance. "I wish I knew. Obviously, someone was out to get me, maybe because Mr. Carson and I are working on the Highsmith murder case. At any rate, I borrowed this gun because I felt like we might be in some kind of danger."

"Is that the way this new job is going to be? I thought you were just like a secretary or something."

"Office manager," I said. Then I laughed, but Kai didn't see anything funny.

She said, "Mr. Carson asked me if I thought Mark Banner could've done this. I told him I didn't think so. People are saying that Mark isn't even in town. He's supposedly off somewhere with Linda Armstrong."

I thought briefly about the fact that Linda was another of the slingshot-toting, cat-murdering gang, but I couldn't say anything about that.

"Those two are pretty tough, Mom."

"We really don't have much of an idea who did this. We've had some threats from some other men who are in town, but it doesn't seem likely that they did this either."

"Threats from men? These things don't happen in Sage Landing. It's like some TV show about Los Angeles or New York. If people can't be safe out here in the middle of nowhere...."

I had nothing to say to that. I tucked the little pistol in my purse and said, "Just so you know where it is."

Kai nodded her head and left the room.

Before I could finish dressing my daughter returned with a surprised expression on her face. "Mom, Mrs. Banner is here to see you."

"Your principal?"

"I haven't done anything at school, I swear."

I thought about her lying to the P.E. teacher and skipping class, but that was probably not why Gail Banner was here. "I'm sure you haven't. This probably has nothing to do with you. I want you and Len to stay out of sight. You don't want to embarrass Mrs. Banner by being around."

I threw on jeans and an old sweater over my T-shirt, ran a brush through what little hair wasn't covered by bandages, and walked into my living room without shoes. As it turns out, I needn't have worried about my appearance because Gail Banner looked worse than I'd ever seen her—maybe even worse than I'd ever seen *me*. She stood by the front door wearing a sweatshirt and wrinkled slacks, normal weekend attire for me but entirely out of character for her. Her hair was worse than a mess. She was wearing yesterday's makeup, and it hadn't held up well through the crying she had obviously been doing.

She turned to greet me. "Mrs. Manymules, thank you for talking to me. I know that you must think that my son has done this to you."

I gestured toward an easy chair, and she sat down as I answered her. "Actually, I don't think he did. It doesn't make sense that he would." I sat on the end of the couch nearest her and continued. "It's no secret that he's a suspect in the Highsmith... thing. While I work in the law firm that is defending Ellen Highsmith, I'm just the office manager. I doubt that Mark even knows anything about me."

She nodded without saying anything.

I waited a moment before asking, "Who else knows about Mark's earlier ...trouble involving slingshots?"

She shrugged. "I don't know. We tried to keep things quiet."

"It's possible that someone could be trying to set your son up." I considered pursuing the idea that Dr. Banner might have done it, but then I remembered Lucille Farneth. The doctor would have no reason to frame his son because he already had a good alibi if he needed it.

Gail Banner interrupted my train of thought. "Pardon me for saying so, but couldn't your client have an interest in doing just that?"

"Ellen? You don't know her," I said. "Ellen isn't the kind of person who could have killed her husband, and she's not the kind who could frame an innocent teenager for murder. Besides, how would she know about the slingshot?"

Gail looked at me and said, "Well, how did *you* know about it?"

I didn't answer.

"You see my point. It's a small town. Eventually everybody knows what no one is supposed to know."

"My kids don't know about it."

She paused a moment and then said, "I see… well, sometimes parents are the last to know."

I nodded agreement. "Sometimes we sure are. No doubt about that. And that's probably true in my house as well as yours."

"But you hope not. And you don't think so, not really." She made direct eye contact. "I realize that you've been in a position to know quite a lot about my household recently."

Several sarcastic responses came to mind, but now was not the time. I held her gaze and said, "In the first place, that's none of my business, and I make a point of remembering that. Second, I haven't learned anything that makes me think that your son is out to get me."

She looked like she was about to cry again. "He's missing, you know? He's been gone for several days."

"This must be terrible for you," I said. "Do you think he's in danger?"

Her hands were shaking as she opened her purse. After a quick search, she extracted a pack of cigarettes and a lighter. "Do you mind?"

I *did* mind, and I did not allow smoking in our house. "No, go right ahead," I said. She was the principal, after all. And, like her or not, she was going through hell.

After she lit up, she said, "I hope he's just hiding out from all of the embarrassment. Linda Armstrong is probably with him although she's been seen in town since he has. He's pretty self-reliant. He knows how to take care of himself, and he's got a truck and a g… I'm sure he's okay."

"A gun? Weren't you about to say that he had a gun?"

Gail Banner looked embarrassed, but didn't answer.

I said, "That's another reason that he probably isn't the one who shot me with the slingshot. If he wanted to shoot me and had a gun, I'd be dead."

She stalled her answer by dragging on her cigarette and exhaling slowly. I suppressed a cough in reaction to the cloud of second-hand smoke. Finally she said, "I guess you would."

"Tell me about the gun."

"Mark has a revolver with him. His father told me that after looking over the gun case. We agreed not to say anything. I'm sorry." She took another drag and then looked around for an ashtray. Finding none, she cupped her hand under the ash.

Not quite sure what to say about her apology, I spotted a crumb-covered sandwich plate on the end table and moved it to where she could use it as an ashtray. She nodded, not looking at me, and tapped the ash onto the plate.

I stayed silent for quite a while before I answered her. "I'm sorry too. You realize that what you just told me is important information? If you don't go to the police with it, I'll have to, I'm afraid. It's better if you do."

"I know. I'd decided to do that anyway." She paused. "I have a difficult question for you."

Good lord. Could this get any more awkward? "Go ahead."

"If Mark *had* done this to you, it would help your friend Ellen, your client, wouldn't it?"

I sat in silence for a bit, mentally sorting through the nuances of confidentiality. On the one hand, she was just looking to confirm what anybody could see. On the other hand, though, I had no business discussing anything about Ellen's case. Certainly not with Gail Banner.

"Honestly, I am in no position to speculate about that."

She nodded her acknowledgement, but continued, "My question is, do you think that Mr. Carson would try to make it look like... could he have done this?"

"With the slingshot, you mean?" I almost laughed.

"Could he... is he that kind of... how well do you know Grant Carson?"

I was shocked at the question and even more shocked at myself for never having considered that possibility. I'd learned that Carson was, as a matter of fact, a bit unscrupulous.

I didn't answer, and Gail Banner continued, "He has a reputation for being…unconventional at least."

Not only did I know that, but I had been benefiting from his disregard for convention, at least as it applied to the typical definition of a job like mine. The suggestion that he might have injured me himself in order to help a client stunned me. It took a moment to wrap my mind around the idea, and just a heartbeat or two more to reject it completely. Gail picked up on those extra heartbeats.

"It's possible, isn't it?" she said. "He's not exactly an exemplary attorney."

"No. I mean, it isn't possible. Listen, Mrs. Banner, Mr. Carson is a good man. He wouldn't frame anybody, and he wouldn't have hurt me. I'm pretty sure that your son didn't do this, but I'm damned sure that Grant Carson didn't."

"I'm just saying... well, he's pretty notorious in some ways."

I fixed her with a cool stare, and she got the point.

"I know, I'm somewhat notorious myself, but not…"

I just continued to stare at her, and she shut up. I decided to speak my mind. "Forgive my pointing it out, Mrs. Banner, but you are a suspect in this murder. Grant isn't. As for your personal lives, you may be in about the same league. He may be an unorthodox attorney, but he's not a crooked one." Well, I thought, not a *really* crooked one.

We had little more to say to each other after that.

~ ~ ~

I was still airing out the house, trying to purge it of cigarette smoke, when Jack Miller called. He offered to buy me lunch. I was surprised that he suggested meeting openly in Sage Landing's only Mexican food restaurant. Apparently he felt that the need for clandestine meetings was behind us.

I was unwilling to leave the kids alone in the house even in broad daylight on a bright Saturday afternoon. Asking him to bring lunch to the house wouldn't work, either, because I didn't want to talk with Jack where they could hear us. Fortunately, I remembered Wanda saying last Monday night that her brother's washing machine had given up the ghost. She'd laughed saying that he hated going to the Laundromat but couldn't use her machine because he was seriously allergic to her cats, "…and I'm damned if I'm going to do his laundry for him!" she'd told me. I hoped he wasn't allergic to dogs, too.

A quick phone call later, Dwayne was at my house, loaded down with enough laundry to keep him there all day, watching various sporting events on television with my kids as he washed, dried, and folded what looked to be his whole wardrobe. He looked over his shoulder to be sure the kids were out of earshot and whispered that Wanda had already filled him in on my "situation," as he called it, and he solemnly assured me that no one was getting near the house while he was there. "Not even a Girl Scout bringing a case of Thin Mints," he swore, crossing his heart for emphasis. That sounded fairly reassuring.

I removed most of my bandages, leaving one small band-aid over the actual hole in my scalp and arranging my hair to cover it. Then I walked from home to what passed for Sage Landing's shopping district, arriving just before noon at Pedro's Hideaway, a rowdy family restaurant. The place was very far from being a hideaway in spite of its name. It consisted of just one big noisy room with a glass front facing the parking lot. You couldn't have "hidden away" a stick of chewing gum in the whole place. Jack and I took a table in the back corner to avoid as much of the busy Saturday lunch noise as we could. I didn't have much hope for a quiet and confidential conversation. Pedro's was well known for welcoming families with loud and ill-behaved children, and today appeared to be no exception. Nevertheless, Jack launched right in as soon as we were seated.

He leaned forward and tried to talk just loud enough for me to hear him without anyone else listening in. "So, what's Carson's current thinking about Ellen? Surely he can see now that she's innocent."

I leaned even closer and tried a loud whisper. "I haven't seen him since yesterday," I said. When I saw that Jack had cupped his hand around his ear to show that he couldn't hear me, I raised my voice. "The last time we spoke, he didn't seem in favor of a plea bargain anymore."

Miller sat back and nodded. "What does he think about the fact that the Banner boy is missing?"

I leaned forward to be heard above the crying baby ten feet away. "I don't know what he thinks about it, but *I'm* beginning to think it's just a coincidence."

"Naomi! Have you gone crazy? Mark Banner almost killed you. Why do you think he did that if he's not involved in this murder?" Unfortunately, Jack said this way too loud, and about twenty people turned their heads.

I leaned over and went back to a whisper. "I talked to his mom. I don't know. Let's say for the sake of argument that he…did…you know, Highsmith. Even if that's the case, I'm certainly no threat to him. I'm not Ellen's attorney, and I'm not a policeman, and I've never met Mark Banner personally. He's just got no reason to come after me."

"Who can tell why a murderer does anything, especially a crazy kid like that?"

"On TV, they always have a reason." I thought that I saw a woman at the next table nod in agreement.

Jack sounded disgusted. "On TV? On TV, they are smart and calculating, in line for a lot of money. That's not the way it really is, believe me. Usually a killer is some stupid moron who got pissed off. They're irrational, and they make lots of mistakes."

The woman who had been listening stiffened and turned away upon hearing the term "pissed off." I noticed that she was eating the same thing I always order—the Hideaway Enchilada and a tamale. I almost raised a thumb and said, "Fuckin' A!"

Suddenly Grant Carson appeared beside our table. He had impressive bandages on his right hand, a wrap of gauze around his forehead, and three plastic bandages on his face. There were dark circles under his eyes and bruises decorating the few square inches of face between bandages. His lip was sporting several stitches. He appeared to be in a bad mood.

Without invitation, he turned one of our chairs around, straddled it, and sat down. He looked at me and said, "They're bringing Ellen Highsmith back in. I think we ought to go over there."

I've translated that for you. What he actually said was, "Dey bing enn hisnit ba en. Ee aht go dere."

"Who's bringing Ellen in? In where?" I said loudly. That quieted the room down a bit.

Jack Miller answered before Carson could. "I'm betting it's the tribal police, right?"

"Yeah. Dey bing huh back. You know bout dis?"

Jack shook his head. "No, but it just makes sense. I figured all along that she'd gone out to her grandfather's place. Looks like the chief figured it out, too. She'd have to be picked up by the tribal police because the place is out on the Rez. It would've taken a little while to work out the paperwork, so the chief probably got on this some time yesterday. He didn't say a word to me."

"You oder lun yet?" Carson asked in his new dialect.

"We just sat down," I said, realizing that I was about to miss lunch.

"Den leth go."

"I can't go with you," Miller said. "I've got to keep a low profile on this or I'll get put back on vacation."

Everyone in the restaurant tried to pretend they hadn't heard that.

～ ～ ～

By the time Carson and I got to the jail, there was a tribal police cruiser in the parking lot. Mike Rodriguez was waiting for us in the lobby.

"Hold on a minute, counselor," the chief said. "She's still processing-in back there for her bail violation, and you won't be able to see her for a while. I wanted to talk to you anyway and fill you in."

We followed Mike back to his office, and everyone got seated as comfortably as was possible in his cramped enclosure. Rodriguez stared at Carson's damaged face so long that it became embarrassing. "I heard about that,

Grant. I can't say that I was happy about it. We don't like to have the tourists attacked by our local lawyers if we can avoid it, and I told you to stay away from them." He paused for a moment and then added, "He sure did a number on you."

"Yeah, ut you shoo see da oth guy."

"I did see the other guy. He looked like shit too. I'll admit that. I went out to see him at the hotel—our third chat, mind you—after I heard about this. I caught them just as they were checking out. Rice said that their presence was just confusing the issue on this Highsmith murder, and they had nothing further to gain by staying around. They could have filed charges, you know?"

"Did you mention that to them?" I asked.

"It didn't come up. Rice asked me if I had seen Larry Sabano recently."

"He athk uth th thame thing a couple time." Carson said.

"What about Ellen?" I asked. "We saw the tribal police cruiser outside."

"Not good, I'm afraid. They found a weapon when they picked her up," he said with a note of tired resignation in his voice. "It was an old .30-06 deer rifle. She says it was her grandfather's."

Carson shook his head and looked discouraged. "Loaded?"

"Fully loaded. There were two extra boxes of ammunition in the cupboards. The rifle had been recently cleaned."

"I assume there was a warrant," I said.

"The tribal police are very thorough, Naomi. They knew what they were picking her up for, and they took the precaution of getting a search warrant from the Federal Magistrate. Her being a Navajo and on the Reservation raises a whole bunch of jurisdictional issues. We might end up with the FBI in on this."

"FBI!" I said. Visions of Ellen being helicoptered away to some secret federal compound filled my head.

"She's on the rolls—a member of the Navajo nation," Rodriguez said. "If she commits a felony on federal land or on the Reservation, it's out of our hands. U.S. law demands that she go to federal prosecution in that case."

"But this was in town!" I realized that I might sound like I thought she was guilty. "Whoever did this was at the edge of town."

"Maybe. Or maybe on the lake. The lake is a national park—Bureau of Reclamation land borders part of it. Or maybe on the Rez—the boundary is just east of here. Still, if she weren't a Navajo, the jurisdiction might be ours."

"But she is," I said.

"Since she is, she has to have been in town limits for the case to be ours. I'm not so sure about where Highsmith had to be. It's complicated."

"Well it's moot," I said, "because Ellen didn't do it."

Carson cut in, speaking slowly enough to be understood. "Making it federal could help her, though."

"How's that?" I asked.

He went on, pronouncing each word at a painfully slow pace. And you would think that he'd therefore say as little as possible, but you would be wrong. "The Feds have a lousy conviction rate in Reservation felonies. They don't have the staff they need out here—not even close."

"That's true," Rodriguez said.

"Anything else? Any trouble at the arrest?" Carson asked.

"No. She met them at the door, invited them in. Pretended she had no idea why they were there."

"Maybe she didn't," I said. "She was just out at her grandfather's place. She goes out there all the time, thinks of it as her home."

"I think she understood the terms of her bail, Naomi," Rodriguez said.

"I don't think so," I said. "If she meant to jump bail and run, she sure as hell would have gone further than five miles away to a place where everyone knew she spent a lot of time. Surely you can see that she didn't think of that as violating her bail."

Rodriguez looked from me to Carson with a *You're seriously going with that?* look on his face.

"Thath ow thory, and we thicking to it," Carson said quickly. Then he slowed way down and pronounced everything much more clearly. "It didn't occur to me that you would think she was jumping bail if she went out to her grandfather's house."

"Are you telling me that you knew where she was?"

"Of course!" Carson answered slowly and distinctly. "I thought everybody knew where she was."

Rodriguez let his jaw drop open and sat back in his chair. "I told you that she'd jumped bail."

Carson managed to look as if he was shocked at the statement.

I jumped in with an answer. "No, you did not! You told us that she'd left her home here in town. When we found out later that she had gone out to her grandfather's place, we assumed you knew it. We assumed everybody knew it."

"Don't try to minimize this, Naomi."

"Don't try to make a federal case out of it, then," I said.

"Is that supposed to be a joke? Because it's a stupid one." Rodriguez smiled in spite of the tension in the room.

Grant answered slowly and painfully. "Oh. The federal warrant. I see what you mean. No, it's just that there's nothing to this, Mike. So she was staying out at her grandfather's? So grandpa had some old deer rifle? So what?"

I sat in silent amazement at my boss. He'd managed to make it sound like he could see no connection between a deer rifle and the shooting of Willard Highsmith.

Rodriguez wasn't buying any of it. "Come on, Grant. This may not be much of a bail jump. I'll agree with that, but the rifle is significant. It's the right kind of weapon."

I piped in again. "Are you kidding? Can you imagine what it would be like standing in a bobbing speedboat in the dark with an old deer rifle?"

"Not from a boat, no. It might be pretty good from the cliffs at the edge of town, though. Don't you think?"

"I thought you said she shot him from their ski boat. As I remember it, you said she did it with her pistol, assuming it was *her* pistol. Isn't that how you got your arrest warrant in the first place?"

"Stop it, Naomi, you're wasting my time."

I leaned over hit the desk with my palm. "That's exactly what I thought you would say. It seems to me that you're willing to change the scenario any old way as long as you keep Ellen Highsmith in the center of the picture."

"That's unfair." He looked at Carson in hopes of a different response.

"Thath exact wha *I* wath abou' to thay, Mike," Carson mumbled.

There was a sharp knock on Rodriguez's door. Peggy opened the door and stuck her head in. "Chief, Gail Banner is here to see you."

CHAPTER EIGHTEEN

WELL, *now* we had a conflict of interest. We had come to the jail to see Ellen, but before we could do that, one of our other murder-defense clients showed up. It turned out that she knew we were in the building, and she had already asked for Mr. Carson to be present while she talked to Mike Rodriguez. I sat there wondering what Carson was going to do, and it was obvious from the look on the chief's face that he wondered the same thing.

"What are we waiting for?" Carson asked slowly. "Let's go see what the woman wants."

Mike Rodriguez just nodded at Peggy Thomas, who said to Carson, "Room three."

I started to follow along, but he looked at me and gestured toward Peggy. I turned and followed her to her desk. I took a seat across from her and said, "When do you think we'll be able to see Ellen?"

"It shouldn't be too long." As she said this she looked around to be sure that no one was coming and then turned a file folder around on her desk so that it faced me. She opened it and leafed down through a few pages. Then she stood up. "Coffee?"

"I could use a cup, but what I really need is some food. My lunch was interrupted before I could order it. Aren't you guys required to keep dough-nuts around here?"

She walked down the hall, and I leaned over to look at the file. It turned out to be Mark Banner's juvenile record. The page she had opened to was a copy of a certificate of accomplishment. It was from a Boy Scout camp and stated that Mark had achieved the designation of expert rifle marksman. It went on to say, in fact, that he had been the number one marksman at camp that year. I'd closed the file by the time Peggy returned.

She carried two cups of coffee, but no doughnuts.

"Interesting," I said.

"What's that?"

"Nothing."

Handing one of the coffees to me, she sat down and said, "Let's play police detective and defense attorney for a minute." She lowered her voice. "I'll play the police detective. It will be good practice. This is the way the prosecution will come at you."

"So I'm the attorney?"

"You're the attorney," she said. "So Ms. Manymules, let's review the evidence against your client."

"Okay, let's."

"First, she cannot convincingly explain her whereabouts on the night of the murder."

"But she had no motive," I lied.

"That's bullshit, counselor." She snorted and crossed her arms.

"Nice talk, detective. You kiss your boyfriend with that mouth?"

She was not to be redirected. Instead, she continued, speaking with exaggerated patience. "Ellen was Willard Highsmith's wife. You can't get any more motive than that as far as I can see, but wait! Just when you thought that was reason enough, there is a new insurance policy to consider. Next, she can't explain the whereabouts of Highsmith's ski boat. And she had a powerful pistol hidden in her house."

I held up my hand to interrupt the barrage. "Okay. How can you prove she wasn't in Tuba City at the time of the murder? The burden of proof is on you. I'm pretty sure she didn't know about the new life insurance. She also doesn't know where the ski boat is, and nobody else does, either. And let's try to figure out how many people in this town had something against Willard Highsmith and also own guns. What would you say? Twenty-five people at a minimum?"

"I think we're ready for my fifth point," Peggy said, ignoring all my questions. "Fifth, she violated her bail. Sixth, it turns out that she had access to a deer rifle, which is the other way that good old Willard might have been shot."

Exasperated, I leaned against the back of my chair and looked toward the ceiling. I didn't want to play anymore. "What's the point of this, Peggy? Whose side are you on?"

"If Ellen is going to get out of this, you and Carson are going to have to be able to counter all those points. Convincingly. I'm trying to help you."

"Like I said, there are other people who are just as likely. Motive, guns, everything. One of them is in the other room with Mike and Grant right now."

She laughed. "Are you using one of your clients against another one?"

I had to laugh, too. "Practically everyone in town is some kind of client related this murder, Peggy. They just keep showing up."

She started laughing again. She didn't like playing the prosecutor arguing the case against a friend any more than I liked playing defense attorney against a pile of circumstantial evidence. I relaxed a little. But my growing sense of dread didn't go away.

~ ~ ~

It was an hour and a half before I saw Carson again. By that time he'd talked with both of his clients. Apparently all that talking had limbered up his face, because he'd become a lot easier to understand. As we drove away he told me that he didn't think things looked much different for either of them at the moment. Maybe Mike Rodriguez was looking a little harder at Mark Banner, but Ellen Highsmith was still at the top of the suspects list.

"What about the federal jurisdiction angle?" I asked. "If it comes to that, would Ellen be better off with the Feds?"

"Probably, like I said, they're understaffed. The state always prosecutes murders, but the Feds sometimes don't. If we highlight the domestic violence—presenting it as a version of self defense—they might not give it much attention."

"And if they did?"

I got no answer until he'd turned left into the parking lot of the little shopping center and pulled up in front of the drugstore. He parked, turned off the engine, and pulled the key out of the ignition. Looking through the windshield at the faded storefront, he said, "Ellen could face the death penalty in either jurisdiction."

Death penalty. It was the first time I'd heard those words spoken aloud in connection with Ellen – the words Carson had avoided saying before, when he warned me that her kids could lose their mother after he'd talked with her in the police station that first time. He hadn't just been talking about losing her to the prison system.

He opened the door of the truck and climbed out. I stayed in the pickup, worrying, while he went into the store. From where I was sitting, I could see my residential street, and I sent up a silent prayer for my kids to be safe, and for Ellen to be okay.

Carson returned to the truck with two black coffees. He handed me mine and opened his without starting the engine. He just sat there as if we were in some comfortable café. "Funny thing is," he said, "Gail Banner was sounding like she was about to make some sort of admission about what happened to Highsmith. She was beating around the bush when Mike asked her why she'd come in, and then she said she'd like a few minutes alone with me."

"Which she got?"

"Yes, Mike left us alone. She started by asking what might happen to her if it turned out that she'd shot Willard in a struggle on the boat—defense of her honor."

The shock of this made me take my first gulp of coffee too fast, burning my throat before sputtering, "She killed Willard?"

"I seriously doubt it, but we didn't get any further down that path because she suddenly interrupted herself and asked why I was at the police station."

"For that matter, how *did* she know you were at the station?" I asked.

"She said she'd been trying to find me and finally went back to your house. Why didn't you tell me she was at your house this morning?"

"When would I have had the chance? Between Jack at the Hideaway and half the police force at the station, we've been surrounded."

He sat silently, waiting for the rest. I took a deep breath and said, "Okay, besides stinking up my house with cigarette smoke, she told me that Mark has a revolver with him. And she asked me if you were a double-dealing jerk-face who shot me with a slingshot in order to make her son look guilty."

"Holy hell, Naomi! She asked what?"

"Well, I paraphrased, but I told her no, you weren't, and no, you didn't. And I told her if she didn't tell the police about Mark and the gun, I would. So, you're saying that Gail went back to my house and..." I waited for the rest of *his* story.

He stared out at the drugstore *OPEN* sign for a long time before saying, "Kai told her that I'd come by looking for you and that I wanted you to go to the police station." He looked over at me. "Maybe you could try telling your daughter to say, 'I don't know,' more often."

I shrugged and took a more cautious sip of the coffee. "Maybe. But a mom doesn't really want to encourage her child to start lying to the principal. Anyway, so Gail went to the station..."

"And then, in the middle of asking her plea-bargain question, it occurred to her to ask why I was there."

"So you told her Ellen had been arrested again."

"Of course not. But she figured it out before I could think of something plausible to say. Anyway, then, suddenly, she clammed up. She just said, 'Oh,' and had nothing more to say. She sat there until Rodriguez came back. Then she said that her business with me could wait, and she left."

"That's all she said?"

"Well, she said it was too bad about Ellen killing her husband."

"She said that while Mike Rodriguez was in the room?"

"Yep."

"That bitch." I sat silent for a moment and then shifted into my see-I-told-you-so posture. Actually the posture is pretty hard to perform when you're seated right beside someone, holding a cardboard cup of coffee that's still too hot, in the cab of a small pickup truck.

"Conflict of interest!" I said. "We had Ellen in the clear, but your conflict of interest screwed it up. You think maybe that's why they have those rules?"

"What conflict of interest?"

"At least four suspects for the same murder think that we—you—are their counsel. Our first client—one of my best friends, by the way, and who did not do this, by the way—was about to be cleared by another one of your clients who, by the way, wanted to confess to killing that rat-bastard Willard Highsmith. But..."

"You don't understand, Naomi," my boss tried to interrupt.

"But nooo!" I said. "You had to have your fingers into too many pies, so now my friend is back on the hook."

Carson looked confused. "I don't think that mix of metaphors works at all, but, anyway, Gail Banner didn't kill Willard Highsmith. I'm pretty sure of that."

"Then why in hell would she be ready to confess?"

"Probably because she thinks that *Mark* might have done it. And now I can see why she might have reason to think so."

I paused and thought about that. "Yeah, and she might be right," I said. My head was starting to hurt, but it was impossible to tell whether it was because of the steel ball that had dented my skull or the conversation we were having. I needed a color-coded diagram to make sense of it all.

"He might've done it, yes." Carson said. "Anyway, I was just telling you why Gail stopped talking at the station. As soon as she realized that Ellen was back in custody, she was done."

I jabbed my finger at him, sloshing some coffee onto the truck seat in the process. "And she found that out from *you*. And she found that out from you because of conflict of interest."

Carson raised his hands next to his shoulders and said, "Hey, they're all innocent until proven guilty. And I didn't tell Gail Banner anything. Besides, I don't think she did it."

"What about Mark? He's an expert shot, you know."

"I know. Maybe." Carson sounded skeptical.

"What now?"

Carson hesitated. "Well, I have to tell you that I hinted to Mike that we might like to talk about a plea-bargain at some point. I made it clear that I didn't think Ellen was guilty, of course, but sometimes a plea down is better than a jury trial."

I glared at him. "I really wish you'd get it straight in your mind that Ellen is innocent. I don't think it was either Gail or Ellen." I thought about the secret information that Kai had shared with me and added, "Still, I guess it wouldn't hurt to explore all the options." After all, I told myself, innocent people do get convicted sometimes. Talking about a plea bargain didn't necessarily mean we thought Ellen was guilty. It just meant we were doing all we could to avoid seeing the worst happen to her.

Carson reached down and started the truck. As he eased onto the street, he changed the subject. "Let's go out to the boat and tell Three-Steps that Rice is out of town."

I attempted a cheery voice. "That should make his day. Do you think we should stop and get some more food?"

"Hell no. He should get off my boat now," Carson said. "But we should stop anyway. I'm sure I'm out of beer by now."

"I haven't had lunch."

"Neither have I. That's why I'm getting the beer."

I convinced Carson turn off the ignition and go back into the drugstore to get some comfort food for me at the lunch counter before heading to the grocery store for beer. By the time we started walking down the dock toward the boat, the sun was getting low over the cliffs to the west of the lake.

Since it was late afternoon on a Saturday, there was quite a bit of boat traffic coming back into the marina, and Larry was laying low. Carson thought that it was possible that John Rice or one of his minions might still be lurking around, so he fired up the engines and got out on the lake before letting Three-Steps show his face. He drove the cruiser back to almost exactly the same spot we had sat in the other day. Then he killed the engines.

After opening a couple of beers Carson brought up the subject of Mark Banner as the potential murderer. "We're starting to like Mark Banner for shooting Highsmith."

"No way," Three-Steps said. "He couldn't have done it."

I thought I'd better straighten him out on that. "I know that he's just a kid and all, but he's an expert marksman."

Larry turned to me. "I didn't know that."

"And his mother's relationship with Highsmith is very embarrassing for him."

"Not *that* embarrassing, for god's sake."

"He's been missing for several days, and his mother is lying about his being home on the night of the murder..."

"Couldn't have done it," Larry interrupted. "I know where he was when Highsmith was killed, and it wasn't anywhere near here."

"Were you with him?" Carson asked.

"No, but I know where he was, and I know it for sure. Trust me."

Carson nodded. "Okay, for the moment we'll assume that Mark Banner couldn't have done it."

I thought that my boss had sided with Larry way too easily. "Well, Ellen sure as hell didn't do it. That's all I know," I said.

"What about self-defense?" Three-Steps said. "Say, for instance, Ellen was out here in a boat, and she confronted Highsmith. Maybe he shot at her first. Maybe she had a gun with her—just had one on the boat or something and fired back?"

Carson laughed. "Don't ever become a defense attorney, Larry. That's the lamest story I ever heard, and I've heard a hell of a lot of lame stories."

I wasn't quite so ready to reject that idea completely. After all, I'd heard *two* shots. There was no reason that they'd had to come from the same gun. I knew that Ellen had been in Tuba City instead of on the other boat, so it hadn't been her in the other boat, but I could see how it could've been someone else.

Carson said, "I'm not buying that story, but I do have news for you. We've heard that John Rice has left town. Maybe your problem with him is over."

That news didn't seem to make Three-Steps as happy as I expected it would. He just stared out over the water without any change of expression. "For now, maybe."

"Mr. Carson beat up that thug Rice had with him," I said in an effort to cheer him up.

"I wondered about your face, Carson, but I didn't think it'd be polite to ask."

"You should see the other guy," I said. "He took a good thrashing."

"A guy like that can take a good beating twice a day," Three-Steps said, grinning. "How many more can you handle, Carson?"

Carson chuckled. "I can handle one every ten years or so. I've got to talk my way out of the next one."

Larry's smile faded. "Well, it won't be ten years until Rice is back in town. I wouldn't suggest going up against whoever he brings next time. His guys kill people, Grant."

I decided just to go ahead and ask the question that was on my mind. "Are they going to kill *you*, Larry?"

He looked sad. Of course, it could have just been the long shadows caused by the afternoon sun, but even allowing for the unflattering orange light, Three-Steps Larry looked older than his years, and very grim. "They're sure going to try."

Carson studied Larry's face for a while and finished off a beer. "If you're in trouble with guys like that, what did you think I could do for you? It doesn't sound to me like you think they're going to take you to court."

Larry went below without answering and returned with an open bottle of red wine. He didn't offer to share it, either. I guess he'd decided that the beer wasn't getting the job done. Whiskey would've been more his style, but I didn't remember seeing any in the galley cupboards when I checked them out the last time we'd taken this little trip. He said, "I don't know. It's complicated. I thought I might need a lawyer for something else I was working on. Now, though… the fact that Rice came down here looking for me—that by itself—means that I'm screwed."

"I'm a pretty good mediator," Carson said. "Maybe we can negotiate with them."

Three-Steps took a long pull right out of the bottle. All he needed was a paper bag to wrap around it and the image would be complete. "It's not a negotiable matter."

"This might be a good time for you to get out of town, Larry," I said. "While Rice and Fred are gone, at least for now."

"You have to run fast and far to get away from these guys, Naomi. Even then, eventually…" He didn't seem to have any ending for that sentence.

"You said you knew where Mark Banner was that night," Carson said. "Couldn't the kid explain that to Rice? I could probably set up a meeting or something."

"I said I knew where the boy was, not that I was with him. I want to leave the kids out of this."

"Kids? What kids?" I asked.

"Forget it. I'm not going to have Mark Banner talk to Rice. Just forget all about it, you guys. It's out of your hands. If you don't mind, Carson, I'll stay on the boat till about dawn. Then…"

Carson interrupted him. "The boat's been a pretty good hideout for you so far, Larry. Why don't you just stay put here while we think on this further? I don't suppose you'd like to tell me why Rice is after you."

At first I didn't think that Three-Steps had heard Carson. He was standing on the deck with the wine bottle in his hand and staring around at the cliffs and the canyon and the island. Finally, he said, "I heard through the grapevine that there was some trouble with Carlos Deguerra's operation up the lake a ways—just overheard some talk there at the marina when some guys walked by on the dock, understand?"

Jesus. He was talking about the dead guys on the expensive houseboat. "They would suspect you?" I asked. "Well, considering everything, I guess that's obvious, isn't it? Larry, whatever you were *really* doing—I mean you had to actually be somewhere at the time—you could prove that." I finally took the first sip of the beer I had been handed earlier. "You could even go to the police to get help."

Larry laughed. "You know, I was just thinking that I might have to do that. I don't usually go to the police voluntarily, but who knows?"

"So maybe you *will* need an attorney," Carson said.

~ ~ ~

After that the conversation dwindled. It was clear that nothing more of consequence was going to be discussed. We cruised back into the docks. After making sure that the two of us were seen securing the boat in the twilight, Carson and I walked back up to the parking lot.

We slid into Carson's little pickup. I buckled up immediately, but Carson started fumbling with the visor on his side of the truck's cab. It wasn't properly clipped into its plastic holder. When he had that all tidied up to his satisfaction, he turned the key and started the engine. Then he looked at the visor on the passenger side, which *was* kind of sagging in front of my face. I guess he decided to straighten that up too, but his hand never reached my visor. He was still stretching toward it when the bullet came through the windshield.

CHAPTER NINETEEN

IT's not like in the movies. I didn't hear a bang—I never did hear the shot. In fact, the first sound I heard was the bullet smacking into Carson's shoulder. A split second later I heard the windshield pop—or maybe they were at the same time. I get confused when bullets are flying. The first thing I *saw* that registered with me was blood hitting the dashboard and the inside of the windshield. It didn't make sense to me, and at first I didn't react. I just sat there staring at the drops of blood running down the inside of the windshield as little cracks started radiating from the small hole near the center, and my mind went blank. I don't know how many seconds it was before I turned to look at Carson.

He'd already grabbed his right shoulder with his left hand and was looking down straining to see the wound. "Get down! Get under the dash," he shouted.

I wedged myself down toward the floor and pulled him over. "*You* get down! They're shooting at you, not me."

He didn't argue.

Nothing happened next. That may sound funny, but when you're expecting something nasty to happen and it doesn't, it seems like the *nothing* that is happening is an event in itself. I was very happy to have this particular event happen. No more bullets came through the windshield. No one jerked open the car door and shot at us. No tires squealed away into the distance.

Carson continued to bleed, though. That was something, and it came to my attention. It sort of ended the nothing-happening phase and started me moving again. I tried to get up, but I was wedged down with Carson leaning against me. He tried to get up, but it took him a moment to figure out that he was going to have to use his left hand to pull himself up. After he did that, he opened his door and passed out on the pavement with his right hand on the .45 that was still stuck behind his belt.

I struggled out onto the parking lot through the open door and found myself lying on top of him. How that happened, I didn't have a clue.

I sat up and noticed that a young couple had just emerged from a car twenty feet away. "Help," I said to their startled faces. They hustled away toward the hotel.

Then I got to my feet and pulled out my little .38. I got it out in front of me and pointed it toward the front of the truck. The bullet had come from that direction, and I was determined to shoot the bastard who had fired it.

The problem was that there was no such bastard in sight. There were lots of empty cars in the deepening gloom. Further out beyond the parking lot, the land sloped steeply up a long, bush-covered hill to the west. As far as I could see, nothing was moving.

When I heard a siren coming out from town, I put my gun out of sight under my shirt, reached in to turn off the engine, and locked Carson's .45 in the glove box. Then I sat down on the pavement beside my boss.

I was at the hospital until midnight. Having finished his laundry, Dwayne had brought Kai and Len over to join me, so I endured several mini-lectures from both of the kids about getting out of the paralegal profession. Their arguments actually sounded pretty good to me until I thought about the hundreds of dollars a week I was now earning with Grant Carson.

News finally came out to the waiting room that Carson was going to be all right. The bullet had entered below his collarbone and had punched a neat hole in his scapula on its way out. The shoulder blade hadn't fractured other than that, so now he just had a clean hole through the thin, flat surface of the bone. He also had the same hole through a couple of muscles in his shoulder. The young doctor who explained this to me actually drew diagrams. He was pretty cute, too.

Carson was still under sedation and wouldn't be able to see visitors until the next afternoon, so I went on home with the kids. If I were truly a good and properly concerned office manager, concern for his welfare probably would've kept me awake all night. But I just felt exhausted and helpless so I went to sleep. It wasn't until I woke up in the morning that I realized how good this shooting had been for Ellen's case. Since she—and her rifle—had been in custody at the time of the shooting, we had a strong argument for her innocence. Besides that, no evidence had yet placed her at the scene of her husband's murder.

I lay in bed thinking that if I were Grant Carson, I could probably have used this information to force Ellen's release—if not on that Sunday, at least on the day after that. But I was not the attorney, just the sort-of paralegal, and I wasn't sure that Grant himself would be in any condition to do anything, even by the next day.

Then I began to wonder again who'd shot Carson. Obviously it wasn't Ellen—she never could have done such a thing, anyway. Mark Banner came to mind, but, again, couldn't see what his motive would've been. The most obvious candidate was John Rice or one of his lackeys. After the hospital parking lot incident, we could certainly categorize him as an enemy, but other than being generally pissed off at Grant, I couldn't see any real motive for him either.

Then I decided to give Wanda another call. I wanted to see if she'd tell me more about the Bull Banks shootings, being the supervising park ranger on the case. If it had anything to do with John Rice, that might help me to understand why he was down here messing around in our business. And I wondered again if there was any possible connection between him and Willard Highsmith, beyond my profound dislike of both.

I would have to try to catch Wanda at home because I didn't want to talk about any of this at Stitch and Bitch on Monday night. I realized as I got out of bed that I was about to use up a part of Wanda's weekend, and that I'd be using up most of my own weekend on work, one way or another, instead of spending it with my kids. I hadn't originally thought of this as being part of a paralegal's job. Maybe my kids were right.

The woman who greeted me in my bathroom mirror was a fright. She looked about twenty years older than I was and had really messy hair. I decided that I would need a good shower and more than my usual modest swipe of mascara just to leave the house. It took nearly an hour of dedicated grooming before that image in the mirror and I merged into one tired-looking, but thirty-something, paralegal. Before I could leave the house, though, I had another problem. Now more than ever I didn't feel safe leaving my children alone at home, what with slingshots slinging and guns firing and glass shattering and who knows what else. Dwayne didn't need to do any more laundry, and I couldn't think of another excuse to get someone to stay with the kids.

Staring numbly out the front window, I noticed my neighbors loading up some aluminum camp chairs and the biggest ice chest I'd ever seen. Quickly shoving my feet into sneakers, I opened the door and walked as casually as I could over to their driveway.

"Hey, Naomi, how are you feeling?" Pete unfolded the chair he was holding and set it down right behind his old Suburban. "Here, have a seat." His wife, Bev, walked over to hug me without saying anything.

I gave her a quick squeeze and took a step back to smile at them both. "Thanks, I actually feel a lot better than I look. What kind of adventure are you guys getting ready for?"

Pete said, "We try to get up to the North Rim about this time every year."

"And today's the day, huh?"

Bev nodded. "Usually we make a weekend of it, but we couldn't work that out this year, so it'll just be a very long day trip for a picnic near the lodge. Come with us, why don't you? You and the kids?"

I was sorely tempted. The North Rim of the Grand Canyon is utterly perfect in October, and it was far away from whatever the hell was going on in town and uplake. But escaping like that wouldn't do anything toward getting Ellen's name cleared. Until that happened, I was going to keep working at it. Reluctantly, I shook my head.

"I can't, but it would be great if Len and Kai could join you. I'd hate for them to miss seeing the deer grazing at the lodge."

Pete and Bev looked at each other and then at me. It was clear that they knew exactly why I'd want the kids to be away from Sage Landing just now, out of the line of fire.

Bev spoke first. "Of course, honey. We'd love to have them. The Martins and their kids are meeting us up there, so it'll be a real party."

Pete said, "I hate to pry, but are you going to be okay here?"

I sure hoped so. Giving them an even brighter smile than before, I said that I'd been okay so far and had no plans to be otherwise. Then I dashed back to my house and in fifteen minutes flat had the kids dressed, fed, and out the door.

After waving them off, I phoned Wanda's house and caught her making pancakes with her kids. I asked if she could meet me at Carson's office later, for just a few minutes. She said that she'd be at her office in a little while, catching up on a massive stack of paperwork, and I could come over there if I wanted. Sounding harried, she told me to wait an hour or so before heading over, because it'd take her at least that long to scrape pancake goo off the stovetop and mop up the syrup puddles. Yum.

When I got to the Park Service building, the outer door was propped slightly open with a fold of the rubber doormat so that I didn't have to make noise to get her to let me in. I pulled the door open and kicked the mat down into place. Then I walked in, gently closed the door, and made sure the latch clicked.

She'd said that no one else would be working in the building, so I was surprised to hear her voice from down the darkened hall and wondered who she was talking to. I walked quietly toward the open door of her office. When I peeked around the door, though, I saw that she was alone, sitting at her desk and talking animatedly on the phone. She looked up and motioned me into the office, pointing at one of the ugly but sturdy government-issue chairs intended to keep visitors from getting too comfortable.

I couldn't hear whoever was on the other end of the line, but I also couldn't help listening to her side of the conversation. It was kind of like watching a Bob Newhart comedy routine. She had the receiver squeezed between her right shoulder and ear, and she was scribbling notes on a steno pad. "How many guys saw them loading up the houseboat?... Okay, that's good... Two suitcases? ... Big ones? Are you sure?...Well, I mean, did you ask them separately? ... Okay, and they both said two... two big suitcases, yeah, got it. And a big ice chest. You mean besides the one we saw when we went up there? It was kind of dinky... Okay, well. Now, where the hell did all that stuff go? Yeah, I know. I was searching the houseboat, too, remember? But two big heavy suitcases and a big ice chest don't just evaporate. Not to mention whatever was inside them." She listened for a while longer but didn't say much before hanging up, a look of frustration on her face. She sat back in her chair and crossed her arms. With considerable feeling, she said, "Shit."

All in all, that seemed to sum it up. Somehow the isolated lake region over which she had oversight had become a hotbed of crime and intrigue. Highsmith had been murdered. Two men had been shot up at Bull Banks. Local teenagers were more-or-less missing. I had been attacked. Carson had been shot. Menacing strangers had been prowling around, hunting persistently for a local. There was practically no end to it all.

Naturally, Wanda was already thinking about possible connections. She was positioned to see the big picture, too, being a supervising law enforcement officer as well as a trainer with the Tribal Police. And she was part of several large, informal networks for keeping up to date about legal and illegal activities in the area. Three, at least.

I was part of only one of them. Her letting me hear half of a conversation about the houseboat was a good start, but I wasn't exactly sure what else she could share with me. "Can I ask you some questions?" When she didn't answer right away, it was clear that she wasn't quite sure about that either. So I added, "Wanda, I realize you probably can't tell me everything. I don't expect that. But whatever you can add to what I already know might be really important."

Wanda looked a little relieved. "Right, well. Go ahead."

"What can you tell me about what happened at Bull Banks Bay?"

"Not a whole lot, actually. There was a private houseboat. An expensive one."

"Belonging to a bad guy named Carlos Deguerra?"

She raised her eyebrows. "How did you know that?"

"I'm a paralegal now. I hear things."

"Yeah, Deguerra probably owns the boat through a chain of corporations. We have it in impound while we investigate."

"And?"

"And there's a second boat."

"An inflatable," I said, nodding.

"Sounds like you know almost as much as I do. We've impounded that boat, too. Off the record, really, Naomi. There were minute traces of cocaine in the carpet and marijuana resins in the smoke residue on the bulkheads—the walls, you know—of the houseboat, but that stuff might've been there for years. There were no narcotics aboard. Actually, there was very little of anything on board. A couple of fishing rods, no tackle. A small ice chest, still cold, with iced beer."

"But it sounds like something...several things...were maybe *removed* from one of the boats? The houseboat, probably?"

Wanda was sifting through the notes she'd taken. She raised one shoulder slightly and tilted her head toward it, like a teenager acknowledging a point without coming right out to say it.

"What about the bodies?" I asked.

"Yeah, odd. FBI forensics has put together a possible scenario. Strictly off the record—way too early to say anything for sure."

"Understood."

"They think maybe the two guys shot each other—multiple times. There were 9mm shell casings all over the place and at opposite ends of the main salon with lots of blood spatters."

"So two people shot each other?"

"There was a 9mm pistol in each guy's hand."

"You sound like there's some doubt."

"Maybe…maybe. One of the forensics guys said it looked staged. The other one disagreed. I don't have enough training to have an opinion."

"So what was that boat doing out there?"

"The insurance company guy that owned the boat said that he'd loaned it to an employee and that he'd become concerned when the man didn't return to work by Tuesday afternoon."

"And he reported it missing?"

"No—too early, he said."

"You didn't turn it over to anyone yet?" I asked.

"The company's attorney, John Rice, has filed a request that the houseboat be immediately released from impound, but we aren't ready yet."

"And that's it?"

"Nope, there's the other boat. On Wednesday, a Utah woman called the Park Service to get help in finding her husband. It seems that he'd left home on Monday evening, saying that he was going fishing."

"But he didn't come home, right?"

"Never returned. His Jeep and boat trailer were found on a remote Utah beach, but he and his inflatable fishing boat had not turned up. We found it drifting not too far from the houseboat.

"Any connection to Rice or Deguerra?" I asked.

"Maybe, maybe not," Wanda said. "The Utah guy was a part-time driver for an ice plant. The plant itself is one of several businesses owned by a holding company in Albuquerque. We haven't managed to determine who owns the holding company."

"It wouldn't be much of a leap to guess."

Wanda shrugged. "We don't get to guess. Another curious thing is that there's no record indicating that the missing man *owned* any boat."

"What about registration?"

"The boat trailer was unregistered so it can't have spent a lot of time on the highways, at least not in the daytime. The wife says that her husband has had the inflatable boat as long as she's known him, which is about two years. She says he went fishing at night a lot. The Jeep turns out to be registered to the company—the ice plant. The wife says she thought it belonged to her husband."

"Maybe the two boats had a collision in the dark, and the men got into a fight."

"Not a chance," Wanda said. "The houseboat wouldn't even have shuddered much if an inflatable hit it. Besides, this is a big inflatable. Nothing can damage one of those. The Coast Guard considers them virtually unsinkable."

"So there's no reason to have a fight over a collision in the dark."

"No. What we've got is a marginally employed man with an expensive Jeep and a deluxe inflatable boat, neither of which actually belongs to him. He goes out on the lake to go fishing at night. He goes missing."

"And he's fishing without a tackle box," I said.

"As far as we know. And then on the same night a luxury houseboat leaves the Arizona side of Bull Banks Bay to go fishing at night, and *maybe* the angler from the inflatable climbs on board. And *maybe* ends up in a gunfight."

Now I picked up the story from the other direction. "Meanwhile, eighty miles away, Highsmith takes a girlfriend skinnydipping off his boat floating at the base of a cliff near , but gets shot to death before he can dive in."

We both sat there gazing at the big map of the lake on the office wall, trying to make it make sense. Wanda said, "Inflatables and houseboats are great boats, but they aren't very fast. I'm damned if I can see the connection."

"Me either. It seems fishy," I said.

"Sort of, yes." Not being a fan of puns, Wanda refrained from acknowledging my bad joke. "This could be a case involving at least three murders, you know? But they are separated by a lot of lake and not a lot of time. Neither of the boats up in the Bull Banks area would've been on the water much earlier than eight o'clock. Neither of those boats could've come down here in time to kill Highsmith."

"So maybe the shootings are related, but could they have been done by the same person?" I asked.

"Right. All we know is that we have three dead men to account for and three boats."

"Maybe four boats," I said. "Highsmith's race boat is missing, and whoever shot him might've done it from that other boat."

"Okay, then. Three bodies, maybe four boats, and nothing but questions to go on."

I was still trying to picture all the moving parts. "And the dead men on the fancy houseboat might've shot each other?"

"That's one of those big questions for sure."

All of a sudden I had one of those mental flashes that interrupts conversation. "Oh my god! I almost forgot," I said as I stood up.

Wanda looked alarmed. "What's wrong?"

"Abe Bingham's wedding! It's today. I'll barely have time to get ready. And a gift! I'll need some kind of a gift."

"You don't mean Abe Bingham, Naomi. Abe is already married. In fact, isn't he sort of over-married? He has two wives—well, rumor has it."

I started rummaging in my purse for my car keys. "Yeah, that's right. This is a third wife, a new one. It's complicated."

"And you get invited to these kinds of things?"

I wondered what she meant by that. Did she imagine that plig weddings were wild ceremonies? And…were they?

"Not usually," I answered, "but Carson and Abe Bingham are good friends. We were doing some... uh, never mind. Anyway, we were invited to the wedding. And now Carson won't be able to go so I'll have to stand in for both of us."

"We *will* expect a full report at tomorrow night's meeting," Wanda said. She looked me over somewhat disapprovingly. "You *are* planning to change clothes and fix your hair, right?"

"I'm going home right now," I said.

~ ~ ~

My efforts to improve my hair and makeup and dress kept getting interrupted by Three-Steps Larry's dog, who clearly intended to stay squarely underfoot no matter what I was doing. By the time I was ready to escape the house and go to the wedding, I'd decided to take the dog with me. Maybe she needed an outing. I'd also decided that the wedding gift would have to wait till Carson had a chance to buy one.

I had only a general idea of where Abe Bingham's house was. He'd said to take the first right into town and then follow the road all the way to its end. But about a mile off the main highway, there was a fork in the road I was on. One road went straight ahead; the other veered sharply to the left. That road appeared to be better traveled, but, like Robert Frost before me, I chose to veer off on the other.

The dirt road I was following became rougher and rougher, less and less like a real road for another two miles. At its end was a dilapidated old shed and a broken-down sheep pen. Beside the shed was a boat trailer parked next to Mark Banner's pickup truck. I wondered if he had been invited to the wedding, but surely this shack was not Abe's house. I thought that maybe it was an outbuilding and someone would be around. Maybe I'd be able to ask directions, so I got out of my car. Larry's dog jumped out with me and ran off toward the shed.

She scurried through a gap in the wall and was immediately out of sight within the little building. As dogs often do, she'd now presented me with a new problem. Not only did I have to find someone who could give me directions, but I had to retrieve the damned dog from the shed. I didn't like opening other people's buildings, especially when I didn't know who owned them, but I walked over to the shed and tried one of its double doors. It opened easily. Inside sat Larry's dog patiently waiting beside the right-hand rear door of an old Subaru. She kept wagging her tail and looking at me as if I were going to open that car's door and give her a ride.

Before I could make up my mind what to do, I heard the sound of music coming from a distance. There was a distinct country-western flavor to the sound, and I wondered whether I'd somehow arrived near the wedding just when I thought I was lost. I followed the music downhill and found myself in a wash that was sloping steeply southward toward the lake. There were numerous footprints going in both directions in the sandy soil, but not nearly enough of them, it seemed to me, to indicate much of a wedding party.

The sides of the wash grew steeper and narrower until I was walking through one of the miniature sandstone canyons for which our lake is famous. The formation got narrower and deeper and finally opened out to a small beach at the edge of the lake.

Then I encountered an example of the nude sunbathing that is so common in the quiet coves of our lake. Below me at the water's edge the long nose of a speedboat had been pulled up onto shore and tied off to a nearby rock. On that same expanse of fiberglass lay a naked man, face up to the sun. Beside him set up an equally naked blond woman who appeared to be trickling water over his forehead from her hand.

Now, I enjoy looking at attractive naked people just as much as the next person, but I also hate to intrude on a young couple's privacy so I started backing quietly up the canyon. Larry's stupid dog, who had joined me about halfway down the canyon, had no such inhibitions. Instead, she started yapping and running toward the couple on the boat.

The young man didn't move a muscle, but the girl turned to face me. It was Linda Armstrong. That meant that the boy was probably Mark Banner.

"I'm sorry," I shouted, "the dog..."

"Princess!" Linda said. "Come here, Princess. Come here girl."

At this invitation the dog ran to the edge of the boat and began several attempts to jump onto it, but she was too small to make any headway. Linda slipped off of the deck and patted the dog before looking up at me.

"Aren't you the woman from Grant Carson's office?" She asked this in the normal tone I would have expected from a person who was wearing some clothes. On the other hand, what choice did she have? There were no clothes in sight. I probably would have bent over and tried to make my hands into adequate covering, but she didn't. "I'm worried about Mark. He's not waking up."

I looked at the young man and then averted my eyes, but not before registering an image of a very fit, very young, man. "Don't you think you should cover him up? I mean... the sun. He's going to burn his..."

"Yeah, sun damage and all that. It's, like, a hell of a place to get cancer. I tell him that and he's all like, 'it takes thirty years to get cancer.' And I'm all like, 'well, you're probably going to live more than thirty years, and then you'll have cancer of the dick, or something.' And he's like, 'not me.' But now he's whacked out and I can't move him. I can't even turn him over."

She reached out and poked the Banner kid's thigh with her forefinger. "Last night I'm all, 'Larry said not to snort any of that until it was cut quite a bit.' But Mark's all, 'it'll be cool. It's just a tiny line.' But I'm like, 'not me, man. I'm sticking to grass.' But then I got stoned, and I didn't notice when he passed out."

"You mentioned a Larry?"

"Three-Steps Larry. He's a friend of ours from town." She was babbling this rapidly with a kind of pleading tone. I walked down to where she stood beside the boat, but I didn't know what to do. Do you put your arm around a babbling naked woman whom you don't know? What do you do for an unconscious naked teenager who is lying there toasting his... equipment? And was it illegal for me to look at him—his being underage and a missing person?

Then I saw the deer rifle lying across the bench seat in the rear of the boat. This was no slingshot, nor was it the revolver that Gail had mentioned. This was serious firepower, able to shoot accurately across long distances. Was I looking at the rifle that had killed Highsmith and damn near killed my boss?

CHAPTER TWENTY

"I'LL get some clothes," Linda said. Then she walked eastward along the shore and I saw their campsite at the edge of the brush about a hundred feet from the boat. They'd pitched a tent and a sun fly. Under the shade was a small folding camp table. Linda went into the tent.

Just when I was pondering how I was going to find out if Mark Banner was still alive, he moved slightly. I figured that was good enough for now so I turned away and waited for Linda, my mind still very much on the rifle in the boat.

When Linda emerged from the tent, she was wearing shorts and a knit tube top. She returned to the boat with a pair of baggy shorts and a dirty T-shirt for Mark. "I don't think I can get these on him," she said, looking at me as if I should take over.

"How long have you guys been here?" I asked, without even a hint that I might try to dress Mark. "All night?" I prompted. This was my clever way of finding out if they'd shot Carson.

"A couple of weeks, off and on. We're in town like every other day, but Mark's afraid to go in now. He's all like, 'They're looking for me because of Highsmith.' And I'm like, 'No they're not. You had nothing to do with that. Besides, they got that Navajo woman—his wife,' and he's like, 'They let her go.' and I'm like, 'I heard they arrested her again,' but he doesn't believe it."

"Did you go into town last night? You or Mark?" I decided that if I didn't question her directly and simply she wouldn't be able to follow what I was saying.

"I just told you Mark won't go into town. But yesterday we started toking up in the afternoon, and about sundown Mark decided to do a line of blow, like I said."

"Cocaine?"

"Yeah. I'm all, 'Larry said not to snort any of that until it was cut,' but he's all, 'it'll be cool. It's just a *tiny* line,' but I'm all, 'not *me*, man.'" She paused. "I already told you that, I think." She spread the T-shirt over Mark's midsection and looked up at me. "Is he going to die?" Her voice wobbled a bit, and she looked like she might cry.

"We should get some help for him, but I don't think we can get him up to the cars. The fastest way to get help would be to take him in to the marina on the boat."

"There may not be enough gas. I filled it up a few days ago, but we've done some cruising around."

Then Mark surprised us by joining the conversation. "I'm not going anywhere." He didn't move as he said this.

"Can you sit up?" I asked him.

He tried. He couldn't. But he did manage to squirm around enough to slide the T-shirt off his body and put himself back in danger of developing the unmentionable cancer. Linda covered him up again. Now that she was dressed, she seemed to have regained some sense of modesty. Well, to be honest, modesty may be too strong a word.

"Let's see if we can get him down into the boat," I said.

We pulled him up into a sitting position and managed to get the T-shirt on him. The shorts were more difficult, but we finally got them on too. Then we more or less rolled him into the boat. We hadn't removed the rifle from the seat first, and he landed on it. That would've hurt a lot if he'd had any functioning nerve endings. As I pulled the weapon out from under him, I asked, kind of off-hand, "Why the rifle?"

"Mark just wanted to bring it," Linda said. "He's all like, 'I want you to borrow Highsmith's boat for me.' He said Two-Steps wanted it."

"How could you get Highsmith's boat?"

"I can get just about anything off Highsmith, and Larry's all, 'and if you can get me a boat, I can take care of you guys *real* good.'"

"Got any other guns?" I asked casually as I helped her push Mark up into a sitting position.

"No. Mark just wanted his rifle. He said he had to practice because he was going deer hunting."

I remembered hearing Dr. Banner say something like that a few days ago and decided to continue my ad hoc investigation. "And it was Three-Steps who wanted the boat?"

"Yeah, it was a good deal. He said he'd give us a hundred and a fat stash of California grass if we could get Highsmith's boat for him." Linda climbed out of the boat and I followed her up to the tent where she retrieved a backpack and a water bottle. "We can leave all the rest of this here," she said, "and I'll bring you back for your car. I'm afraid to take him in to the marina by myself."

I realized that the dog had run off somewhere so I was leaving my car and the dog. I didn't like doing either, but there didn't seem to be any good alternative.

As we walked back to the boat, Linda said, "Three-Steps wanted to go cruising on the lake. I figured maybe he had a girlfriend he was trying to impress."

That surprised me. "So, he wanted the speedboat, not the other High-smith boat?" We pushed off, waded out beside the boat, and struggled up over the side.

Linda rummaged around in the backpack while she answered. "He didn't say, actually. I just figured he meant this boat. It's a cool boat." She found the key she was looking for and stuck it in the ignition.

I reached out and touched her hand before she turned the key. "I won't be able to hear you when you start this thing up," I said. "So tell me more about Larry."

She shrugged and then had to re-insert herself into the tube top. "He came down the canyon like you, except he was carrying a duffel bag with some stuff in it."

"What stuff? Did you see what he had in the bag?"

"No. I asked him where he was going, and he said he was going to try to shoot some deer. We're here with the boat, so Larry gives us a big baggy and a hundred and takes off."

"With the boat and Mark's rifle? Is it deer season?"

She looked quizzically at me. "Not the rifle, just the boat. Mark would never let anyone borrow his precious deer rifle." She was shaking her head. "Next morning, he comes in here about dawn, wakes us up with the boat. He's all nervous like. He's in a generous mood, though." She reached out again to start the engine, but I stopped her once more.

"Generous?"

"Yeah, he's all like, 'let's keep this whole thing quiet,' and he gives us five hundreds and some blow, and he says not to snort the blow 'til we cut it way down. He says a little on the gums is plenty 'til we cut it."

"Then what?" I said, still touching her hand.

"Then Mark decides to ditch school for another day so we take the boat out for a ride. Then I had that appointment with my dad and Mr. Carson, and I heard about Highsmith." She started the boat and the roar of the engine made it impossible to ask her any more questions.

I noticed that the gasoline gauge read about three-quarters full. We made it to the marina at a higher speed than I'd ever ridden in a boat. Luckily, the lake was flat and windless so the spanking of the speedboat on the water gave me only minor kidney damage. While Linda tied up at the public slips, I ran up the dock and dialed for the paramedics. It didn't look like I was going to experience my first plig wedding after all. Wanda would be so disappointed.

~ ~ ~

An hour later I walked into Carson's hospital room to tell him about my afternoon. Then I had to whirl around and walk back out because I thought I might be interrupting something between him and a nurse. I just got the feeling—well, she was leaning over him. It could have been perfectly innocent. Anyway, she came out of the room pretty quickly.

Then I went in as if nothing had happened and told Carson all about stumbling into the campsite of naked teenagers who were very much under the influence, before bouncing across the lake at speeds too fast for ordinary mortals to see, and then navigating emergency medical services for the third time in three days. I ignored the open bottle of lotion on his bedside table.

"Mark's still alive, as far as I know, but the doctors didn't seem very confident when we got him here," I said to finish the story.

"What about his parents?"

"They're both downstairs in the waiting room. I haven't said anything to them. Linda Armstrong is in the waiting room, too, but no one is speaking to her. Actually, no one's speaking to anyone down there."

"Has Linda talked to the police yet?"

"Miller said he talked to her, but he didn't believe her story. He thinks the Banner kid shot me and you and Highsmith."

"You talked to her, Naomi. What do you think?"

"I think I believe her. There's other stuff, too," I said. Then I told him what I'd learned from Wanda about the boats uplake and the dead men.

"If we had suspicious minds, we might think that Larry wasn't just joy riding," he said.

I didn't want to think about that. "What would happen if John Rice heard this? Do you think he could... that he might hear it?"

"No, not likely, probably. And there could be an entirely different explanation for the houseboat shootings."

"For instance?"

"For instance, could be that a couple of Deguerra's boys were sent out on the lake in the houseboat to meet a guy from the Utah side. But instead of doing whatever they were supposed to do, they got into a serious fight. Maybe one tried to pull a heist and the others weren't in on it. If one got away with that, he might have made quite a haul."

"Or if Three-Steps was in on it, *he'd* be pretty well set up."

"Maybe…unlikely," Carson said. "Or he might've had a small part of it in some way. I don't see how he could overcome two or more men in the dark."

"Well, Larry probably didn't shoot you last night because he was still behind us on your boat. And we know Ellen couldn't have done it, and I don't think the Banner kid did. Maybe it was that guy of Rice's—that Fred guy. Getting even, you think?"

Carson was quiet for a minute, staring at the ceiling and absently scratching the stubble on his chin. Then he faced me and said "Tell me again what Wanda thought about where Highsmith might fit in with all this."

I didn't quite see what he was getting at. "It isn't so much that she thought Highsmith was involved. It was just that the timing bothered her."

"Bothered her how, exactly?"

"Well, I think it bothered her because of the coincidence, three men shot all on the same night. And because it couldn't have been the same shooter."

"Because of the timing."

"Right, and the distance."

Carson slid out of bed and stood there facing me. His right shoulder and arm were under the regulation hospital gown. He reached his left hand behind his neck and fiddled with the tie on the gown. Then he shrugged it off his shoulders and started tugging it toward the floor. Luckily he was wearing boxer shorts under the gown. "Watch the hall," he said. "Peggy brought me some clothes that aren't bloody. I'm going to get dressed and get out of here."

I turned away. "You think that's wise? I mean it hasn't been twenty-four hours since you took a bullet."

"I don't think it's smart to stay here where everyone knows where I am. If someone is trying to kill me, I should be harder to find."

"*If* someone is trying to kill you?" I said. "Clearly someone is."

"Not necessarily. They might have been trying to kill *you* again. You were in the seat with me, and someone already tried to kill you. I may have been an innocent bystander."

A moment later I felt Carson's hand on my shoulder. I turned to see him with khakis on and a shirt hanging from his left arm. That's as far as he could get with his right arm and shoulder bandaged up. "The coast is clear," I said, as I rearranged him and buttoned him up. Then I put his shoes on for him. "Where are we going?"

"Let's go out to the end of the wing and down the stairs to the parking lot. We'll figure out the rest later." He paused and looked around the room. "Where's my .45?"

I had to think. "I locked it in your truck last night."

"And was there any windshield left after the bullet went through? Just curious about how effective the lock is likely to be."

Typical Carson, acting like a Monday-morning quarterback. I took a deep, calming breath and spoke very softly so that I wouldn't be hollering at an injured man. "Look, there's just a small hole in the windshield. The doors are locked. Nobody's going to mess with your truck or grab your big gun. It's not just lying there on the seat for anybody to see because I put it in the glove box. I've got my pistol, so we're properly armed. Quit fussing."

He was looking out the door to the hall, and I could see him consider several possible responses to my scolding before he finally said, "Okay, then. Good. Let's go."

We walked confidently toward the end of the hospital wing without drawing a second glance from the people we passed in the hall, and we would've breezed on out if we hadn't seen Jack Miller dressed in casual civilian clothes.

He came out of the elevator and turned down the hall away from us. When he reached the doorway of a room a few steps away from the elevator, he looked through its little glass window and then reached down to open the door. Just before turning the handle, he took the precaution of checking to his right and left, and he recognized us. Then he nodded, turned sharply toward the exit, and left the building ahead of us.

When we reached that same doorway on our way out, Carson looked in the room as Miller had done. "Mark Banner," he said.

"Funny," I said. "Jack can't question him yet. He's still unconscious."

"Funny," Carson said. "Maybe he's just checking to be sure the kid isn't getting away."

"That's probably it," I said. "Jack is sure the kid is guilty."

When we got to the parking lot, Jack was nowhere to be seen, and I remembered that my car was still out at the lake. You'd think I would've remembered that before we were standing dumbly in the hospital parking lot. I told Carson.

"How did you get here?"

"I came in on the boat with Linda and Mark. We came up here in the ambulance. Your truck is probably still at the marina."

"Let's hope so. You came here in the ambulance with me last night too, I guess."

"Yeah, and I walked home with my kids later. Then today I drove my car out to go to the wedding....It's complicated. So now what, Carson?"

"Now we find a phone and call a cab."

"You mean we call *the* cab. There is only one cab in town. On a Sunday evening we're going to catch him at home."

Carson patted his pockets. "You have any money?"

"No. It's out with my car somewhere in Utah. You?"

"There is no wallet in these pants. I wonder where that got to."

"I gave it to the admissions desk last night—insurance and identification and all that."

Carson sighed and looked helpless. "You think the cabbie will trust us? We just want to go out to the marina."

"Billy Farneth owns the cab. His sister's a friend of mine, so he knows me. Maybe he'll take my I.O.U."

~ ~ ~

A half-hour later, with a few rays of sunlight still making it to the lake's darkening surface, Billy dropped us off at the marina docks and shook my hand for security on a twenty-dollar I.O.U. Carson's truck wasn't in the lot so we figured it had been towed on police orders. If we'd known that, we could've walked over and picked it up in town.

Carson had been quiet throughout the ride, but when we didn't see his truck, he pointed toward the docks. "Hiding out on the boat has worked pretty well for Three-Steps. Let's give it a try ourselves while we try to figure out what's going on."

I looked at my watch and figured that Bev and Pete wouldn't have the kids back till nine at the earliest, so I agreed.

As we walked along the dock toward his boat, he said, "Where do you think the Highsmith case would go if Mark Banner died?"

"I don't follow you," I said. "What do you mean?"

"What would Chief Rodriguez think? What would the county attorney do? What about the Feds?"

I thought about that while we climbed aboard. "They might think that Mark Banner did it all—killed Highsmith, slingshotted me, and put a bullet through you."

Carson said, "Actually, there wouldn't be anything like an ironclad case against him, but he would be dead, unable to defend himself. There's the rifle. And he's got that history with the slingshot."

"But Linda Armstrong would testify…"

"Unreliable witness. Drugs."

"Okay, but Larry will testify that the kid was somewhere else."

"Larry isn't going to testify, not if Mark Banner is dead. Why would he open himself up to a narcotics investigation?"

Larry's voice came up out of the salon. "Mark Banner is dead?"

I answered, looking at Carson as if I were talking to him. "No, Larry. We're just talking about how the case would go if he died. He's in the hospital."

Carson started the engines, and for a moment we couldn't hear anything else. As we backed out of the slip, I opened the cabin door and stuck my head in. "Overdose. You son of a bitch."

"I told them not to use that stuff until they cut it," Three-Steps said, as if that made any difference.

I thought that if I had a gun I'd shoot him. Then it occurred to me that I *did* have a gun—it was parked right there under my shirt in the middle of my back. So I *could* shoot him. I even wondered for a moment if it would be considered justifiable homicide, which was ridiculous, but certainly a pistol whack to the head or—even better—to the nose would be pretty easy to justify. I slid my hand back to at least touch the pistol, but before I reached it, Carson clamped his hand around my wrist.

"I'm glad you have that, Naomi. I'd rather have mine, but it's safely locked in the truck." He smiled at me. "Why don't you give me yours for the time being?"

Grant was shaking his head no, but he was still smiling. I handed him the little pistol. He slipped it into his pocket and kicked the engines up a notch. "Come on up," he called to Larry, who climbed up and stood beside him next to the helm. I stumbled over to the bucket seat closest to them, so that I could watch their faces and hear most of what they said.

Carson raised his voice above the engine noise to tell Three-Steps about Linda and Mark and the trip to the hospital. He also repeated what Linda had told me about the night Highsmith died. Then he added, "If Linda tells that story around very much, John Rice will hear it. That would probably be just about be all he'd need to have you hunted down."

From where I sat, Larry's eyes looked worried. However, because he was Larry Sabano, his lips immediately started lying. "She got it all wrong. I told them, just like I'm telling you—I wanted to bag a big buck, but the herd didn't show up. I went a long ways for nothing."

"So where did all of the money come from, and the cocaine?" I asked, almost shouting.

Three-Steps stared ahead over the top of the windshield, bouncing along with the boat and stalling before he answered. Finally he said, "I gave them a few hundred dollars and some grass. I admit that." He looked from me to Carson and back to me. "But Mark already had the blow from somewhere. I *saw* it. I *tasted* it for them. I *said* not to use it. I *told* them it was too hot. Linda is too messed up to remember what happened."

There was a long gap in the conversation. I channeled my disbelief and disgust into my facial expression and body language. Carson gave the appearance of neutrality, but that he didn't mean that he believed Three-Steps.

"Where are we going?" Larry finally asked.

It was a good question, one I should have wondered about myself.

"Beats me," said Carson. "For now, I'm getting as far the hell away from anyone's gun as we can get."

"Go around the island and head back up toward the Utah shore," I said. "We can find the campsite, and I can get my car." After a moment I added, "I just remembered that Larry's dog is stranded up there."

Three-Steps looked surprised. "You abandoned Princess?"

I couldn't believe his nerve. Now he was judging me? "Actually, Three-Steps, she abandoned me. She wasn't around when we left to take Mark *to the hospital*, you son of a bitch. I guess I'm not such a good dog sitter. Remember that the next time you have to flee for your life."

"She'll be around the camp or up at my car," Larry said, completely ignoring my fury. "Maybe it's time for me to take her and head up north for a while."

"Up north?" Carson asked, sounding interested.

"Been wanting to visit a friend in Vancouver—now would be a good time."

Maybe so, but now was not turning out to be a very good time to be boating on the lake. A stiff breeze had come up, and the choppy surface of the water was making navigation more difficult. Carson still stood at the helm and waved off Larry's offer to take over. He cruised up toward the Utah shore after we cleared the island, and by my reckoning we were a few miles short of where I had found the kids when Larry broke the silence. "Just let me off at the mouth of that little cove ahead."

"We're still a couple of miles away from the cars," I said.

"I can use the walk."

"Are you thinking that someone might be waiting around the camp?" Carson asked.

"What do you think?" Larry said. "It isn't likely, but it's possible."

"We'll keep it in mind," Carson said as he cut back on the engines to take Larry in to shore in the deepening dusk.

Later, as we approached the mouth of the canyon where the camp was hidden from the lake, I said, "Oh, and I missed Abe's wedding. I got lost."

"We'll catch his next one," Carson said.

CHAPTER TWENTY-ONE

THE wind got worse. We entered the canyon, both of us keeping a sharp eye out for any sign that someone was there. Since there was no boat in the cove, we were reasonably sure that no one was around. Still, it was possible that someone might have found the camp and the cars above it, leaving a lookout behind, so we were watchful as Carson nosed the *Deep Inn* into the beach sand.

Inside the tent we switched on an electric lantern and found both the marijuana stash and the bag of cocaine. Carson tasted the white powder and pronounced it virtually uncut. In terms of the measurements I use, there was about a cup of the stuff.

"Larry *was* lying," Carson said. "There's no way those kids could have afforded this much of this grade of coke. He must have given it to them like Linda said."

So much for what Three-Steps had said about Linda's reliability. "No surprise to hear that Larry is a liar, but why would he give them that much? How much money are we talking about?"

A gust of wind rattled the nylon surrounding us. I kept my eyes on the drugs lying on the floor of the tent among the rumpled sleeping bags, tangled clothes, and half-empty potato chip bags. As Dr. Banner had said —when, a week ago? What a mess.

"The grass here is worth a few hundred, but the coke might be worth several thousand. I'm kind of out of practice at valuing this stuff, but I had to deal with it all the time when I was a prosecutor in Phoenix. Mark and Linda wouldn't have the money for this. They wouldn't know a dealer who sold it, either."

"Except Larry," I said. "Obviously. He had access to this stuff." I finished my packing.

"No, he might have some now, but I doubt he's ever been a dealer on this scale. There wouldn't a big enough market up here, for one thing. What we have right here might supply the entire market in Sage Landing for a long time, unless I'm way wrong about the town's few party-type users."

"It's probably not a very profitable place to be a dealer," I agreed. "At least I hope I'm right about that. So why would Larry be so generous?"

Carson switched off the lantern, and we took it out of the tent with us. "And so free with the money if Linda is telling the truth?"

We searched the area around the tent but found no money and no more drugs. We did find Larry's little dog, who came down the canyon to join us. She didn't seem any the worse for having spent the afternoon alone in the wild. She did take an interest in the ice chest that was under the camp table. I opened it and gave her what remained of a package of cheese that I found there. She gobbled it up in three big bites and then trotted to the beach to lap up some delicious lake water. I worried briefly that she maybe shouldn't be drinking that but remembered hearing about dogs drinking from toilets, so beach water should be pretty clean by comparison.

"I've been thinking about Larry's generosity," I said. "He must have had lots of cocaine and money to be so lavish, but it was still a stupid thing to do—giving it to a couple of teenagers like that."

"You'd think he would know better. Did he think they wouldn't show off with it back in town? If he thought that, he was nuts," Carson said. "But there's a nastier possibility."

I thought about that and shuddered. "If killing those kids was his plan, it almost worked, at least on Mark. Do you think Larry could do that?"

"Mark may not recover, even now, Naomi, and with Linda's past it's a miracle that she didn't snort any of this herself."

"Still, I can't see Three-Steps as a cold-blooded killer. I'm betting that he just wanted to get rid of it, all at once. And he was too thick-headed to just dump it in the lake."

Carson looked directly into my face in the near darkness. "Maybe. Actually, that makes a certain amount of sense. There he was with a lot of money and a lot of very high-grade coke. It's a sure bet that he'd taken it away from somebody. Could be it dawned on him that he couldn't start dealing the stuff without the wrong people noticing."

"Maybe he was just part of a scheme with the other guys, like you said."

"If there was a scheme, those other guys would be up in New Mexico or Utah with that inflatable—except they're dead."

"Yeah, there is that."

Another gust pulled at the sun fly. "And then there's the Highsmith boat," Carson said, speaking loudly over the wind.

"Well, he would need a boat to get up there if he was part of it."

Carson started untying the lines that held the shade up. "But why such a fast boat? For that matter, why would the others need Larry at all? They had the inflatable to get away with."

"Linda said he didn't specify that boat. She just assumed that was the one he'd wanted." I helped Carson collapse and fold the sun fly, and we stuck it between a table leg and the ice chest. "But if only one of them was going to pull something off, he would need outside help—maybe."

As we took a last look around the camp, it was hard for me to make sense of everything. Three-Steps Larry seemed too goofy to be part of a hijacking against a crime syndicate. And he seemed too harmless to deliberately set two kids up for death by overdose. But he *had* tried to get Carson to alibi for him for that Monday night, and he did seem to have a lot of new money. He did ask for the boat. He must have given the kids the raw dope, and it *had* nearly killed one of them.

Carson interrupted my train of thought. "I wonder where he is now? Why did he want off up-lake instead of coming back to his car with us?"

"Being super-cautious? Maybe he just didn't want to risk showing his face here. Or maybe his stash is up there somewhere."

"He'll need money if he's going to make a run for it. He didn't take anything with him when he went ashore."

"And he didn't have a gun with him as far as I could tell."

"Yeah, but who knows what he's got hidden up there. I'd like to get out of here before he has time to hike this far, just in case," Carson said. "Should we drive your car back to town or take the boat?"

I thought about my car up the canyon by the shed where Larry had hidden his old Subaru. I didn't really want to try to drive back out of the hills in the dark. More to the point, my kids would be home soon. "I think the boat would get me home quicker, but I want to run up to my car and get my purse."

"It's getting pretty dark to be walking through that," Carson said, gesturing toward the narrow opening in the sandstone that I would have to climb through to get back up to the top.

"Damn." I'd have to leave my purse overnight again. I hoped I'd at least locked the car. "Let's just get out onto the lake and head back in." I looked at Princess, who was now sitting on the beach a few feet away. "What about the dog?"

"Larry seemed pretty sure that he could find his way back here. Let's leave her for him."

The wind was now beating on the tent and making a racket. It was ruffling the dog's fur.

"I don't know," I said. "She's a pretty nice little dog."

"What's your point?"

"Well, I think she deserves someone better, is all."

"Better how? She's his dog."

"He's going to be on the run. That's no way for a little dog to live. What do you think would happen to her if Rice catches up with him?"

"If we take her with us, Larry will get back here and wonder what happened to her," Carson said.

"Screw Larry. Put her on board."

Then I realized that he couldn't pick up the thirty-plus-pound mutt with his one good arm so I hoisted her up to my chest and waded out beside the cruiser. I tumbled her over the side and waded back to shore.

"You'll never get rid of her if you bring her with us now. Don't expect me to take her off your hands. I don't even like dogs." Carson shouldered the bow up to loosen it in the sand while I helped.

Then I remembered the marijuana and the cocaine still lying on the floor of the tent. "Wait, Carson! Wait! The drugs—shouldn't we take them in?"

Carson kept pushing the boat off the beach. "Good god almighty, Naomi. Why on earth would we want to do that?"

Then we waded out nearly waist deep, and I helped him climb aboard.

We cruised out of the cove into wind and gunfire. The term "a hail of bullets" came to mind, but it wasn't all that many bullets—about four, I think.

All four came through the right windshield, though, and in rapid succession. I stood and screamed, but Carson killed the running lights and the engines and hit the deck, dragging me down after him. Once again, I found myself lying beside my boss, and not in a good way. He put his one good arm over me and pulled me closer.

"You okay?" he said.

"Yeah, you?"

"So far," he said. "Help me get the gun out of my pocket. It's stuck." I thought about all the bandages beneath the right side of his shirt and realized that his right arm and hand were under the buttons. He wasn't doing too well in his one-handed condition.

I struggled with the thing and finally got its hammer disengaged from the cloth. I extended it towards him, but he said, "I'm right handed."

"Well, you can shoot with your left hand," I said.

"Shit, Naomi, with that little snub-nose neither of us can hit anything anyway. You may as well hold it. If you can figure out where they are, you might scare them with a shot or two in their general direction."

"This thing only holds five shots."

"They don't know that."

I crawled to the rear of the boat, the stern, and peeked over the side.

Then I saw the other boat bobbing in the choppy water. It was just a little fishing boat, maybe a fifteen-footer. There was only one man in it, and I could make out his silhouette really clearly against the light reflecting off the lake because he was to our west. He was only about fifty yards away, and he was standing up in the boat in spite of its motion.

I decided to shoot him.

I took careful aim along the whole inch-and-a-half or two inches of barrel on my borrowed pistol. I then remembered from lessons long ago that my best shot would be if I cocked the hammer first. I did that and aimed again and took my shot. When I opened my eyes, I couldn't hear anything but ringing in my ears, and the man was gone.

I was pretty goddamned amazed, to tell you the truth. I'd killed the bastard with a snub-nosed revolver in one shot at about a hundred and fifty feet.

I decided to shoot his boat, too. I followed the same procedure, including closing my eyes at the last second, and gave it another shot. After a couple of seconds, there were flames at the back of the little boat—not exactly where I'd aimed, but what the hell.

Boy, those flames had a mind of their own, I can tell you. Within about ten seconds, they were shooting up into the darkening sky. Then there was a whooshing sound and the whole back of the boat was in roaring flames.

I was sold on this gun I had borrowed. I made a mental note to find out what kind it was and buy one as soon as possible.

"What are you shooting at?" He hadn't seen my amazing sniper-like accuracy.

"I shot the guy!" I said. "I shot his boat, too! It's burning right now."

Carson stood up and switched on the deck lights which included a pedestal-mounted green one at the stern.

"That's some shooting, Naomi. Are you sure *you* didn't shoot High-smith?" he turned on a spotlight and swiveled it toward the flaming boat.

"That was someone else's pleasure." I looked out over the water and could see something large churning the surface between us and the burning boat. I raised my pistol again and started to take aim.

"Hold on," Carson said.

I lowered the pistol and stood there watching as the form of a swimmer became more distinct, swimming well and headed straight toward our boat.

"I don't see anything in his hands. I think he lost his gun, but be careful."

Finally, the spotlight illuminated Jack Miller's grim, wet face. He reached up toward the side of the boat, but failed to touch it until he moved closer. "Give me a hand," he coughed.

Carson nodded toward the gun in my hand and then answered, "Show me both your hands, Jack."

Miller raised both hands out of the water. Both were empty. Too bad there wasn't a gun in one of them—I was loaded for bear and eager to shoot again.

"I only have one hand at the moment, so you'll have to swim around to the ladder and climb in. Naomi is holding a gun, and she's a hell of a shot. You understand?"

"Sure, Grant."

While Carson stood by the ladder and helped him aboard, I stepped back and sat down on a bench. "What are you doing out here, Jack?"

"From the look of those holes in the windshield, I'd say he was trying pretty hard to kill us," Carson answered for him. "And I'd say it isn't the first time. Am I right, Jack?"

"Yes and no," he said, out of breath. A gust of wind rocked the cruiser, and Miller rolled onto his back on the deck and lay still. Even in the darkness, I could see that his clothes were the same ones he'd been wearing in the hospital earlier.

Now I was really confused. I looked over at Carson as he kept talking to Jack. "The steel ball that you shot at Naomi wasn't supposed to kill her?"

I was shocked. What made Carson think that? I was more amazed when Jack answered.

"No. It wasn't even supposed to hit her, just scare her and get found in her room."

"Because of Mark Banner's juvenile arrest," Carson said.

I realized that I should have been able to figure that out.

Miller answered. "Yeah, but I'm lousy at using a slingshot, and Naomi was moving around." He sighed and looked at me. Then he coughed up a little water.

Carson raised his voice to be heard over the wind. "What about shooting me last night? That's a pretty sure way to kill a man."

"The bullet was supposed to go right through the front and back windows and end up in the water behind your truck. You jerked over toward Naomi and got in the way."

Princess leaned against my leg and started shivering. That was funny because she was the only dry one on board. I ignored her and my own chilled legs, now angry with myself for not seeing through Jack and his interference with the investigation.

"*You* planted the steel balls at the Banner house?"

"And you planted the Navajo medicine bundle in the evidence room, the one in the box of stuff taken from Ellen's," Carson added.

"The pollen bag, you mean." Not that it mattered now, but I couldn't help setting the record straight.

"Did Ellen know?" Carson asked him.

I stared at him. How could he even ask that?

Shaking his head, Jack went into a coughing fit for a minute. When it had subsided, he struggled to a sitting position. "No. She never—once she was arrested, she wouldn't talk to me at all, wouldn't listen. She didn't know."

I was relieved in spite of myself, but Carson just looked at him and then looked over at me. My brain took awhile to catch up with the whole 'situation,' as Dwayne Polacca would have called it. But when it did finally click into gear, it put two and two together. "He's telling the truth about that, Carson. Jack told Peggy that the evidence he 'found' was a medicine bundle. Ellen would've known better."

But, I thought...*Jack*? I still couldn't believe it. He was a cop, for god's sake. "A few minutes ago—you tried to kill us this time, right? You're just a damn lousy shot and you happened to miss this time."

He didn't answer.

"Well, right?" I needed to hear it from him.

Finally he muttered, "You guys saw me at the hospital. No way around that." He coughed again. "Then you took off in the cab and came out here. It took me a while to get my boat and start trying to follow you."

"So you were at the hospital, so what?" I said.

"He was going to finish Mark Banner, Naomi. He thought we knew that," Carson said.

I looked at Carson. "I didn't think that, did you?"

"The thought occurred to me," Carson said.

"I figured it would," Miller said quietly.

I looked over at his burning boat and asked, "Where did I hit you? You were swimming pretty good for a guy with shoes and clothes on and a bullet in him somewhere."

"You didn't hit me. You probably didn't even come close. I saw your muzzle flash and jumped overboard. One of your shots hit the gas can, though. I lost my rifle in the lake and couldn't get back on my boat because the fire was spreading. After a while I figured that I had to drown or swim over here."

"What I can't figure out," Carson said, "is how you shot Highsmith. I checked your alibi myself."

"I didn't shoot Highsmith. I wasn't anywhere near Sage Landing that night. I know that the Banner kid did it, but no one else seems to think so. I kept trying to show people that."

"I think it's called framing him," I said.

"Rodriguez just kept going after Ellen for it. I just wanted to convince him. I figured the ball bearing through Naomi's window would help change the picture. Then last night I knew the kid was hiding out somewhere so I thought..."

"Why would anyone think he was trying to kill me?" I interrupted. "I'm just a lawyer's secretary."

"Paralegal and office manager," Carson said.

"Assistant to an attorney," I said.

Miller looked at us as if we might be the crazy ones. "I figured the Banner kid might try to stop you guys from defending Ellen. He would want her convicted. The idea was just to get Rodriguez to take a look him. The rest would fall into place if the chief would do a proper investigation."

"Except that Mark Banner is innocent—I mean he's not guilty of shooting Highsmith," I said. It was true that Mark hadn't killed Highsmith, but I wouldn't go so far as to use the word *innocent* to describe him. "There are witnesses. He didn't do it."

We all sat silently in the eerie green light, watching the flames that were consuming Jack's boat. After a couple of minutes, there was a gurgling sound as it disappeared below the surface.

"Foam flotation burned out of her," Carson said.

"What now?" Miller asked, looking up at Carson.

"You owe me for two new windshields—one for the truck and one for the boat. It's an old boat and the parts are expensive."

"Of course, we have to turn you in," I said.

Carson turned to me with a surprised expression. "Don't be silly, Naomi. What would be the point? Jack would get out of this in a heartbeat."

I looked at Carson and sputtered, "How in hell would he beat these charges?"

Miller looked at Carson, his face just as stunned. "Simple," Carson said. "His attorney would just say that he was following up on the obvious narcotics connection with the Banner kid."

I still didn't follow. "I don't get it."

"He'd say that on a hunch, he came out here to check out the camp for drugs. And what should he see but a boat speeding toward him in the darkness."

"That wouldn't give him the right to shoot at the speeding boat," I said.

"He'd say the boat shot at him and he had to return fire. Then the shooter in the other boat sunk his boat."

"But we saved his life. Explain that!"

"We got cold feet and picked him up. And what should turn out to be on board this evil speeding cruiser but a woman with a handgun—recently fired—with a shitload of illegal narcotics in her wake. Then how would we explain ourselves?"

"But we don't have any drugs." All we'd taken from the campsite was a scruffy dog.

Still looking right at Jack, Carson actually laughed. "You can bet that if we'd gotten shot, they'd find marijuana and cocaine hidden somewhere on the *Deep Inn*."

"Okay, but there aren't any drugs on board now. How could he claim there were?"

"Naomi, he wouldn't have to. Our fingerprints are on the bags. He'd say we came out shooting when we heard his boat approaching. It would be his word against ours, and he's the cop."

Gulp. "I never would've thought of that," I said.

Miller still gawked at Carson in amazed silence.

"If Jack got the right attorney, he would think of it," Carson went on. "I'm not even the best attorney, and I thought of it already. I'm not going into that can of worms." He shook his head solemnly.

To me, that seemed less like a can of worms and more like the tip of an iceberg. I stammered, so angry that I could hardly get the words out, "How about shooting me? Shooting you? Trying to frame Mark Banner, and entering... going into... intending to kill him? What about all that?"

Carson crossed his ankles in front of him and leaned back, his hands behind his head. "You can't prosecute someone for having evil intentions, and anyway it would be our word against Jack's about all the rest. Think about it, Naomi. Think about the *whole* can of worms, not just tonight's."

Damn. Damn it to hell, he was right. I was sure that Ellen had had no part of Jack's little plan to clear her, but it still would look very bad. I didn't want that.

Carson waited while I thought all that through and then turned to Jack. "What are you going to do now?"

"I'll take a job down in Tucson," he said. "That's if I manage to stay out of jail up here. As for the Highsmith thing, it's back to square one. How do we prove Ellen didn't do it?" Jack said finally.

The stupid little dog started licking Jack's hand affectionately or pityingly or something. I can't read dogs too well. I thought about how her owner and presumably best friend was a narcotics dealer and likely a murderer. And here she was licking the hand of a bad cop who was also an attempted murderer. I thought about how some people are like that—drawn to the criminal element. So now I had taken in a criminal dog—a dog moll.

Then I got back to thinking about what Jack had asked. "The coyote alibi," I said. It was all we had.

Chapter Twenty-two

Jack Miller drove us in from the marina and dropped me off at my house. Bev and Pete pulled into their driveway about twenty minutes after I got home, and as soon as the kids walked in, I herded them into their rooms with orders to go right to bed—school night and all that. Then I crawled into my own bed without setting my alarm. By the time I woke up the next day, the kids had slipped away to school without waking me. The dog was sound asleep, curled up on Len's bed. My car was still out at the lake, so I walked to the office. I'd assumed that Grant Carson would stay at home and rest at least until afternoon, but when I reached the parking lot, I saw his little pickup, complete with new bullet hole in the windshield.

I found him in his office at his desk. He was hunched over a yellow legal pad and was trying to scribble notes with his left hand. He'd managed to get his left arm into a shirt and drape it over his right shoulder, but his right arm was still bound across his chest with an elastic bandage. He had done up a couple of buttons, rounding off the ensemble with rumpled denims and his favorite sandals. Apparently he was unable to comb his hair with his left hand and had left it to nature.

He looked up and smiled as I entered his office. "Naomi, just the help I need. I can't seem to make any headway with this. Do you mind making some notes?"

"No problem. What are we making notes about?" I leaned over and rebuttoned his shirt.

"Suspects. I'm trying to make a list."

I decided there was nothing I could do about his hair so I picked up the pad and pen and sat across from him. "Good. I've been meaning to map them out, too. Seems like most everyone in town had something to do with what's happened."

"Let's make about four columns. Name, motive." He paused for a moment and looked at the ceiling. "Opportunity, and best defense. Can you think of anything else?"

I remembered wanting to draw dotted lines showing who was connected to whom. But that could wait. "Not yet. Who's on first?"

He chuckled. "No, Who's on second."

I stared at him. "I know enough to understand that that's a line from an old comedy routine, Carson, but it's from before my time."

He frowned as if he didn't like thinking of himself as originating from a time much prior to my own. "Ellen is on first."

"Please tell me this isn't a ranked list"

"No. Maybe it will be a chronological list—depends on my memory. Anyway, it isn't a list of judgments, just data."

I wrote Ellen's name in the top left spot. "As for motive, I guess being married to the rat-bastard would be good enough."

"That will do fine."

He was still frowning, and now he was also looking pale. I said, "You don't look so good, Carson. How are you feeling?"

"How do you think? My shoulder aches. I need a shower, but the bandages can't take the water. I need a shave, but I'm right-handed, and I don't own an electric shaver. My scalp itches, I didn't sleep worth a damn and apparently I'm very old. Want to get back to the list?"

Mr. Cranky needed a nap, but I knew better than to say so. I looked back down at the notepad. "No opportunity. She was in Tuba City about that time." I wrote "NO—Tuba City" in the third column.

"We are going to have to do better than that. Add that she could've been in town in time. In the last column, write that she saw a coyote."

"She didn't just *see* a coyote. She was *obstructed* by a coyote. You're not making this look very good."

"Right, it doesn't look very good. Let's move on to someone else. How about Jack Miller?"

I wrote his name under Ellen's. "I suppose you would say for motive that he was in love with Ellen?"

Carson stared at me for a moment. "Wouldn't you?"

I wrote that down and moved to the "opportunity" column. "He was out of town, right?"

Carson nodded. "Right. It took a couple of hours of calling around Phoenix, but I confirmed last week that Miller delivered a prisoner to the Maricopa County jail at eight o'clock on the night of Highsmith's murder."

"That's over five hours from here."

"More like six from the jail. I don't know if he slept a few hours in Phoenix or came right back up here, but he didn't get very much sleep because he walked in here about eleven the next morning, and he was already working on the case."

I went back to my list. "So the opportunity column says, 'No,' and the best defense says 'confirmed in Phoenix.'" I paused. "Gail Banner?"

"Yeah. Motive would be secret relationship with the rat-bastard. Do I have that right?"

I nodded and wrote it down. "She had the opportunity because she was on the boat with him, and either or both of them could've had a gun. What's her best defense?"

"For one thing, she came forward when no one was looking for her," he said.

"But they *were* looking for her. They were looking for someone who was sneaking through town at midnight."

"Naked."

"That's the fun part," I said. "Anyway, she could've done it. Coming forward isn't a very good defense."

"You're right. She's a viable suspect."

"We should list Dr. Banner, too," I said, "even though I know he didn't do it."

Carson ticked off the four columns with fingers on his left hand. "Dr. Banner…jealousy…no, with someone else… confirmed."

"Do you want me to bother with Frank Armstrong?"

"Sure. He says he's a suspect. Motive was Highsmith's involvement with his then sixteen-year-old daughter."

"Have we ever followed up on his whereabouts when Highsmith was killed?"

"No. We should've."

I made a note. "I think we'll find out that he was with a woman."

"Wasn't everybody?" Carson asked. "What a little *Peyton Place* we have here."

"Again, Carson, I know that there's some sort of cultural reference there, but it must be from way back."

He looked confused. "It's a famous book."

"Never heard of it."

He frowned and got back to the murder chart we were making. "For Armstrong, put 'whereabouts unclear' under 'opportunity.' Best defense is 'with unnamed woman—unconfirmed.' Add Linda Armstrong."

"Linda?"

"Why not? Relationship with rat-bastard. Woman scorned, maybe." He seemed even more sullen now, and I regretted my age-difference remarks.

I smiled as nicely as I could. "I'm betting it's more like 'Gold digger manipulating old guy.' Why would she kill the rat-bastard?"

"Motive could be 'former lover.' Opportunity falls short, though, according to Three-Steps Larry."

I scoffed loudly at the thought of Three-Steps as any kind of reliable witness as I wrote notes. "Is that 'yes' for the third column and 'Three-Steps Larry's say-so—unconfirmed' for the fourth?"

"Definitely."

"Mark Banner," I said.

"Mother's affair."

"And history of violence," I added, "but he was out at the Utah beach."

"Says Three-Steps. And Linda. So that's unconfirmed, too."

I wrote all that. "Who else?"

"Three-Steps Larry."

I looked up from my notes. "He told the kids some bullshit about going deer hunting. Anyway, I'm pretty sure he was somewhere far away at the time."

"And maybe doing something just as bad as killing Highsmith, but it is possible that he wanted Willard dead. He had opportunity."

"But no motive." I said.

"Maybe he had a thing for Gail Banner and wanted Highsmith out of the way."

"Not likely. His best defense is that he was maybe up-lake killing somebody else."

"Write that down," Carson said. "Unconfirmed."

I did. "So who else?"

"There's you." Carson smiled and stared into my eyes.

"Funny."

"I've seen you shoot, and you hated the rat-bastard."

"I was knitting."

"The meeting was over."

"I heard the shots and told what I knew!"

"After Jack came by and confronted you with the news that you'd been seen near the scene of the crime. And you already said that coming forward wasn't a good defense."

I stared back at him, feeling furious. Unjustly accused. And kind of trapped. "Fine. I'll just... put... my... name... right... here," I said as I filled in my columns. I looked up and said, "unconfirmed."

"Okay. Naomi, the way you're feeling right now is the same way that everyone on that list feels—except one."

I nodded. "Which one?"

"Exactly. We don't know. What's your feeling about the list?"

"From the top, Ellen's a no. That's my feeling. Jack's a no. Gail Banner is a strong maybe."

"I'm with you so far."

"Dr. Banner is a no and so is Frank Armstrong."

"And the next two?" he asked, meaning Mark Banner and Linda Armstrong.

"Both are maybe's if Three-Steps was lying."

"Or if he was in cahoots with them," Carson added. "Otherwise, they're clear."

The phone rang, and I picked up. The caller was an officer at the bank who wanted to speak with Carson. He took the phone, and I waited. "Perfectly legal," he said. "I understand your concern," he added after a moment, "but that's completely within her rights." He continued listening until a minute or two later, when he said, "It bothers me too, George, but that's the way it is, I'm afraid. Thanks for calling." He hung up.

"Trouble?"

"Not for me. Linda Armstrong has just made a big withdrawal from a joint account she has with her dad. I'd bet she's leaving town."

"And with Mark Banner still in a coma, maybe. How much money is she taking?"

"Twenty thousand. Only about half of what was in that one account. She has access to other accounts, too, but so far, she isn't touching them."

"How does this affect your thinking about the suspect list?" I asked.

"It doesn't change a thing if Larry Sabano is telling the truth."

I rolled my eyes. "And what, exactly, are the chances of that?"

Let the record show that Grant Carson had no answer.

The list completed for now, I walked back to my office and turned on my computer. Then I opened the front blinds. Out in the parking lot, a car had parked beside Carson's truck. It looked like the Subaru I'd seen in the shed in Utah, and it looked like someone was sitting in it.

"Speak of the devil," I said.

Carson came out and stood right beside me. Against me, actually, but he probably just needed a little support. Poor old guy. After a few seconds, he said, "Maybe you should go get us some coffee." He fished a twenty out of his pocket and handed it to me. "Make it three."

"Hell, no!" I said. "I'm not going to miss this."

"I won't let him say anything until you get back," Carson promised.

I was back in ten minutes with the three coffees, but it was another five before Three-Steps Larry emerged from the car and started a slow walk toward our office. He came in, nodded at me, and walked through to Carson's office and closed the door. I heard him sink down into one of the chairs. His coffee was waiting for him in there.

"So, Larry. I see that you got back to your car all right."

I could just picture Larry nodding vigorously as he said, "Yeah, I did. It was right where I left it."

"Good, good." My boss was being very chipper. "Naomi got you some coffee," he added. *All part of the service*, I thought.

"Yeah, thanks." Larry paused to take a noisy slurp. "But I couldn't find Princess. She wasn't by the shack, and she didn't come when I called. I hope she's okay." I felt just a little guilty, but she really did deserve someone better than him. And I thought back to how happy she looked this morning, snoring on the comforter that topped Len's bed.

"She's fine, Larry. We brought her back with us, since we weren't sure how long it would take you to get back to the campsite. Naomi will look after her until you figure out where you're going next. Vancouver, was it?"

"Um, maybe. Look…"

Carson interrupted him. "Where are the drugs now, Larry?"

"What drugs?"

With more impatience in his voice than seemed wise to me—Three-Steps didn't respond well to impatience—Carson said, "The marijuana. The cocaine. You tasted it, remember? Surely you aren't…foolhardy enough to have them on you. Where are they now?"

"Oh. Okay, well, they're gone."

"I kind of figured that they wouldn't be in the tent anymore, but where are they?

"I don't know. When I got to the campsite, they weren't there. Some hikers must be really happy right now." He sounded just this side of convincing.

The room went quiet for a while. Then Carson sighed loudly and asked, "What's up, Larry? Why are you here?"

"I need to ask you how to turn myself in for accidentally killing Willard Highsmith."

I held my breath.

"Be careful now, Larry. Are you admitting to me that you killed Willard?"

Yet again, I silently cursed the wall that made me miss seeing this.

"Accidentally," Three-Steps repeated.

"Okay. Explain how this *accident* happened."

"This is in confidence, right? And I may be confused about some of it."

"It's just between you and me," Carson said. I heard some shuffling around as he found a pen and one of his legal pads. "So you may later need to... revise some parts of what you are about to say?"

"Right, but it was like this." Larry was silent for several seconds. "I was crossing the lake in a boat I'd borrowed. I was just cruising around. Understand?"

"I'm with you so far."

"It was pretty dark. I was going to go up that canyon that runs east of the power plant. I was out to hunt some deer."

"You have a license and a tag to help with this story?"

"No, I didn't bother," Larry paused and then added, "which was mildly illegal so I didn't want to be seen by anybody."

"Okay, go on."

"Well, when I got to the mouth of the canyon, I stopped to grab a beer out of the cooler. And then I saw this other boat and killed my engine. I just sat still in the dark for a while—maybe ten or fifteen minutes. But the guy in the other boat—it turned out to be Highsmith—he did see me, finally." Three-Steps went silent again.

"Then what?"

"Well, the boat I'd borrowed was *his* boat, but I didn't borrow it from him. So he recognized the boat, I guess. It's a special boat. Kind of flashy." Another silence.

"And?"

"You got any coffee creamer or anything? This coffee's a little bitter."

"No. Don't complain about a free cup of coffee. Highsmith saw you and …?"

"Okay, well, yeah. He must've thought I'd stolen his boat…and he took a shot at me. And then I shot back. I thought I'd scare him, maybe, or something, but I hit him…accidentally."

"Did he fall into the lake?"

Larry paused for a few seconds. "I think so. It was dark."

"And his gun?"

"I told you, it was dark, but yeah, that must have fallen in the lake, too."

"Was he alone?"

"What?"

"Was anyone with Highsmith when you shot him?"

Larry was quiet for a long time before answering, but Carson gave him no prompts. Finally, Three-Steps said, "I didn't see anybody. But I drifted up along the canyon after the… the accident… and I couldn't see the boat anymore from there."

"What did you do with the gun?"

"What? Oh, my gun. I threw it in the lake."

"Why did you… never mind. It doesn't matter. Then what did you do?"

"I sat still and did nothing. I was in the shadow of the cliff, drifting further up the canyon. I waited a long time to be sure that no one was around."

"How long?"

"Maybe a half hour. I don't know."

"Then what?"

"I took off. I just drove the boat around for a long time. Then I took it back to where I borrowed it."

"What happened after that?"

"Well, I wasn't going to tell anybody, but then this other problem—the one that you know about—that thing came up, and I had to sort of lay low. I couldn't talk to those guys about whatever they wanted because I was afraid that it would come out—what I did to Highsmith—if I talked to them."

Carson waited for a moment and then asked, "So why are you here now? Why not just leave town?"

"Well, it's good for your client, right, that woman…Highsmith's wife? She shouldn't take the fall for what I did."

I sat back and smirked. How noble of him. What a great guy.

I heard Carson's chair creak as he shifted his weight. "Naomi has this crazy theory that you didn't kill Highsmith because you were way up the lake killing some of Deguerra's drug runners instead. I think John Rice has the same theory."

Three-Steps choked on his bitter coffee.

No one said anything for a long time. Finally, Three-Steps spoke up. "Would twenty-five thousand dollars in cash be a sufficient retainer for representing me during my confession and all that?" A brief silence followed. "I have it with me."

Carson answered Three-Steps after another silence. "It *would* be good for Ellen Highsmith if you confessed to this accidental shooting. Very good for you, too, I'm betting."

"Good for me?"

"Proves you weren't up at Bull Banks like Rice thinks maybe you were."

"That's just a coincidence—and for the record, I did not shoot those guys …anyone up the lake."

Carson answered, "But this won't work—the Rice part of it—if the prosecutor doesn't buy your Highsmith story."

I heard Larry shift forward in his chair, making a little squeaking sound on the floor. "Why wouldn't the County Attorney believe me?"

"It won't be the County Attorney."

"What? Why not?"

Both of you were on the lake. Park Service jurisdiction, FBI stuff."

"Shit!"

"And there were maybe other witnesses."

"Other witnesses? Naomi heard the shots. Yeah, I know."

"And maybe others. And there's a strong possibility that the prosecutor won't go for accidental death. It'll sound more like manslaughter to him."

"Manslaughter?"

"Death in a fight."

"No, no, no," Larry said. "Self defense, maybe. Can't you find out before I go in?"

"Mr. Sabano," said Carson, "you need more specialized legal expertise than I am able to provide."

"Wait! You're my lawyer."

"No, Mr. Sabano, as of right now, I no longer represent you. I will give you the contact information for someone who better meets your needs."

"But you're my lawyer."

Carson's voice was gentle but quite firm. "No, I'm not your lawyer anymore. Daniel J. Larson should be your attorney. I'm writing down his phone number on this card, and I suggest that you contact him before talking to the police or anyone—anyone—else."

~ ~ ~

An hour later, Carson and I were talking with Gail Banner in the waiting room at the hospital, where Mark was still unconscious.

After listening to the suggestion that maybe Highsmith had been shot from another boat and that he'd maybe opened fire first, Gail said, "It doesn't sound quite right to me, Mr. Carson. I didn't see any other boat, and, as far as I know, Willard didn't have a gun on board." She paused. "I've heard that Rodriguez thought that Ellen Highsmith might have been out there with their speedboat, but the Armstrong girl cleared that up."

After a pause, she seemed to catch on to the new picture that Carson was presenting.

"Didn't you say you'd heard other boats passing in the dark?"

"Yes, I did, but I don't remember hearing anything that close."

Patiently, Carson went on. "Apparently the other boat was already in the area when you and Willard arrived. It was floating in the shadows of the canyon, hoping not to be seen."

Gail still looked skeptical, but I could tell that she was thinking through the events of that night, trying to sort out the timeline.

Carson continued, "There's this person willing to swear to this story—to confess to the killing."

"And get Ellen Highsmith off the hook," she said, with a real edge to her voice.

Carson paused. "Investigation of several people would come to an end."

Gail Banner stiffened. "Including me, you mean."

"And including your son," Carson said.

Gail looked at me and then at Carson. "You don't really think that Mark did this."

"What is important is which way the prosecution might take the investigation. Until they can close it, a lot of people are still possible suspects. The longer it goes on, the messier it gets for everybody."

She looked down at the floor for a moment and then looked at me. "How does this fit with what you saw and heard?"

"I heard the shots. I never saw you, but I heard you swimming away because you were right under me. I saw Highsmith after he fell. I didn't see any other boat, but I wouldn't have seen it if it was in the shadow of the cliff."

"So you can't corroborate this man's story?"

"Or disprove it."

She looked at Carson again. "Why would this man confess if he didn't do it? It's first degree murder."

"First, maybe he did shoot Willard. He says he did, and no one can say for sure that he didn't. Second, no, he isn't confessing to murder. There's no basis at all for premeditation. He says it was an accidental shooting. I've told him that the prosecution probably wouldn't settle for less than manslaughter. I think the most they could conceivably go for is homicide during the commission of a crime. I doubt they'd try for it."

"Are you representing him?"

Like you're representing every other possible suspect in this case? I mentally added.

"If his story is correct, this is a federal case. I have no credentials for a federal felony case."

Ms. Banner reached down into her purse and pulled out a cigarette. Then she remembered where she was and put it back. "What do you think are the consequences for the man?"

"He might get five to ten—parole in no less than three, but I really don't know. He has a record."

"As a drug dealer," I added, and she looked over at me. I held her gaze and said slowly, "He's been convicted of selling drugs."

Gail Banner glanced down the hallway toward her son's room. She clenched her jaw. Then she said, "Who knows? One possibility, of course, is that he *did* do it." She swept her gaze from me to Carson.

I looked away from her, but Carson said, "As far as I can tell, you could say that about half a dozen people."

"But not Ellen Highsmith?" Gail said.

"Ellen didn't do it," I said. "She was in Tuba City at the time."

CHAPTER TWENTY-THREE

Amonth later the weather had turned. An overcast sky shrouded the canyons and would stay that way until the winds of March. The lake had given up its warmth, and the last of the tourists were gone. Sage Landing's appearance showed only one discernible change—the sign over the door of the furniture store now read simply, Ellen's Family Furniture.

That change had involved us in new corporate paperwork, and we'd been paid to draw it up. It had been processed through the State Corporation Commission in Phoenix and had now returned to our offices.

Three-Steps Larry had already begun serving a five-to-ten year sentence in a minimum-security federal prison. The judge who'd administered the plea bargain had added the stipulation that there would be no parole in fewer than three years. I was stuck with the dog for at least that long, and I was not at all sure that Larry would ever return for her. My son, Len, had renamed her Three-Steps, mostly because it occasionally gave him an opening to tell an amazing story. He took his time whenever he told it, and it held an audience pretty well. The dog didn't seem to mind.

We heard through the rumor mill that Linda Armstrong had rented an apartment in Tempe and was registered for the spring term at Arizona State. Frank Armstrong had survived his surgery for only eight days. It was his heart that got him in the end.

Jack Miller had stayed in Sage Landing for only one week after Ellen's release. Then he'd moved back down to Tucson and rejoined the Tucson police force. According to Carson's sources, Jack had taken a regular patrol assignment, a step down for him. With the Highsmith case wrapped up, any investigation into the assaults on me and Carson seemed to fade away. And, as far as I knew, Jack never paid Carson for the windshields.

~ ~ ~

On a Tuesday morning in late November, John Rice walked into our office and waited for me to announce him. Then he walked into Carson's office and didn't bother to close the door.

"Surprised to see me?" he asked.

"Not at all," Carson said. "I knew it was just a matter of time until you read the newspaper and came over here to check the facts."

Rice laughed. "Actually, I'm over here to check on a boat that's for sale at the marina. But as long as I was in town, I thought I'd drop by and touch base. I've already checked on the facts that you mentioned." I heard him sit down in one of the chairs.

"And what did you find out?" Carson asked.

"It's a pretty wild story—Larry Sabano ending up killing a philandering husband in some kind of shootout. He was fortunate in being able to afford expensive, specialized representation. Otherwise, he might have had a much longer sentence."

There was a pause before Carson said, "Did you know that Sabano had prior convictions?"

"Oh, yes, I knew that before I came to Sage Landing. Actually, we've known his criminal record all along. It is an odd set of circumstances, though—having that particular man's speedboat."

"You can say that again!" Carson agreed. "It was a surprise to me too—I think there's a hidden story there. I'm guessing some sort of love triangle thing."

"Ha! Sabano and who?"

"The guy he shot was quite a man about town, so it's anyone's guess. Did you ever get a chance to talk to Larry while you were over here before?"

"No, we never managed to locate him. Actually I came in here today to ask you just one question about something that came up at the sentencing."

"What was that?"

"The judge mentioned narcotics. The transcript shows that the judge was under the impression that Larry had given drugs to the teenagers who provided the boat. Where do you think Larry Sabano got those drugs?"

"Yeah, I checked into that. Hearsay has it that he was a small-time dealer and that he had some history of selling drugs to teenagers here in town. I believe he told the prosecution that he had traded them some marijuana. I wasn't present when he said that."

"But the boy, Banner, he was hospitalized. I heard that he was in a coma following a drug overdose. Marijuana doesn't do that."

"I heard that rumor too, but I have no access to hospital records. I understand that the young man has left the area and is now in a rehabilitation clinic in California. As for the drugs that he took, I suspect methamphetamine. It's very nasty stuff, and I think that some of the kids around here know how to get hold of it—maybe even cook it."

Rice was quiet for a minute, apparently deciding not to take issue with what Carson had said. He went on, "There was a young woman involved as well."

"Yes, she testified about the marijuana but consistently denied that there were any hard drugs. Frankly, I didn't believe her. She has also left the area. She did come back for the hearing, but she no longer lives here."

"I understand that her father died. Sad."

After a moment, Carson asked, "Did you ever straighten out your land transaction, or whatever it was that you wanted to see Mr. Sabano about?"

"No. We are looking for some other people who might be able to shed some light on the situation, but no one has turned up. It's beginning to look like a dead loss."

"A small one, I hope."

"No, rather a large one."

Carson, of course, said nothing. After a moment I heard Rice stand. "I've got a long drive ahead of me, Mr. Carson, and I don't want to take up any more of your time." He walked out of Carson's office, nodded at me again, and left. As he drove away, I realized that it was the first time I'd seen him without Fred. I wondered if Fred got canned because he took a licking at the hands of a lawyer who was nearly a senior citizen.

~ ~ ~

On Thursday morning that same week, we prepared a package of corporate papers for Ellen Highsmith, some for signatures and some just for delivery. Carson and I went together to Ellen's Family Furniture and found that she wasn't in her office. The store manager told us that Ellen was restocking her grandfather's place with sheep and that she was out there much of the time. We thanked him and picked up doughnuts at the bakery. Then we drove toward the Reservation.

I remembered the way to the ranch from when Ellen and I went out there as kids. The drive took us less than thirty minutes, nearly half of it on a dirt road. Finally, we found the late model double-wide manufactured home nestled into a quarter acre of nice landscaping. Surrounding that, of course, was red sand and sparse vegetation in all directions. There were no cars parked at the house. After a brief wait to see if anyone would come out, we concluded that no one was home.

"I still think I should have knocked on the door," Carson said as he started his pickup.

"I told you. We don't do that, at least not out here on the Rez. It would be extremely rude to barge into the front yard and knock on the door. Out in this kind of terrain, if someone's home, they'll know you're coming at least five minutes before you've arrived. The next move is up to them. If they want to talk to you, they'll come out. That's the custom. Deal with it."

We noticed a dust trail down a dirt road to the east.

"Ellen?"

"Could be," I said.

"Is it all right to drive over there and see?"

"Sure. Let's go."

A few minutes later, we drove up behind Ellen's new pickup truck. It was parked next to newly-built holding pens which contained perhaps two dozen sheep. Scattered across the high desert in the distance were another twenty or so sheep, and in the distance was another small pen. Ellen was standing next to a watering tank, dressed in denim pants and shirt—a rancher's outfit, complete with boots. She turned to face us as we got out of the smaller pickup. She smiled.

"Got some papers for you," I said.

"You didn't have to come all the way out here."

"Yes we did. You don't seem to be in town when we try to find you there. How's the sheep business?"

"Well, I imagine that the furniture business will probably have to support the sheep business, but I like the sheep business better."

"How do the kids like the sheep business?" I asked.

"They don't come out here much—too busy with school activities. But they'll appreciate it when they're older. In our family, the sheep have always been at the heart of what we did. Well, up through my grandfather's time, anyway. These days, I'm a furniture seller, and one of my brothers is an accountant. My mother is a retired clerk, and my father is still with the coal mines. My grandfather was the last full-time sheep herder."

"It's nice out here," Carson said, extending the package of papers toward Ellen.

She turned away and balanced the package on a post to read the cover sheet. "Do I have to go through these now?"

"We can't finish some of the filings until you sign them, but..."

Just then Ellen looked up from the bundle of papers and stared out over the desert to the east. She stiffened for a moment and then whirled around and ran to her truck. She jerked open the door, tossed the papers on the floor, slid a rifle out from behind the seat, and started trotting back toward us. When she reached the sturdy railings of the pen, she bolted a round into the chamber and rested the rifle on a post. A second later she fired into the distance, and the penned sheep beside us fled to the other side of the corral.

She jerked her head up from its rest on the rifle butt and looked over the top of the barrel as she slammed in another bullet. Then she held her breath and fired again. In the distance I could see a coyote spin around and sprint till he was out of range. She jacked in another round but did not fire. After a moment she relaxed.

"Got him running now," she said.

"What was it?" Carson asked.

"I'll show you," she said. She walked back to her truck and disarmed the rifle before placing it behind the seat again. "Come on!"

We climbed into the truck beside her, and she started driving out over the trackless, bumpy desert. When we'd traveled less than the length of a football field, she stopped the truck and got out. We followed her to where the coyote had stopped and fled. His tracks in the sand were all that remained to show that he'd been there.

He'd almost made it to a small enclosure where several lambs were shivering next to their mothers.

She walked over to calm the sheep, speaking to them softly in Navajo before walking back to where we stood. Carson was watching her closely, but when she spoke, it was to me. "When they go after the lambs like that ... well, you just have to shoot. Once they manage to get hold of a lamb…"

"I know," I said, "you have to protect…them."

Carson stared at the coyote tracks for a moment and then turned and looked back to where his little truck was parked. "Hell of a shot."

"You've got to be good at it if you're going to run sheep in this country." She kicked at the coyote tracks in the dust. Then she turned and started back toward her new truck.

"It's not so bad this year," she said, "Because the sheep haven't been out here very long. The coyotes are just starting to notice them." She hefted the rifle. "I'm hoping I convinced that one to forget where my sheep are."

Involuntarily, I glanced at Carson, but he just headed back to Ellen's truck and climbed in.

After Ellen dropped us off at Carson's truck, we drove back toward town in silence for a couple of miles. Finally, he said, "She could have nailed that coyote at that distance."

"Maybe. But beliefs about coyotes are complicated, remember?" I went on, "Many Navajos would prefer not to kill them. Even some sheep herders."

He nodded. "Really? Learn something new all the time out here." A moment later he said, "It sounded like maybe you guys weren't just talking about protecting wooly lambs."

I hesitated for a minute and then shrugged. "Lots of things need protection."

Keeping his eyes on the road, he waited, not wanting to ask the question.

I watched the road for a few breaths before saying, "The night I got hit in the head…Kai told me some stuff." I paused and then added, "He hadn't done anything, really…."

"Yet," Carson said with a clench jaw. "Not yet."

"Not yet," I echoed.

He tapped his fingers in a drumming rhythm along the top of the steering wheel for a moment. "Good thing Three-Steps shot the rat-bastard, then."

"Damn good thing," I said.

About the Author

J. & D. Burges are a husband-and-wife writing team in Virginia. Having lived for many years on the edge of the Navajo Nation, they write with cheerful authority about open spaces, big lakes, and the unique mix of cultures captured in their Sage Landing stories.

Their mysteries are now hatched in a cottage in the woods near a lake. It's a great place to plot light-hearted homicides. When they're not doing that or working out, they might be dancing. There's also some knitting and woodworking going on.

They can't resist interfering in each other's work. It's often hard for them to remember which story idea originated where and whose words made it into the final draft. Each of them claims that the best lines belong to the other.

Check out their web site at www.jdburges.com

Made in United States
North Haven, CT
24 June 2022

20578061R00171